# HEART MELTER

## SOPHIA KNIGHTLY

## DEDICATION

With much love to my daughter, Gigi, the talented songbird who inspired this story. May you always sing and spread joy with your beautiful voice.

## Acknowledgements

Huge thanks to Martha Paley Francescato for your many reads and encouragement during the writing of HEART MELTER. I'm so happy you loved Natasha and Ian's story from the start.

To Maggie Dove, many thanks for the laughter and fun times in plotting, and to Marcia King-Gamble for your feedback and always lending an ear.

A big shout out and thanks to my wonderful beta readers and to the amazing Sophia's Sirens led by our fabulous team leader, Amanda Brown!

Lots of love to my daughters, Gigi and Jacqui, for your boundless enthusiasm and support. *Gracias* to my Mom, the original storyteller whose tales held me spellbound as a child.

And finally to my husband, Paul, for your heart melting love.

\*    \*    \*

# Ian and Natasha - Heartthrob Series, Book Two

Scottish surgeon, Dr. Ian MacGregor, has no desire to see his ex-fiancée again. But when the dazzling Broadway star lands in his office wounded, the healer in Ian can't turn her away.

Natasha White has no idea why anyone would knife her on a crowded street in Times Square. At first she thinks the cut on her thigh is an accident, but as frightening events unravel, she learns the mob is after an incriminating flash drive they think she has. She's grateful when Ian whisks her away to his castle in the Highlands, far from the mob.

Irresistibly drawn to her, Ian tries to deny the sexy sparks that ignite as he becomes her fierce protector. Their hot chemistry deepens into strong feelings as they dodge impending danger and he fights to keep her safe. Ian will do anything to guard Natasha, but will their love be strong enough to survive the shocking secrets revealed?

Dear Readers,

*HEART MELTER is a story very dear to my heart. Years ago, I traveled to Scotland and was captivated by its valiant history, the warm and friendly Scots and the magic of their land. I always wanted to set a romance there, and now I'm thrilled to share Ian and Natasha's love story with you. I hope you will root for them and fall in love with them as much as I did.*

*Happy reading,*
*Sophia Knightly*

# CHAPTER ONE

"You're flat," Simon called out from the third row of the dark theatre.

"No, I'm not." Natasha White gritted her teeth and raised a challenging eyebrow at the director. Her hands curved on the waist of her fawn satin teddy as she tamped down her simmering temper. Simon Worth was referring to her pitch, not her breasts, although he had spent most of the morning ogling them while she danced. It was the third time he'd rudely interrupted her song, and he'd made Freddie the choreographer change her tap number so many times, her muscles were screaming in protest. But she ignored the pain; it was worth having the starring role of Legs LaRue in "The Bee's Knees", a new roaring twenties musical sure to be a Broadway hit.

Simon was pushing hard during dress rehearsal—unfairly so. But what else could she expect from the control freak who had written the songs and lyrics of "The Bee's Knees" and was also directing it? The thirty-nine-year-old musical genius was temperamental and rude, but that wouldn't have stopped Natasha's mother, legendary Broadway diva, Anitra White, from letting loose a rant that would have singed Simon's bushy black brows. Where her acerbic mother would have screamed, Natasha held her tongue, even if she felt like strangling Simon. She didn't want any comparisons with her drama queen mama, not now, not ever.

"She was pitch perfect," her accompanist, Bruce, said instantly. Her white-haired defender pushed his horn rimmed glasses up on his high-bridged nose and glared at Simon. Bruce was an experienced, old school Broadway accompanist and nobody dared contradict him, not even Simon.

"Sounded gorgeous to me. Piss off, Simon." Freddie the choreographer's jaw clenched beneath his trim salt-and-pepper goatee as he sent a supportive nod Natasha's way. He had already had a meltdown this morning over Simon's intrusive meddling in his choreography. His compact dancer's body was coiled tightly, ready to spring on the director if he continued to bully Natasha. Not that she needed protecting. If she could handle her mother's tough criticism all those years growing up, she could certainly endure Simon's.

"Thanks, guys," Natasha said, blowing them kisses. She alternately rolled her neck and shoulders, and then peered into the theatre, her gaze zeroing in on her understudy, Lisette Raye, who watched with rabid ambition.

It was no secret Lisette was hot for the starring role—and the director. The pushy twenty-one-year-old actress and Simon were already sleeping together. Once he'd plowed through the ensemble and slept with most of them, Simon settled on Lisette, who eagerly pleased him in *all* areas. Well, she could have the pompous gasbag. Musical genius or not, he didn't appeal to Natasha, and she'd be damned if she'd sleep her way to the top. She'd seen too many failed "showmances"—mostly hook-ups that thrived during shows, but rarely made it past the last curtain call. Hanging around backstage as a child during her mom's Broadway shows had taught her to steer clear of romances in the business. It had also toughened her enough to let Simon's insults slide and not affect her performance.

"Let's take it from the top, and this time make sure your E makes me weep," Simon drawled caustically, ignoring the collective groans from Bruce and Freddie.

An hour later when Elisha, the stage manager, called lunch break, Natasha fled the theatre intent on grabbing a bite to eat and taking her Pomeranian puppy, Evita, for a quick walk. Evita was a gift from her childhood friend, Ronnie, and Ronnie's gorgeous new husband, Nick Cameron. They'd given her the puppy before leaving on their honeymoon. The moment the puppy emitted a melodious, crooning howl while Natasha sang, she promptly named her Evita, after the musical.

Natasha hurried across Times Square, her nerves frayed from Simon's heedless interruptions and unwarranted criticisms. Something wasn't right; she could feel it in her bones. Thinking back to her horoscope this morning, maybe she should heed Sydney Taggert's advice: *Keep an eye on your back and an eye toward the future.*

She zipped her tan leather jacket against the blast of ice cold air swirling around her. A bit early for such frigid weather in October, but everything this month seemed off. She usually made her way home at a brisk trot, but today her leg and butt muscles quivered from the morning's repetitive variations of the same dance. She was used to grueling workouts, but Simon had gone overboard. It was almost as if he were trying to push her to the breaking point. Well, it wasn't going to happen. He had underestimated the kind of grit she had developed over the years. She wasn't about to relinquish the plum role of Legs LaRue to a greedy newbie like Lisette.

With her head bent forward and her heavy dance tote slung across her chest, Natasha wove through the teeming crowd of tourists. She was two blocks away from her apartment when she felt a firm jerk on her dance bag. As she grappled to hold onto it and not lose her footing, a sharp pain sliced across her outer right thigh.

"Ouch!" She craned her neck to the side to see where the jab had come from. A quick glance at her leg made her gasp at the slash in her jeans and the long red line on her skin revealed by the gaping fabric. Within seconds blood rose to the cut's surface. With shaky hands, Natasha pulled her long knit scarf off her neck and tied it tightly around her upper thigh, forming a tourniquet to stop the bleeding.

She stepped onto the curb and frantically hailed a taxi. Within seconds, a cab drove up and she clambered inside.

"Where to?" the driver asked, turning to stare at her when she didn't answer right away.

Natasha could barely breathe, let alone speak as she stared at the driver. She swallowed and said through trembling lips, "Take me to the closest emergency clinic."

*No, that wouldn't do.* If she went to an emergency clinic, she'd be there all day. With Simon's foul mood and Lisette itching for her starring role, Natasha had to get back to rehearsal ASAP.

When the driver turned on 40th Street onto 6th Avenue, she remembered Ian's medical clinic was on that street. Her heart leaped at the thought of seeing her ex-fiancé again and it brought an onslaught of painful memories. Given the way they'd split up seven years ago, would he even agree to see her? At this crucial moment, who cared? She needed his expertise and who better than brilliant renowned cosmetic surgeon, Dr. Ian MacGregor, to treat her wound and not leave a disfiguring scar?

Knowing Ian, he'd take care of her too. He was a doctor first and foremost. Years ago, he'd been strong and protective of her...and they'd been passionately in love. Did she really want to go there after struggling for seven years to get him out of her heart? How would he react to her unexpected visit? She'd soon find out, she thought, quaking inside as she made a rash decision.

When she recognized Ian's building, she told the driver, "Stop here. Please. I'm getting off." She handed him a ten dollar bill and bolted out of the cab.

Inside the building, Natasha gulped air and tried not to look at her wound as she pressed the elevator button. Thankfully, it was empty and she rode up to Ian's office alone. But the moment she entered the reception area, she panicked at the roomful of patients waiting to be seen. Summoning strength—and courage—she limped toward the counter and tried not to put too much pressure on her injured leg.

"Excuse me," she said to a gray haired woman whose narrowed gaze was fixed on the computer screen before her. "I need to see Dr. MacGregor."

"Do you have an appointment?"

"No, but it's an emergency."

"I'm sorry. Dr. MacGregor doesn't take walk-ins," the woman replied briskly. Her name tag said Carla and Natasha wondered if she was the office manager.

"But I'm hurt," Natasha said, her voice rising in anguish. She motioned to her injured leg, hoping Carla would take pity on her.

"You're bleeding! You need to go to an emergency center. Now!" Carla said with a disapproving shake of her head.

A collective gasp sounded behind her and Natasha didn't need to turn around to confirm that all attention was riveted on her, from the buzzing voices of waiting patients to the concerned faces behind the glass reception counter.

She leaned forward and clutched the counter. "I don't feel very well. Please tell Dr. MacGregor that Natasha White needs to see him. He knows me."

"I can't interrupt him while he's with a patient," Carla said firmly.

Natasha closed her eyes and drew in calming breaths. How on earth was she going to get past Ian's gatekeeper to see him? *Desperate times called for desperate measures.* She swayed on her feet and collapsed, making sure to land carefully on her uninjured side. Good thing her acting classes had included pratfalls, she thought wryly, as she lay on the floor pretending to be unconscious.

Carla rounded the corner immediately. "Good Lord! She fainted. Get Dr. MacGregor. Quick!" she yelled, patting Natasha's cheek.

Seconds later, Natasha heard a deep male voice say, "What's going on, Carla?" He reached Natasha's side in seconds. "Tasha? Oh God. What happened?"

The hairs on Natasha's arms stood on end and butterflies swarmed her belly at the sound of Ian's rich voice, resonant with a Scottish burr. She opened her eyes and slowly met his—silver-green wolf eyes densely rimmed with sooty black lashes. Her heart pounded riotously as his arresting gaze locked with hers and a familiar weakness overcame her making it hard to breathe.

Ian's sheer male force engulfed her, held her in thrall as she lay before him, almost sick with anticipation of his next move. A jumble of potent emotions blindsided her. Longing, excitement, trepidation, despair. She hadn't realized how much seeing him again would affect her and she needed a moment to pull herself together.

Natasha closed her eyes and let her body go limp again.

Muttering "bloody hell", Ian lifted her up and carried her down the hallway and into a room. She didn't dare open her eyes. *Please let him think I'm unconscious,* she thought, mortified she'd had to resort to fainting like a damsel in distress. Before Ian, of all people.

He gently deposited her on the examining table and made short work of removing her jeans with the help of a nurse named Judy. While the nurse cleaned the wound, Ian examined it and Natasha kept her eyes closed the whole time.

"It's superficial. I'll take it from here, Judy. Please go to Mrs. Phillips in room six. I'll be there shortly."

"Yes, Doc," Judy said and hustled out of the room.

"Nobody faints for that long. Open your eyes, Tasha," Ian said in a voice laden with irony.

*Tasha*. Hearing Ian's pet name for her made Natasha's heart squeeze. Her lashes fluttered as she blinked at the bright lights and focused on Ian's face. He loomed above her, handsome as ever with a straight, aristocratic nose, a firm jaw and sensual lips that rivaled any Michelangelo statue. Thick dark brows formed straight slashes above narrowed crystal green eyes that raked over her with concern. Ian's vibrant wolf eyes stirred her blood and a tremor coursed through her as his steady gaze held her immobile.

"Ian." Natasha took a deep breath of the sterile air in a fruitless attempt to calm her racing heart. "I...I..." she stammered.

Ian arched one brow and stared at her meaningfully.

She rubbed her arms against the shivery sensations he aroused, fervently hoping he couldn't tell how unhinged she felt. She stared back, trapped in his penetrating gaze. For the life of her, she couldn't think of anything to say. He had to be wondering if she'd lost her marbles.

"I'm sorry I passed out and bled all over your carpet out there. I'll have it replaced," she finally managed to say. She held her breath and waited for Ian to do something. A smile, a frown—anything to break the crackling tension between them.

Ian's mouth tightened. "I don't care about the bloody carpet. Let's turn you on your left side so I can tend to the cut." He placed a supporting hand on Natasha's upper back and carefully eased her onto her side.

The moment his warm skin touched hers, gooseflesh spread on Natasha's sensitized skin and zips of excitement shot to her pleasure points. It had always been like this with him. Ian's touch or a look from his heated eyes was all it took to set her aflame.

She huffed for air before meeting his gaze. "I probably shouldn't have come here, but I don't trust anyone else with my legs. You're the best." The moment the words left her lips, she regretted it. Where was her filter for God's sake?

Ian raised a sardonic brow. "Oh?"

This was no time for modesty, but she couldn't help feeling utterly exposed in nothing but her blouse and bikini panties. A light blanket was draped over her hip, but her legs were bare to his gaze from thigh to ankle. He kept a blank expression, professional as a doctor should, but still...

She gave a shaky laugh. "Wait, that didn't come out right. I meant you're the best physician." She cleared her throat and looked at her thigh. "Is the cut very deep? How bad is it?"

"It's not deep at all. You're lucky your jeans were in the way or it would have been worse." Ian's angular jaw was set in taut lines and his clipped tone spoke volumes.

Natasha lifted her eyes to meet his steady gaze. She was still reeling from his touch and the electrifying moment their eyes had met after so many years. Now the sexy sound of his Scottish burr and his nearness were making her heart pound and her senses buzz. This wouldn't do. Ian's intense gaze wreaked havoc on her composure as she wondered what lurked beneath the stillness.

She shivered inwardly, dropping her gaze to compose herself. He could read her like a book and he wouldn't tolerate any artifice or acting on her part. He knew her too well.

"Are you going to stitch it up?" she asked, finding her voice.

"No. I'll close the wound with tissue glue. It should heal without a scar."

"No scar? Oh good." She heaved a sigh of relief. No stitches and no scar. Now if she could just get him to smile, she'd feel a lot better.

"Be sure to keep the area clean and dry for 24 hours."

"I will. Thanks, I appreciate it." Ian's expression didn't soften when she smiled at him. With a sigh, she stared at the unyielding set of his mouth. The same mouth that had once smiled at her with heart-melting tenderness, had crooned Scottish endearments while making love to her, had kissed her *everywhere* into quivering acquiescence. All of it had been wonderful until seven years ago when she'd broken off their engagement and he'd thundered, *"Stay out of my life!"*

"How did you get cut like that?" he asked, jarring her from her musings.

"I don't know. One minute I was rushing home on my lunch break, and the next I felt a tug on my dance bag. When I pulled back, something sharp sliced across my thigh."

He touched her leg again and she jerked in response.

"Hold still," he said firmly. One masterful hand held her thigh immobile as the other treated the cut. "Are you in pain?"

"A bit."

He slanted a sympathetic look her way. "I'm almost done. I'll give you something for the pain before you leave if you still need it."

Natasha nodded and bit her lip. It wasn't so much the pain that was jolting; his touch was making her heart race and awakening every nerve portal of her body. She closed her eyes and cast aside the thrilling memory of his hands caressing her legs when they'd first made love. *Think of him as a doctor, nothing more.*

When he finished tending the wound, he straightened and folded his arms over his chest. "When was the last time you ate?" His keen eyes bored into hers.

"I had breakfast this morning. Why do you ask?" She drew aside the light blanket to inspect the large bandage wrapped around her thigh

He studied her with thoughtful deliberation. "You passed out earlier and you're thinner than I remember. Have you been on some crazy diet?"

"No, of course not," she said, wincing as she sat up. "It's all the dancing I've been doing." She wasn't about to divulge that Simon had rudely told her, "Better not lose those round tits and ass, babe. The role calls for it."

Ian's dark brows furrowed. "You used to love food." His elegant surgeon's hand turned her face toward him and his eyes settled on hers with the familiarity born of intimacy. Their eyes locked like lovers, electrified by the memory of their ill-fated passion years ago when his mere touch could set her on fire. The feel of his long fingers gently touching her face made Natasha's heart hurt. His unswerving gaze was fathomless as he stared at her.

"I still do." She drew in a heavy sigh and broke eye contact as she struggled to tether unraveling emotions. Did he remember how amazing it had been between them? Even in his sterile office, and despite the sharp headache budding behind her eyes, Ian aroused turbulent emotions inside her. She felt hot and cold and shaky at once reliving the memory of their heartbreaking split.

He'd been her first and only love. No man she'd dated since had filled his shoes...or captured her heart. Especially not the last guy she'd dated. Tony Martin had been the exact opposite of Ian. Try as she might to forget Ian by dating Tony, it hadn't worked—especially when Tony revealed his violent personality. After he unleashed his nasty temper on her, she ended things right away.

Natasha's phone beeped with a text message bringing her back to her present predicament. On the way to Ian's office, between panicking and fighting nausea, she'd texted the stage manager and alerted Elisha that she'd had a minor accident and would be late.

"Will I be able to dance tomorrow?" she asked, fighting the urge to check the text.

"No. Not for several days."

"Several days?" Her shoulders slumped in spite of her resolve to be strong.

He frowned. "Do you want the wound to open again?"

"No, but..." How could she tell him this show was crucial to her career, when it was her career that had been the catalyst of their break-up?

"Follow my directions and you'll be as good as new. When was your last tetanus shot?"

Natasha shrugged. "A long time ago. Just before summer camp." A vision of Simon's snarling face suddenly made her frantic to leave. She swung her legs over the side. "I have to get back to rehearsal."

"You're not leaving until you get a tetanus shot. And you're not going to rehearsal today." Ian's steely eyes brooked no arguments. He was annoyingly authoritarian, yet a brilliant physician and a born healer. She had a scrapbook filled with newspaper and magazine articles about Dr. Ian MacGregor, the eminent laser surgeon and dermatologist, who worked magic removing disfiguring scars and birthmarks. His recent laser invention had catapulted him into celebrity status and garnered him billions.

But it was his work with underprivileged children and adults that made Natasha's heart swell with pride. Since she'd last seen him, he had traveled extensively with Doctors Without Borders and The Smile Train, removing the stigma of disfiguring cleft palates and port wine birthmarks for those who couldn't afford it. Ian would insist on not letting her leave until he could "fix" whatever was wrong with her, but she couldn't stay a moment longer.

"I don't want a shot. I have to leave now!" Not going to rehearsal was out of the question.

Ian's silver-green eyes darkened to gun metal grey as they zeroed in on her with such ferocity she fought the urge to squirm. "What in bloody hell is going on, Tasha?"

She lifted her chin. "I'm starring in a new show and we start previews tomorrow. If I don't get back to dress rehearsal, I'm going to get fined, and possibly replaced."

Ian's lip curled as he shook his head. "Nothing has changed. The show must go on. Comes before everything. Right, Tasha?"

His ironic tone irked the hell out of her. "Yes, that's right. Just like your patients always come first," she retorted. His accusation rubbed a raw spot as they faced an impasse. He was right. Nothing had changed—he was as stubborn and narrow-minded as ever when it came to her.

Natasha inched toward the edge, ready to get off the table, when his hand clamped down on her shoulder.

"Don't get up. Tetanus shot first," he said, turning to the table beside her.

She twisted her neck to see if the syringe was there, but she couldn't see over his broad shoulders. "Fine, I'll take the shot. In my arm and from someone other than you."

"I wasn't planning on it," he said coolly. "Judy will be in shortly." He turned and stalked away.

Natasha got off the examining table when he shut the door. She promptly called her agent, Marty Cranshaw, only to get the bad news that Simon had replaced her temporarily and called a put-in rehearsal for Lisette.

"No sense in going to the theatre now. Most likely they'll be there all night. Go home and rest, hon," Marty said in a caring voice.

"I will, but make no mistake, Marty. I'll be back on that stage stronger than ever for opening night," she said fervently.

Marty chuckled. "I know you will. Have I ever doubted you?"

"Nope, and that's why I love you. Bye, Marty," Natasha said, hanging up with a smile.

A smiling, middle-aged woman walked in holding a pair of blue scrubs in one hand and a small metal tray with a syringe in the other hand. "I brought these pants for you to put on after I give you the shot. We keep a few extra pairs in the office for the nurses."

"Thanks. That's very kind of you. I can't exactly leave here in a leather jacket and panties," Natasha said grimacing. "Which arm do you want? Right or left?"

"Neither. Doc ordered it in your gluteus muscle. Bottoms up," Judy said cheerfully.

14

"Great." Natasha rolled her eyes and privately cursed Ian. "Let's get it over with then."

"First a tiny jab, then a bit of stinging as the liquid goes in. Relax your muscles so it won't hurt," Nurse Judy said. She pulled on plastic gloves and lowered the edge of Natasha's panties, rubbing alcohol on the spot she'd inject.

Natasha gritted her teeth and silently endured the needle even though it hurt when the liquid went in.

"Okay, we're finished, dear. If the area gets sore or swollen, put an ice pack or a bag of frozen veggies on it. That should take care of it," Judy said reassuringly.

With a nod, Natasha turned over and reached for the scrubs.

"I love your hair color. I want to dye mine the same shade of red, but yours looks natural," Judy said, patting her short curly brown hair.

"It is." Natasha smiled. "You should go for it. It would look great on you."

Judy grinned broadly. "Thanks, I think I will. You're the Broadway actress aren't you?" she asked as she helped Natasha into the drawstring pants.

"Yes. Do you like musicals?"

Judy's big brown eyes sparkled with enthusiasm. "I *love* musicals. They're my biggest indulgence. I heard you're starring in 'The Bee's Knees'. When is it—"

A few sharp raps on the door interrupted her question as Ian entered. "All done?"

"Yes. All done, doc." Judy winked at Natasha and left the room.

"Are you planning any more surprise jabs before you let me go?" Natasha inquired with a sleek lift of one brow.

Ian's lips twitched. "You needed the shot, so don't complain. You can leave now, but you'll have a hard time finding a taxi at this hour. My car service will take you home."

"Thanks, that's kind of you," she said, grateful for his consideration.

"Are you still in pain?"

Natasha gave a half-shrug. "Not too much. I'll take a painkiller when I get home if it feels worse."

He handed her two prescriptions and written instructions. "Come back in a week for a recheck. I'm leaving for London tomorrow. Carla will give you an appointment with my partner, Dr. Delacorte."

Natasha hid her disappointment. He didn't intend to see her again? Ian was acting so detached, it made her nostalgic for the Ian of before—the young man who'd told her she was his first love, his only love. If he hadn't been so dead set on making her leave everything behind to join him in Scotland, things would have worked out between them. It was ironic he was still in town. *All that time wasted apart.* He had been too damn proud and stubborn to take her calls afterward, making her withdraw and immerse herself full force in her career to heal the pain of their split.

"Tell me something," she said, on impulse. "Why are you still living in New York when you were so eager to make Scotland your permanent home?"

A flash of annoyance hardened his features. "I intend to move back as soon as my clinic is ready. It's taken longer than I'd planned," he said in a strained voice.

"Oh. I'm sorry to hear it," she said softly. Natasha recalled his Aunt Maggie, whom she'd stayed in touch with over the years, telling her that Ian's inheritance was still unresolved. Was it because of that? *Better not go there.* The shuttered look on Ian's face silenced further questions.

Ian's eyes narrowed on Natasha. She might sound concerned and have a kind heart, but there was no room in it for him. Her fair cheeks glowed pink and her wide blue eyes were clouded with disappointment, yet he felt no compunction to feed her curiosity. Not now, especially when reclaiming Glenhaven was so close at hand.

The first time he'd set eyes on Natasha was when she'd visited from the States with her parents. She was a dreamy-eyed dazzler, recently graduated from Juilliard and ripe for romance. Ian's father, Malcolm, and her father, Walter, had known each other since they were students at Oxford, but it was the first time Ian had met Natasha. From that moment on he couldn't get enough of her. Her warmth and sparkling wit were just what he'd needed during the lowest point of his life when he'd learned many disturbing things about his late father. Drawn into the cocoon of her beautiful heart, Ian had immediately set out to keep her in Scotland as long as he could and make her fall in love with him as rapidly, and completely, as he had with her.

She'd stayed the whole summer and captivated not only Ian, but also his Aunt Maggie and Uncle Ranald, the caretakers of Glenhaven Estate. Tasha had embraced Scotland as if she'd always lived there. He had loved sharing his homeland with her and she'd been as delighted as a kid at Disneyworld. She'd wanted to explore every castle, sample the local food and fine Scottish whiskey and meet his friends and neighbors. By the end of that glorious summer, he wanted to keep her with him forever, but they embarked on a long-distance romance for two long years, taking numerous passion-filled trips back and forth while she performed in America and he finished his doctoral degree in biomedical science. The moment he graduated, he proposed and she accepted, tears of joy flowing down her cheeks.

Sharp desire made him shift his stance as he stared at Tasha, a stunning woman now. More enticing than ever.

"If anyone can solve this, it's you, Dr. Who," Natasha said, jolting him back to the present.

Ian stiffened at hearing her nickname for him and the teasing intonation in her voice.

"Don't you remember I used to call you that?" she said, a soft smile playing at her rosy lips.

"No," he lied, looking away from her tempting mouth. Of course, he remembered. Tasha had loved the popular British sci fi show since she'd first seen it.

"I think you do." The tiny dimple at the left corner of her mouth deepened seductively. It was the same dimple that had lured him to kiss her for the first time. Ian's palms grew damp while he scrutinized Natasha's face. *Still the face of an angel—a wayward one.* Her creamy complexion, flushed pink now, was framed by long, burnished copper curls. Luminous, curly-lashed blue eyes tantalized him, and her mouth, lush and pink, held his attention. It was the sweetest mouth he'd ever kissed—and the most deceptive.

*I want a chance to make it on Broadway. Theatre is my life. I love you, Ian, but I would be miserable without performing.* She'd said those words when she'd broken off their engagement—after telling him for months that she loved him and couldn't wait to be his wife! He had offered his love and a wonderful life complete with a castle and servants in Scotland, but she had made an immediate about-face right after her controlling mother had interfered.

Anitra had flown to Glenhaven from New York the previous day to muck things up between them. He recalled their meeting as if it were yesterday. The witch had laughed mockingly in his face as she'd spewed hateful words. *Natasha needs to spread her wings. She's destined to be a Broadway star like me. You didn't really think she'd give up her career to marry you and move to Scotland, did you? To be a country doctor's wife surrounded by sheep? My daughter adores the theatre, much more than she'll ever love you!*

Ian had barely held onto his temper and hadn't given into the urge to drag Anitra's bony behind out of his castle for good. Unfortunately, her harsh words were confirmed the next day when Natasha ended their engagement—by phone. He'd never forget the feeling of being gutted by her and he wasn't about to waste another second trying to figure her out. Impatient to end their little visit, Ian took hold of her elbow and helped her down from the table.

"Does your mother know you're injured?" he asked curtly.

"No, and I plan to keep it that way. I'm not the same girl you knew seven years ago. I've made it on my own, *without* Anitra's help."

"Still not calling her mum?" he said with a shake of his head.

"Nope. As far as Anitra's concerned, she's too young to have a thirty year old daughter," Natasha said ironically.

Ian snorted. "So that's how it is. Pity that."

"I don't want to talk about Anitra. Can't we make peace, Ian? Or are you going to continue scowling at me?"

Natasha's gaze was direct as she waited for his answer. Now that she'd brought it into the open, he couldn't summon the initial bitterness he'd felt at seeing her again. He just felt empty inside. She had once held the deepest part of his heart and soul captive and he'd loved her ardently, but they had no future together.

Ian headed toward the door and said, "Time to go, wee *nyaff*."

"Just a minute." Natasha grabbed his sleeve and faced him with fiery blue eyes as she tossed her flaming curls. "Don't call me an irritating little person!" She thrust her chin up and smiled slyly. "*Dunderheid*," she retaliated, daring to insult him.

Ian stifled the rumble of caustic laughter rising in his chest. They hadn't spent more than an hour together and they were already trading insults. Tasha had a way of getting under his skin and provoking him more than anyone else could, yet her quick wit never ceased to entertain him.

Striding out the door, he squashed the powerful urge to turn and grab the maddening redhead and kiss her senseless. And that wasn't all he felt like doing.

# CHAPTER TWO

Natasha stood in front of her apartment door and tried to shake off the profound yearning her visit with Ian had stirred in her heart. If she'd ever imagined them reuniting, he had dashed her last hope today. A wave of dread swept over her as she turned the key in the lock to enter her lonely apartment. The only bright spot would be her puppy waiting to greet her. She could hear Evita barking on the other side.

When she opened the door, Evita flung herself at her barking frantically. Startled, Natasha cradled her in her arms. "What's wrong, baby?" she crooned, kissing the top of her furry orange head. "I'm sorry I'm late. You must be starving."

Evita gave a shrill bark and convulsively jerked her little body back and forth. The second Natasha set her on the floor, Evita sprinted into the living room barking wildly. Natasha ran after her and caught a whiff of a putrid odor as she passed by the kitchen. She froze and her heart nearly stopped when she caught sight of her ransacked living room. Her sofa was turned upside down with the lining in tatters. The pale apricot silk wing chairs were upended, their shredded insides resembling linguini. Her treasured art and dance books formed a messy pile at the base of the built-in shelves. Even her ferns were tipped over, their dumped soil forming little hills on the wood parquet floor.

Rigid with fear, she racked her brain on what to do next. Check what was causing the foul odor in the kitchen? No way. It could be a dead body. Terror snaked up her backbone as she scooped up Evita and ran into the hall. She rode the elevator down to the floor below and got out in the hall as she dialed 9-1-1 on her smartphone. After she reported the emergency, they kept her on the line until two detectives arrived at her apartment.

She rode up the elevator and met them in the hall. "I'm so glad you're here," she said when she saw them..

"Ms. White, I'm Detective Carson," a tall, fit woman in her late thirties said, "and this is Detective Peterson." She indicated a young, athletic man with a blond buzz cut beside. They both flashed their police IDs. Neither wore a uniform, but they held guns.

"Stay out here," Detective Peterson said. "We'll check things and let you know when it's safe to go inside." Moments later, he stepped into the hallway. "You can come in now."

"Thanks. I have to check my room," Natasha said.

Detective Peterson nodded. "We'll be in the kitchen."

On unsteady legs, Natasha entered the bedroom and gasped when she saw her queen sized mattress flung off the box spring and slashed like her living room furniture. Feathers were scattered everywhere, torn from the inside of her goose down pillows. She ran to the dresser and found her black lacquer jewelry box exactly where she had left it.

She set Evita down and opened the mother-of-pearl inset lid and exhaled a blast of relief when she saw the South Sea pearl necklace and earrings Ian had given her on their first Christmas together. With trembling hands, she lifted the jewelry out of the box. She slipped the pearl studs in her earlobes and placed the pearl choker necklace on her neck with a grateful sigh.

Why hadn't they taken her most valuable set of jewelry? There was no sign of forced entry and as far as she could tell, nothing of value had been stolen. Thank God, her laptop was where she always kept it, in the bottom zippered panel of her dance bag.

Natasha's heart plummeted when she saw the reprint of Gustav Klimt's "The Kiss" in shambles beside the bed. The print wasn't valuable, but the shattered memories of when Ian had bought if for her made her terribly sad. Squatting beside it on the floor, she checked to see if there was any way to salvage it.

Detective Carson called out to her. "Ms. White, come to the kitchen."

As she approached the kitchen, Natasha smelled the foul odor again. She joined the officers and saw every cabinet open and her groceries and non-perishables strewn on the counters. She glanced in the sink and clapped a hand over her mouth when she saw a hunk of brownish green rotting beef. A metal skewer stuck out from the raw meat and brown blood seeped from the gaping hole. On the skewer a paper with letters glued on it said, "Fork it over or this will be you."

Natasha gripped the kitchen counter as a surge of nausea made her gag. "I don't get it. Why the raw meat?"

Detective Carson studied her gravely. "The Capelli family just staked your apartment as their property. The rotting beef is their trademark. Looks like they've targeted you."

"Me? But why? I don't even know them." Natasha's eyes ached and her head pounded as a million thoughts raced through her mind, none of them making sense. The only thing certain was that someone was out to get her and she had no idea why. Thank God, Evita was safe!

The officers exchanged a grim look and Detective Carson cleared her throat. "You'd better sit down," she said, righting a fallen chair for Natasha. "We've been investigating Tony Martin's murder."

"*Murder?*" Appalled, Natasha sank into a chair before her legs buckled. Her heart ricocheted against her ribs as she said in a quiet voice, "I thought it was an accident."

"It was no accident. We believe a member of the Capelli mob ran Tony's car off the bridge to kill him," Detective Carson said. "They left rotting beef in Tony's apartment on the night he was murdered."

Natasha's stomach lurched. "I can't believe it. Why would they kill him?"

"Your boyfriend had important information on the syndicate," Detective Carson said.

"Tony wasn't my boyfriend. We dated for a while— that's all. I didn't know he had any connection with crime."

"Are you sure?" Detective Peterson demanded.

"Yes, of course I'm sure. I wouldn't have gone out with him if I'd known he was even remotely involved with the mob."

Initially, she'd been attracted to Tony because he was handsome and darkly exciting. But a few weeks before he'd died in the accident, she'd cut him off when he had unleashed his violent temper on her. He had pushed hard for sex without a commitment, and Natasha had stalled him. At first, he'd teased her about being a prude, but one evening he lost his patience and his temper exploded. He slapped her face and slammed her hard against the wall when she said she wanted to take things slowly. She kneed his groin and narrowly escaped being raped as she ran away from him. Staggering forward, he had roared after her. *It isn't over between us. It never will be. I'll be back for you!* That night she changed her phone number and told the doormen not to allow Tony in the building.

The next day, her back and shoulders were badly bruised where they'd hit the concrete wall, courtesy of Tony's shove. He had been back a few times to see her, but her doormen hadn't let him in the building. She had thought about getting a restraining order, but shortly afterward she heard he was dead.

"Tony had been working with the D.A.'s office to convict the Capelli mob. They run the largest family crime syndicate in the city," Detective Carson said.

"What does that have to do with me?"

"They're looking for a flash drive he had at the time of his murder. It incriminates the entire Capelli family and their employees on illegal activities," Detective Peterson said.

"But we had stopped dating weeks before he died. I don't have any of his things here."

"They must think you do," he said.

"I can't imagine how they got up here. The doormen are very strict, and there's a camera in every elevator."

"We're looking into it," Detective Peterson said. "Be on your guard at all times and find a safe place to stay for the next few days until we contact you. They're ruthless."

It was suddenly too much to bear. First the cut on her thigh followed by the emotionally draining visit with Ian and now this. Had the street attack on her leg been random…or on purpose? Should she tell the detectives about it? Not yet. They might think she had more going on than she actually did, even a connection with the mob. It was insane and alarming at every level.

Natasha's throat locked and her chest compressed with panic. Her stomach heaved at the sickening smell of rotting beef and she couldn't take it a second longer. She thrust Evita in Detective Carson's arms and bolted to the bathroom where she vomited in the toilet bowl.

When she finally raised her head and was able to control the heaves, she rinsed her mouth, brushed her teeth and joined the officers in the living room. Too agitated to sit calmly, she paced the room with Evita in her arms while Detective Carson filled out a report and Detective Peterson worked the crime scene.

In a daze, she waited until they finished and left before she ventured back to her bedroom. She set Evita in the middle of her bed and petted her until she settled down. "Stay here, baby, while I get my important papers together. Then we're off to Aunt Ronnie's apartment."

Evita yipped in agreement and rewarded Natasha's hand with licks.

Kneeling next to the bed, Natasha searched for the plastic accordion file case underneath where she kept her important documents and passport. She found the empty file tilted sideways and papers strewn everywhere. She slid under the bed and gathered the papers, her heart leaping with relief when she found her passport.

With no time to waste, she threw an overnight bag together and searched for Evita's favorite toy, a fuzzy white goose that made a funny honking sound. She packed the toy goose, Evita's leopard fur comforter, her little camel cashmere coat, her rust and tan tartan collar and leash, and a chewy toy inside her carrying kennel.

Now to face the kitchen. On leaden feet, Natasha dragged herself there. The detectives had taken the rotting beef and the note as evidence, but the kitchen still stank horridly. She popped a peppermint in her mouth and tied a clean scarf around her mouth and nose to block the smell as she disinfected and scoured the sink with bleach. She grabbed the small bag of dog food and added it to Evita's traveling kennel before leaving the kitchen.

Looking around her trashed apartment, she wished she could put everything back to order, but she had to leave immediately. With the accordion file under one arm and her dance bag and overnight bag slung over her shoulders, she carried Evita in the kennel and headed for Ronnie's apartment.

It was the perfect place for her to sleep tonight. Ronnie and her new husband, Nick, were honeymooning in Bali and Natasha still had the key to Ronnie's apartment from when she had housesat for her several months ago. Thankfully, the newly married couple had decided to keep Ronnie's apartment in New York after their marriage and Ronnie's relocation to Starfish Island.

She'd met Ronnie Whitcomb (now Cameron) and her other close friend, Teddy Behr, at Camp Merry Cascades in North Carolina as a child. They had forged a lifelong friendship and called themselves the Heart Sisters. She wished one of them was nearby to keep her company tonight.

That night, Natasha tossed and turned in bed while Evita snored softly beside her. Every time she closed her eyes, disturbing images of Tony thrashing about in murky water and gasping for air invaded her subconscious. She relived the violent way he'd assaulted her and realized that was mild compared to what a crime syndicate was capable of doing to her. She had a cut on her thigh to prove it! There was no doubt in her mind now that it hadn't been a random act.

The following morning, the cut didn't hurt and there was no redness around it, but her hip was sore from the shot. At least the wound was healing well. Natasha hastened to get ready and tried not to think of how emotionally draining it had been to see him again.

When she arrived at her apartment, she was shocked to find Rico Gamberi, Tony Martin's partner, standing beside the entrance of her building. She took a step backward as Evita growled at the tall man. Looking suave in tailored black Italian suit and polished Bally loafers, Rico leaned forward and she got an unwelcome whiff of cologne mingled with cigar smoke.

"Rico. What are you doing here?" she said, recoiling instantly. Rico owned half of Tony's jazz club and Natasha had never trusted him. He was a smooth operator and now he was the sole owner. Could he have something to do with Tony's death? Did he know who had destroyed her belongings looking for the flash drive?

Rico's flinty eyes narrowed. "We need to talk."

"About what?" she asked cautiously.

He grabbed her elbow. "Not here. Let's go to your apartment."

"Let go of me," she said, struggling out of his grip. "Whatever you have to say, you can say here."

"Where's the flash drive?"

Natasha glared at him. "What flash drive?"

"Tony's flash drive. Don't act stupid."

Evita growled deep in her throat and bared her pointy teeth at him. Natasha petted Evita's head and stared at Rico, taken aback by the aggressive side of him she'd never seen. He'd always gone out of his way to be friendly the few times she'd gone to the nightclub.

"I don't have Tony's flash drive or anything else that belonged to him," she said frantically. What kind of connection did Rico have with the Capelli family? Did he work for them?

"Stop playing games, bitch. You're lying," he said in a chilling voice.

She swallowed hard. "No, I'm not!"

Rico grabbed Natasha's shoulders in an iron grip and shook her. Although lean, he was strong as Hercules.

With a voracious snarl, Evita lunged forward and nipped Rico's arm.

"Shit! Fucking little turd." Rico grabbed Evita by the nape and squeezed hard, making her whimper in distress.

"Let go of her," Natasha screamed, making people on the sidewalk stop and turn around.

Rico's eyes turned lethal as he released Evita's neck. "Give up the flash drive or it'll be your neck next time. Tony found out the hard way," he snarled before darting across the street.

Natasha ran into her building as Evita barked ferociously all the way to the elevator, ignoring the doorman's confused look.

On the elevator ride up, Natasha cradled Evita close and said soothingly, "You're safe now, baby. I'm sorry that bastard hurt you." Inside the apartment, the pup calmed down and curled up in her little bed. After a few dramatic groans, she was out.

Natasha's stomach roiled remembering Rico's words. *Give up the flash drive or it'll be your neck the next time. Tony found out the hard way.*

She anxiously raced through her apartment gathering things. What was she going to do? She didn't want to leave, but if she stayed in the city and continued in "The Bee's Knees", she'd be risking her life and she'd have to hire a bodyguard to protect her. That was out of the question.

If she left the city, she'd be safe, but it might be career suicide. Marty would have to negotiate getting her out of her contract and her professional reputation would be tarnished. It was no cliché that on Broadway the show must go on, no matter what.

Natasha's ringing smartphone jolted her from her thoughts. Weird, there was no number on the caller ID. She didn't answer and waited until it went to voice mail where she listened to a muffled man's voice say, "Give it up or you're next. Better watch your ass. And your ugly mutt's too."

The caller's voice didn't sound like Rico, but he could have been disguising it. What connection did he have with the Capellis? Natasha's belly did a sharp somersault of fear. The mob had already murdered Tony because of the flash drive.

She and Evita might be next. They had to get out of NYC fast!

# CHAPTER THREE

Natasha stared at Evita peacefully asleep in her little bed. Thankfully, they hadn't destroyed Evita's things. She couldn't bear the thought of any harm coming to her little fur baby, even though Evita was far from helpless. She must have put up quite a fight, barking and growling. It was a miracle they hadn't harmed her, she thought, her stomach churning.

Natasha couldn't imagine spending another night fearing for their safety. She was making the right decision. After toiling long hours perfecting her musical theatre talents, putting up with aching feet, strained vocal chords and a weary body, she was on her way to the top. But her newfound success would have to be put on hold. Now that she had to choose between her life and fame, life took precedence.

Her smartphone rang again, spooking her. She jumped and her hand trembled on the phone as she checked the number. She felt a surge of relief, then surprise, when she saw it was Ian's Aunt Maggie calling. Maggie Duncan was the closest thing Natasha had to maternal love, and she cherished their warm relationship. Even after her split up with Ian, they had stayed in contact.

Why would Maggie be phoning if they had chatted and caught up just last week? She glanced at the time. 10:15 a.m. in the States, which made it early afternoon in Scotland.

Natasha drew in a deep breath and steadied her voice. "Hi, Maggie. How are you?"

"Weel, I'm a wee bit worried, lass," Maggie said in an uneasy tone.

"You are? About what?" Natasha asked, surprised.

"I had a nightmare last night. About you." She paused. "I have a sixth sense about things. Are you all right?"

Natasha hesitated. She didn't want to lie to Maggie, but she didn't want to worry her either. After a moment, she said, "I'm fine, Maggie."

"You don't sound fine to me. I can tell in your voice," Maggie persisted. Natasha could just imagine the stubborn tilt of her chin and her round cheeks puffed up with conviction.

"I don't want to worry you..." Natasha said with a sigh, suspecting Maggie wouldn't stop until she pried it out of her.

"Too late. I'm worried already. Would you rather tell Ranald about it? He's tugging on my sleeve wanting to speak with you, lass. Or shall I call Ian?" she inquired slyly.

"No. Absolutely not." There was no fooling Maggie and she sure knew which buttons to press. "Okay, I'll tell you, but promise me you won't contact Ian."

"Well now. I don't like promising that, but I will," Maggie said resignedly. "What's going on?"

Natasha couldn't very well tell her she was terrified of the Capellis. She hadn't slept a wink last night worrying they might try to break her legs so she couldn't dance, or damage her throat so she could never sing again. She shuddered when she remembered the rotting meat they'd left in her sink and what the detectives had said it meant. The Capelli family was capable of viciously terminating her thirty year old life, like they'd done to Tony.

"Are you there, lass? I can't hear you," Maggie fretted.

"Yes, I'm here." Natasha swallowed hard. "This may sound convoluted, but…uh…." She drew in a deep breath and said, "I have to go into hiding. The mob is after me."

"Whaaat!" Maggie exclaimed.

Natasha heard Ranald talking in the background and Maggie saying, "Wait, Ranald. Let the lass explain and then I'll tell ye what's happening." Getting back to Natasha, she asked, "Why on earth do you think they're after you?"

"I don't just *think* so, Maggie, I know so. They think I have damaging evidence against them."

"Why would they think that?" Maggie sounded utterly perplexed.

"Because Tony, the guy I was dating a while ago, had incriminating information about the mob on a flash drive that he was going to turn over to the Fed."

"Why is the mob after you if Tony has it?"

"Because Tony is dead and the police think he was murdered. But that's not all. Someone trashed my apartment yesterday looking for the flash drive."

Maggie gasped. "The good Lord above have mercy on us! Have you gone to the police?"

"Yes. They're investigating it, but they can't guarantee my safety 24/7. I'm going to have to leave here."

"You bet!" Maggie cried. "Come to Glenhaven. Ranald and I would love to have you here again."

"Thank you for offering, but I can't put the two of you in danger."

"Och, don't be daft. Glenhaven is verra far away from New York. Even if it were close, the thick stone walls of the castle would keep you safe. You must come." She paused. "*Dinna fash* about Ian. He's traveling to London tomorrow and won't be coming to Glenhaven."

Natasha knew that already, but she didn't want to get into her injury and the fact that she'd been to Ian's office.

Maggie continued, "The lad has pressing business in London, but he said he had return to his patients in New York."

*Lad* was not the word Natasha would have chosen for someone as formidable as Ian, but his Aunt Maggie would always see him as a lad since she'd helped raise him after his mother's death. He was the son Maggie and Ranald never had, and Ian loved them very much.

"Stop *swithering* over it. You must come right away," Maggie urged.

"I'm not sure I can. I still have to find a place for Evita."

"Bring her with you. Aren't I her godmother?" Maggie said with mock offense.

"Yes, you are," Natasha said with an indulgent smile. Maggie hadn't even met Evita, but right away she'd appointed herself as her godmother.

"When you have your flight information, email us. Ranald will meet you at Inverness Airport and drive you to Glenhaven."

"That's very kind of you. I can't wait to see you and Ranald again. Thank you so much!"

"You're welcome. I can hardly wait too, lovey. Everything will be fine once you're back at Glenhaven."

Natasha hung up with nostalgic eagerness to see Maggie and Ranald again…and the splendor of Glenhaven Castle.

Whoever said life got easier as you got older? Oh yeah, Dad. Dear Dad who always looked on the bright side of life, unlike his difficult wife. How could two opposite people who constantly fought still be married? Why her easygoing Midwestern father ever married high strung Anitra in the first place, Natasha would never know, but they remained married, living separate lives while Dad taught in Boston and Anitra currently performed in the West End in London.

Turning her thoughts away from her puzzling parents, Natasha drew in a deep breath and dialed her agent's number.

"Hey hon, how's the leg?" Marty said, the minute he answered.

"It's healing. But I have another more pressing matter I need your help with, Marty," Natasha said.

After she explained her complicated and dire situation, he agreed to re-negotiate her contract with a leave of absence. He wasn't happy about it, especially since it involved a loss of revenue for both of them, but he agreed that her safety came first.

Relieved that Marty was looking out for her career, Natasha sent emails to her dad and her younger brother Robert, telling them she had a minor leg injury and needed to leave the show to recuperate. Next she dialed Anitra's number in London. There was no getting around it. Soon the news that she'd been replaced by Lisette would hit the media and Anitra would come barreling forward to intervene. She wanted to avoid that at all costs. Anitra was a control freak and barely tolerated, but revered, in the performing world because of her numerous Tony Awards.

When Anitra didn't answer and her recorded message came on, a dull ache settled in the pit of Natasha's belly along with vast relief that she wouldn't have to deal with her. The only time Anitra seemed interested in her was if it concerned Natasha's career, and that's exactly when Natasha wanted her to butt out. When she first realized Natasha had inherited her extraordinary vocal range, Anitra had tried to groom her as a mini-me, urging her to dye her hair black like her own, but Natasha wouldn't have it. She didn't share her mother's ruthless ambition or her huge ego.

Natasha had spent her youth trying to live up to her mother's stringent expectations until the fateful day she ended things with Ian. In a moment of panic, Natasha had heeded to her mother's words. *You'll be stepping back in time a hundred years if you move to Glenhaven. Think! Do you want to throw everything away you've worked so hard for? You're young and destined to be a star. Act like it! If he truly loves you, he'll let you fly.*

The moment Natasha broke off her engagement with Ian, she regretted it, but it was too late. The damage had been done and Anitra had swept in like an avenging angel, facilitating Natasha's entry into stardom. Caught up in the glory of her first role on Broadway, it was a while before the glamour faded and Natasha realized how urgently Anitra had fought to separate them. When Natasha had tried to talk to Ian, he'd refused her calls.

He'd also returned her letters unopened, breaking her heart with his stubbornness.

Shaking off the wretched memories, Natasha packed two suitcases, one for herself and one for Evita, and then concentrated on searching the Internet for flights to Inverness.

In the midst of her search, Michael the doorman called. "Natasha, a Dr. Ian MacGregor is here to see you. Should I let him up?"

*Ian was in her building?* "Okay, but please ask for his ID before you let him up." After the break-in yesterday, she wasn't taking any chances.

Natasha stepped into the hall and waited for Ian to come up. The moment he emerged from the elevator, her pulse pounded wildly. Impeccably dressed in a dark olive bonded Burberry trench coat, his thick dark hair was tousled from the wind and his sharp cheekbones were tinged pink from the crisp autumn air. Natasha shivered at the purposeful glint in his silver-green eyes as he strode toward her.

"Ian. Why are you here?" With shaky hands, she closed the door behind her and stood with her back to it, summoning as much composure as she could in spite of her pounding heart.

"You have to ask?" His unswerving gaze held her hostage as he closed the distance between them. "Your injury yesterday wasn't an accident, was it?"

"I honestly don't know," she said, dread inching up her spine when she realized she was going to have to tell him about Tony…eventually.

"Why didn't you tell me you were in trouble?" he demanded, his voice low and controlled.

Her chin shot up. "I'm not in trouble."

Ian's hands closed over her shoulders and squeezed just enough to get her attention. "Well, you're definitely in danger." When she remained silent, he searched her eyes intently. "Are you all right, then?"

"I'm fine." Natasha swallowed against the lump in her throat brought on by his kindness and interest in her well-being. But who was she kidding? He'd obviously been sent by his Aunt Maggie to check on her.

"Darn that Maggie," she said, flushing. "She promised she wouldn't say anything to you until I got things sorted out."

Ian released her shoulders and shook his head. "It wasn't Maggie. Ranald had the sense to call me the minute Maggie hung up with you. You should have told me what was going on, Tasha," he chastised.

What kind of game did he think she'd been playing with him? "That's not fair. All this happened *after* I went to see you!" she said, her hands clenched at her sides.

"Have you packed your bag yet?"

"Yes."

"Is your passport up to date?" he asked briskly.

"Yes. Everything's in order. I've traveled before, you know." She gave him an exasperated look.

"Get your things. I'm taking you to Scotland. The executive jet is waiting."

Astonished, she reared back and gawked at him. "But I thought you were going to London."

"I am, after I drop you off in Inverness," he said simply.

Natasha was speechless. He would be going out of his way to take her there first and then backtrack to London. Why?

"Are you ready?" he said, his words tinged with a Scottish burr.

*Was she ready?* Natasha privately rejoiced at the unexpected turn of events, but jittery nerves quivered deep in her belly. Ian's vibrant energy flowed straight into her vulnerable heart as she stood there helplessly staring at him. It had only been hours since he'd doctored her wound and he was already taking charge, protecting her and getting to her in ways that only he could.

"What about my puppy? I have to take her with me," Natasha said.

"Aye. Maggie told me about Evita. You can bring her too." Ian put his hand on the doorknob and turned it.

"Wait!" Natasha put her hand over his, but snatched it back the second her palm grazed the back of his hand, eliciting tingles that spread through her like electric currents. "You can't come inside. I'm sorry if that sounds rude, but I'd rather you wait out here while I get my suitcase...and Evita," she said in a rush. She hadn't had a chance to put things in order, and she didn't want Ian to see how badly they'd ransacked her apartment.

Surprisingly, he nodded in resignation. The fierce protectiveness in his eyes made her want to melt into his strong arms. She released her half-held breath and with a bittersweet sigh turned the doorknob. "I'll be out in a few minutes."

Natasha wondered about Ian's plans as she gathered her suitcases and Evita's travel kennel. As soon as she opened the door and joined him in the hall, Ian took the kennel from her hands. He lifted the barking and agitated Evita out and held her gently as he spoke to her in a quiet tone. Openmouthed, Natasha watched as Evita calmed down almost instantly.

"Way to go, Ian. Evita is pretty feisty. You're better than the dog whisperer," she said, unable to hide her delight. Who could blame her puppy when she went limp in Ian's hold and licked his hand? That's how compliant Natasha felt at the moment, and Ian hadn't even whispered the soothing Scottish words he'd said to her pup.

"Let's go." Ian placed Evita in the kennel and handed it to Natasha before lifting the other suitcases and heading to the elevator.

Following behind, Natasha smiled at the solid set of Ian's broad shoulders and straight back as she tried to keep up with his pace. In spite of the dire circumstances for their impromptu trip, she was looking forward to having eight long hours with him in close quarters.

"As soon as we board, we'll have a lobster dinner." He casually threw it out there, but his words tempted her like no other man could, and she was certain he knew it.

"Oh," she said, suddenly hungry. "I have a weakness for lobster." *And you*, she silently added.

"I know." His silver-green wolf eyes glittered enigmatically. The only sign that he might be feeling as off-kilter as she, was the blank look he steadfastly kept on his face to hide his emotions.

Before leaving, Natasha told the doorman she was going out of town. On the ride to the airport, she called Detective Carson and gave her an email address and Maggie's phone number in Scotland, in addition to her cell phone.

She settled back in the plush seat of Ian's hired sedan and glanced at his striking profile as he checked his emails on his smartphone. She couldn't believe they were on their way to his homeland. A frisson of exhilaration shot through her as she thought of staying at Glenhaven Castle again. It was built like a fortress and remotely hidden in the lush, misty Highlands. To soothe her jumpy nerves, Natasha summoned images of salmon-filled crystalline Scottish lochs and blue-green grass, of grand mountains covered in heather and winding glens.

But it didn't work. Glenhaven held bittersweet memories, especially Ian's castle where he had first made love to her. Now he was being protective and cordial, but his body language told her he wanted distance. Ian could be tough and uncompromising—she knew that only too well. But long ago, he'd been tender and loving. She wanted that Ian back more than anything in the world, but she had been the one who had cut him off.

Gazing at him now, she knew he was studiously ignoring her. Natasha's heart ached with longing as she turned her gaze away from him and looked down at her hands clenched together on her lap.

It was high time they healed the rift.

# CHAPTER FOUR

Aboard the flight, Ian watched Natasha fuss over Evita, wrapping her in a leopard fur blanket and smothering her in kisses. "You're such a smart doggie, and brave too. Who's my cute little pom pom? You are, Evita," Natasha cooed.

"Oh brother," Ian groaned, rolling his eyes.

Natasha ignored Ian and continued her baby talk to Evita. "Now go to sleep and when you wake up, Mommy will have a surprise for you." She placed her pup back in the kennel and Evita licked Natasha's hands as she gazed at her through adoring chocolate brown eyes.

"Where'd you get that silly blanket for her?"

Natasha glanced up and grinned. "Hey, don't judge. It makes her relax. Look how she fell right asleep. It was a gift from my friend Teddy, who I'll have you know has fabulous taste and bought most of Evita's wardrobe."

He snorted in disbelief. "Your dog has a wardrobe?"

Her chin shot up. "Yes, and she looks smashing in everything."

Long copper waves framed Natasha's creamy complexion as her eyes sparkled radiantly. Keeping his expression bland, he studied the pearl studs in her dainty earlobes and the string of pearls around her slender neck. The jewels he'd given her adorned her in places he liked to kiss—to own—the warm pulse behind her ears, the soft, bare skin of her nape beneath her glossy hair. His gaze dropped to her right hand where she pointed to the kennel, her slender fingers pale and unadorned except for garnet nail polish. She'd once worn his engagement ring on that soft hand.

A young brunette flight attendant approached them with a friendly smile. "Hi, my name is Lori. What would you like to drink with your dinner today? I can offer you white or red wine, soft drinks, juice, coffee, tea or mineral water."

"I'd like a glass of mineral water. Flat, no bubbles please," Natasha said.

"Same for me. And please bring us a bottle of chardonnay," Ian said.

The flight attendant nodded and left.

"Are you comfortable?" he asked.

"Are you kidding? This plane is gorgeous and so big. A lot of people could ride here," Natasha said.

"Nine to be exact."

She slid her hand across the cushion and patted it. "White leather and mahogany paneling. Nice. Is it yours?"

Ian nodded. "Yes. Some might find it excessive, but this plane was worth every cent."

"What kind of an airplane is it?"

"It's a Bombardier Challenger 300 jet. It's efficient and cuts my traveling time in half."

Natasha gave a throaty chuckle, the sound pleasing to his ears. "You don't have to sell me on it. After this, it'll be hard to fly commercial again."

"How is your wound? Did you remember to take your antibiotic?"

"Yes, doc."

"Did you feel any itching or see redness this morning?"

"Nope. It looked fine. But another part of me is sore," she grumbled.

His mouth twitched. "Can't help you there. I'll take a look at the cut later."

She eyed him with a humorous lift of her brow. "This is hardly the place to examine my thigh. You'll just have to take my word for it."

Natasha had taken her leather jacket off earlier and was wearing a chocolate silk blouse with camel-colored cigarette pants and brown ankle booties. She bounced back lightly on the leather divan and the motion made her breasts jiggle. His palms grew damp as he remembered their soft fullness in his hands years ago. He turned his gaze away from temptation and cleared his throat.

Fluffing her hair, Natasha leaned back and closed her eyes. "Ahhh," she sighed pleasurably, "the leather feels wonderful against my skin. I didn't sleep very well last night." She lowered her chin and watched him through her long lashes, her blue eyes as soft as velvet. Her mouth parted and she licked her plush lower lip as her chest rose and fell with shallow breaths. Entranced, he watched the tiny pulse beat at the hollow of her throat.

*Was she trying to drive him crazy?* When they'd boarded the plane earlier, Ian had sat across from her, but after she'd settled Evita in her kennel, she'd joined him on the divan. Seated close beside him, Natasha smelled like fresh roses. He inhaled deeply, sorely tempted to wind his hand in her lustrous hair and pull her on top of him for slow, deep kisses.

"That looks comfortable." Natasha indicated the two reclining seats down the aisle covered by white down comforters. She stretched and arched her back, and the first button of her blouse strained between her round breasts. He willed it to pop open when he saw the outline of her nipples through the thin silk. "I think I'll stretch my legs and nap there later," she said, gazing at him with a dreamy smile.

"Be my guest." He couldn't control the strain in his voice, taunted by an image of Natasha nestled beneath the comforter, her supple curves naked, sweet nipples wet and pink from his greedy kisses. Hot desire inflamed his groin, making him irritable and frustrated at the strong physical power she had over him. Clamping down his jaw, Ian opened his briefcase and forced sensual images of Tasha firmly out of his mind...and memory.

"Are you going to work now?" she asked, sounding disappointed.

"Aye, I need to prepare for tomorrow's meetings." He pulled his laptop out and turned it on.

"Oh." She grew silent and watched him with curious eyes.

"What?" he said at last.

"You haven't asked me any questions about...you know. My situation." She caught her lower lip between her teeth and waited.

"I heard enough from Ranald," he said tight-lipped.

One graceful brow lifted. "Maybe you should hear it from me."

"Not now. I can't discuss it without wanting to throttle you. What were you thinking getting involved with a shady nightclub owner with connections to a crime syndicate?" Ian shook his head in disgust.

She sucked in an outraged breath and glared at him, blue eyes sparking. "I didn't know he was a shady nightclub owner with connections to a crime syndicate!"

"You were naïve and reckless to date the *scunner*," he said curtly.

Natasha's chin shot up with high indignation. She opened her mouth to retort, but shut it when the flight attendant approached with their drinks and dinner trays.

When Lori left, Natasha said, "I had no idea Tony had ties to the mob. It came as a total surprise. I also didn't know he was murdered. I thought his death had been an accident."

Her revelation slammed into his gut. "Murdered? I didn't know that part."

"Well you do now, and for your information, I stopped dating him way before it happened," she huffed. "That's all I care to talk about. Let's eat."

"Fine," he grunted, spreading the white cloth napkin on his lap.

"Fine," she repeated, taking a long swig of wine. Natasha buttered a piece of crusty roll and chewed it slowly. Ian watched her dip a chunk of meaty lobster in drawn butter and relish every bite. Her lips glistened as she finished both lobster tails, focused on her meal, not Ian

She might not want to talk about it anymore, but one thing was certain. He would make damn sure Maggie and Ranald didn't let Tasha out of their sight while she was in

Glenhaven. Her situation was even grimmer than he'd suspected.

They ate in weighty silence and when they finished, Natasha took off her boots and snuggled under the comforter on the recliner. She turned on her side and fell asleep, her slim and curvy back facing Ian as he worked. He stared at her red-gold hair, her delicate shoulders and the graceful line of her spine for a long while.

He wouldn't have a moment's peace until he knew she was safe again.

When they landed in Inverness, Ian thanked the two pilots, Ron and Jeremy, and Lori, the flight attendant, before deplaning. They went through the formalities at the airport and cleared customs in no time.

Feeling awkward, Natasha quietly stood beside Ian outside Inverness Airport. His unfair criticism and accusations earlier had aroused frustration in her. Now she felt regret as she gazed into his earnest eyes.

"Stay at Glenhaven the whole time you're there. Don't venture into town unless you're with Maggie and Ranald," Ian said firmly.

She looked heavenward. "Isn't that going a bit overboard?" From the resolute angle of his jaw, he didn't seem to think so.

"Promise," he said, his steely voice inflexible.

"Okay, I promise. Dinny get yer knickers in a twist," she said, affecting a Scottish burr.

Ian chuckled in spite of his somber mood. "Look, there's Uncle Ranald."

Ranald drove up in a white Land Rover and parked it beside them. He enveloped Natasha in a bear hug first and then hugged Ian effusively. Shorter than Ian by several inches, Ranald was nevertheless strong and sturdy for a man in his mid-seventies. His long face split into a wide grin.

"Welcome back, dearie. Isn't she a wee bonnie lass, Ian?" Ranald's green eyes twinkled as he beamed at Natasha.

"Aye," Ian said good-naturedly. "That she is."

"Thank you, Ranald. You're too sweet," Natasha said, kissing the older man's weathered cheek.

"I have to go now. I'm leaving Tasha in your care, Uncle Ranald. Keep an eye on her. She likes to roam when she's in Scotland," Ian said, giving Ranald a private wink.

Natasha rolled her eyes. "You make me sound like one of your sheep."

"Nae, a lamb," Ranald quipped as he opened the trunk. He and Ian loaded the suitcases while Natasha lifted Evita's kennel.

"Is that the famous Evita, then?" Ranald threw his head back and laughed when he got a good look at her. "Will you look at her get up?"

Evita lifted her proud little snout and barked at him. She looked fabulous in her cashmere coat and little plaid collar and she knew it. The camel colored coat complemented her orange sable fur perfectly.

"I have to go now," Ian said.

Natasha peered up at him and smiled. "Thank you for everything. I appreciate it very much," she said sincerely and deposited a kiss on each of his lean cheeks, European style. She wished she could linger longer, but she noticed Ranald's eyes dancing as he watched her.

"You're welcome. Mind what I said and be extra careful," Ian said with a meaningful look. "Good bye, Uncle Ranald. I'll call tomorrow."

Natasha watched Ian's strong, proud back as he retreated to his jet and climbed the gangway. Tears stung her eyes when she realized it might be the last time she'd see him. She blinked rapidly, hoping Ranald hadn't noticed her momentary weakness. Ian was returning to New York from London and he hadn't said a word about seeing her again.

With a dejected sigh, she straightened her spine and tried not to look morose as they drove away. Evita cuddled on her lap and licked her hand, sensing Natasha's melancholy mood. Good thing they were riding next to Ranald, who was easygoing and great company. He would keep her distracted with amusing accounts of the village's latest news. Ian had once said his chatty uncle was the only man he knew who loved to gossip.

"So what's the hottest news this week?" Natasha said in an attempt to chase away the blues at parting from Ian.

Ranald handled the steering wheel with one hand and scratched Evita's ears with the other. "Let's see now." He pondered the question for a moment. "Bettina Roberts just had cosmetic work done in Glasgow and she looks verra different."

"What did she have done?"

Ranald's hand left the steering wheel as both his hands made a circular, bouncing motion in front of his chest.

"A boob job?" Natasha giggled at his pantomime.

Ranald nodded and grinned devilishly. "It's no secret, but don't tell Maggie I told you."

"Is Bettina still after Ian?" Bettina was a cute and outgoing masseuse in her mid-thirties who was Ian's ardent admirer. She came to Glenhaven twice a month to give Maggie and Ranald Swedish massages—Ian too, when he was in town.

Ranald chuckled and shook his headful of shaggy white hair. "Aye, that one won't give up, but Ian has had a girlfriend for two years now."

*Girlfriend?* It caught Natasha unaware, but why should she be surprised that he had a girlfriend? Most women would consider him a hot catch, with a capital H.

"Who is she? What's her name?" Natasha tried not to act distressed, but it wasn't working.

"Danielle Parkhurst." Ranald didn't take his eyes off the road as he concentrated on the winding path. "She's a dermatologist who worked with him in Doctors Without Borders."

"Oh." Natasha strove to keep the disappointment she felt out of her voice and off her facial expression. "So they've been together for two years you said?" she asked in a light tone.

"Aye...but it's been on again off again because she lives in London. They keep breaking up and getting back together." Ranald rubbed the tip of his ruddy nose. "Rather complicates things because Ian has been working with her to build his clinic in Edinburgh."

"Are they back together now?" Natasha's stomach tightened with jealousy. Not only were Ian and Danielle lovers, but they were working together on realizing Ian's dream.

"Maggie said they haven't been getting along lately, so maybe it's off again." Ranald shrugged. "You should ask him."

"No, thanks." She touched Ranald's shirtsleeve. "Please don't tell Ian I was asking. I was a little curious…that's all."

Ranald's weathered hand gave her shoulder a fond pat. "Ian is closed-mouthed about his love life. Maggie and I don't dare ask him much about his women."

*His women?* "How many women are you talking about?" Natasha was embarrassed to ask, but she couldn't help it.

He tilted his head and his brows drew together as if he were counting them. "A few, but none have mattered as much as that Parkhurst girl," he said after a long moment of deliberation.

Natasha flinched. She couldn't bear hearing about Ian's love life, especially when it didn't involve her. She had just spent several hours with him on his private jet, hoping to reconnect, but everything had gone downhill after they'd argued. She had hoped to open communication with him after she woke up from her nap, but Ian had been less than talkative. Even during the continental breakfast they'd shared later, he'd been brooding and pensive. When she'd tried to draw him into conversation, he'd said he was preoccupied with the upcoming meetings in London. Now she wondered if part of his pensiveness was the expectation of seeing Danielle.

"Och, listen to me ramblin' on. How was your trip over, lass?" Ranald turned to peer at her warmly through olive green eyes.

"Amazing. I'd never been on a private jet before. The food was wonderful," she said.

"What did you eat?"

"Ian arranged for a fine lobster dinner and then later, a nice breakfast."

"Did he now?" Ranald chuckled. "Jolly good. I'm glad the two of you have made amends. Maggie and I couldn't be happier."

"Don't get too excited. I wouldn't exactly call it amends. Ian didn't talk much, and I slept most of the way over."

"He's not one for conversation when he's preoccupied," Ranald said, nodding.

*Preoccupied with Danielle*, she thought, her heart sinking like a stone in water.

They lapsed into amicable silence for the remainder of the drive as she looked around her, enchanted by the scenery. The Scottish Highlands were breathtaking in October. Purplish-pink heather mantled the moors in splendor, while clouds hung mistily over the fir trees and Highland peaks. Natasha never tired of the countryside with its verdant, sheep-covered mountains, jagged cliffs and resplendent glens. There was something entrancing about the volatile history of this magical land and the stalwart Scots who had defended it over the centuries from every type of invasive attack.

When they reached the winding road to Ian's home, Natasha's heart leaped at the first sight of Glenhaven estate. An enchanting arch formed by two thick rows of tall larch trees lined the dirt road. She closed her eyes, momentarily memorizing the beauty of Ian's ancestors' land. She opened them wide just in time to see the turreted front of the fortified castle.

"Oh, Ranald, everything is just as I remembered. So beautiful!" she murmured.

He nodded. "Aye, lass, it is." Ranald's craggy face creased into a lopsided grin as he regarded her warmly.

When they pulled up the drive, Maggie ran out of the heavy castle doors toward them. Natasha handed Evita to Ranald and threw her arms around Maggie, exuberantly embracing her ample body. Natasha loved the comforting feel of her girth, so unlike Anitra's stick thin figure. They hugged and rocked from side to side for several moments while Evita yipped and howled. Maggie pulled back and studied Natasha, her soft brown eyes brimming with happy tears.

"We've missed you, lovey," Maggie said, wiping her eyes as she gave a rueful shake of her short, salt and pepper curls. "You shouldn't have stayed away so long! You're always welcome here."

"Thank you, Maggie. I've missed you and Ranald so much too…and Glenhaven, of course."

Maggie turned her attention to Evita. "So this is my little god-doggy. She's a redhead like you, lovey. Did you plan it that way?"

"No, but my friend Ronnie did." Ronnie had delighted in telling Natasha that Evita looked just like her, except for the brown eyes.

Evita emitted a soulful howl. "And she sings too," Maggie said, her shoulders shaking with mirth.

While Maggie fussed over Evita, who rewarded her with happy licks, Natasha stared at the moss-covered, dark stone dwelling before her, awed by the magnificence of Glenhaven Castle. Bathed in misty rain and morning fog, the 16th century castle was peacefully cloistered from the noise and havoc of the 21st century. Natasha inhaled deeply of the cool, damp Scottish air to refresh her travel weary body.

"Come inside." Maggie's pretty face was radiant as she ushered Natasha through the high-beamed, wood-paneled foyer into the warmth of centuries-old, Scottish grandeur. She led the way up the spiral staircase to the master bedroom while Ranald followed behind, huffing as he carried her suitcases.

"Here, let me help you carry it. I'll take one end," Natasha offered, shifting Evita's dog carrier to her other hand.

"You'll do no such thing," Ranald blustered. "Ian told us you're a wee bit knackered. He said you are here to rest and rest you will, my lass."

Natasha wryly shook her head. Ian was already mandating from afar and everyone was scrambling to obey—as usual.

When they reached the second floor, Natasha stopped in front of the large portrait of Ian's mother, Fiona, dressed in a jade evening gown, her dark hair swept back from her beautiful face. Studying Fiona's alabaster complexion, rosy cheeks and serene smile, Natasha didn't find much similarity between Ian and his mum except for the eyes, almost haunting in their silver-green intensity and framed by inky lashes.

"I wish I could have met her," Natasha said. "It's a pity Ian lost his mother when he was only a boy."

"Aye," Maggie said. "He was verra close to her. Ian is just as passionate as Fiona was when it comes to his home."

"Glenhaven is in his blood," Natasha said. "I didn't come to realize how much until it was too late."

"It's never too late," Maggie said with conviction.

"We'll see," Natasha said, remembering what Ranald had said about Danielle.

Natasha followed Maggie into the master bedroom and watched her approach the tapestry-covered north wall. A vivid memory of the first time she'd laid eyes on the medieval tapestry of courtly love above the massive bed came rushing back to her. The memory so vibrant she could almost smell Ian's clean, evergreen scent, feel his warm skin on her, taste the desire in his ravenous kisses. The laird of Glenhaven's compelling presence filled the room, even if he was miles away.

"I had the hidden chamber prepared since I know it's your favorite. Do you want to sleep there?" Maggie's motherly voice held a hint of hesitation as she watched her.

"Sure. Ian isn't here, so it's fine," Natasha said, tamping the shiver of excitement at staying so close to his master quarters.

Maggie pushed aside the colorful Flemish tapestry. "Verra well, then."

Underneath the tapestry was a hidden pocket door that Maggie slid into the wall. They walked through a dark corridor leading to a bolted door. Maggie unlocked the ancient wooden door and led Natasha inside the secret, little-used room.

# CHAPTER FIVE

Maggie turned the lights on when they entered the cozy alcove. A four-poster bed, covered in a luxurious cream silk duvet, was in the center of the room, flanked by two dark mahogany carved tables topped by brass candle lamps. A rich sky blue, mint green and rose Belgian tapestry of flora and fauna hung on a burnished brass rod above the bed. Maggie briskly fluffed up the bed pillows and turned down the duvet.

"You may place your things in here." Maggie unlocked the intricately carved mahogany armoire and handed the key to Natasha. It was a massive piece of furniture, large enough to store her suitcases.

"Thank you. Everything is lovely. I feel right at home." Natasha slipped the key in her pants' pocket and stood still, marveling at all the homey touches in the beautifully decorated room. She had always loved the secret chamber and how it felt like a serene cocoon. Quiet and incredibly peaceful, it was the perfect place to sing.

She could sing as high as she wanted or belt a tune as loud as she wished without disturbing anyone.

"Ian had a bathroom installed in this chamber last year, complete with a shower and bathtub. There's running hot water too," Ranald said proudly as he put the bags down beside the bed.

"A warm soak in the tub would be heavenly. Thank you for the beautiful flowers," she said, indicating the crystal vase brimming with freshly cut crimson poppies on an antique vanity in front of the bed. "And for the ride over."

"You're welcome. Maggie has been in a tizzy ever since your phone call," Ranald said. "Wait till you see the sweater she knit for Evita."

Maggie waved him off with a scolding look. "Och, Mr. Duncan, now you spoiled it. It was supposed to be a surprise!" She turned to Natasha. "You must have a wee bit of jet lag, lovey. Rest now. Tea is at four and dinner at seven. If you'd rather sleep than have tea, that's fine."

Natasha smiled. "I wouldn't dream of missing your tea."

"Good." Maggie took Evita out of the kennel and cuddled her to her bosom. "The wee one and I are going to get acquainted now. See you in a bit." She gave Natasha a jaunty wave and shooed Ranald out before her.

When they left, Natasha bathed in rose-scented water and washed her hair before donning a soft chenille robe. She lit the candles beside the bed and wallowed in the luxury of the candle-lit glow. Filled with wonder, she gazed at the fireplace. Tonight she'd sleep blissfully in a toasty room and leave her New York worries behind. She reclined on the eiderdown comforter, closed her eyes and gave into the jet lag that overtook her.

When Natasha awoke, the room smelled of melted wax. She turned on the chandelier above the bed and checked her watch. 3:30 pm. She couldn't believe she'd slept so long and so deeply. She had just enough time to get dressed and run downstairs for tea.

Natasha found Maggie in the patio garden, surrounded by clusters of wild flowers flourishing in the cool, vaporous weather. Bluebells and honeysuckle, many varieties of thistle and a splendid display of roses filled the garden with vivid color.

"Come sit beside me." Maggie patted the space next to her on a dark green wrought iron bench. "Dugie prepared some treats. Are you hungry, lass?"

"Yes. Everything looks delicious." Natasha's stomach rumbled at the tempting sight of assorted tea sandwiches, plump currant-studded scones, clotted cream and homemade raspberry jam set out by the cook. Dugie had been the MacGregor family cook since Ian was born. She had started out as the kitchen maid and was now running the kitchen with the help of her daughter, Emma.

Maggie poured Earl Grey tea into delicate porcelain teacups and handed her a steaming cup.

"Thank you." Natasha took a sip of the fragrant, perfectly brewed tea. "Where's Ranald?"

"He won't be joining us. He's giving Evita a grand tour of the grounds. She's already gotten more kisses from Ranald in one day than I have all month," Maggie said with a snort. She handed Natasha a porcelain dish and offered her a scone.

"Thanks." Natasha broke off a piece and slathered a spoonful of cream and a dab of raspberry jam on top before devouring it in two bites. "Oh, yum. It's so good!"

"Dugie will be happy to hear it. She's had her wee daughter on a tight schedule. Emma's head has been in the clouds since she got engaged to young Colin last month."

Natasha smiled. "That's nice. I remember Emma. She was sweet and quiet as she followed Dugie around," she said, recalling the shy girl.

"It's hard for her to get a word in edgewise. Dugie's bossy and verra outspoken," Maggie said, chuckling. She pointed to a coppery-orange rose and looked at Natasha expectantly. "Do you remember those roses?"

Natasha nodded quietly.

"And the name Ian chose for this hybrid?"

"Yes, he named them after me," Natasha said with a pang. Maggie seemed to think everything was fine between her and Ian now. Sadly, it wasn't the case.

Maggie laid a gentle hand on Natasha's forearm. "Why so glum?"

"I didn't realize I looked sad, Maggie. I guess it's because I wanted to make peace with Ian before coming to Glenhaven, but he still hasn't forgiven me for breaking off our engagement. I've missed him terribly."

Maggie patted Natasha's shoulder. "Don't give up, even if Ian pushes you away. After your break-up, the lad was a mess. He had dark circles under his eyes from not sleeping and his cheeks were gaunt from barely eating. He was in a foul temper for weeks. Ranald and I were beside ourselves."

Natasha drew in a ragged sigh. "What did you do?"

Maggie's wise eyes glowed with zeal. "I badgered him so much to open up, he finally did, just to quiet me. Ian felt torn apart inside. He had planned a life with you here and you betrayed him when Anitra intervened." She shook her head unhappily. "Those were his words, not mine."

Natasha blinked back tears. Her shoulders slumped as she set the scone on the plate, her appetite gone. "I didn't mean to betray him, Maggie. I couldn't be in a marriage that was so limiting. I had just graduated and was eager to spread my wings with music and follow my dreams—dreams Ian couldn't share."

Bittersweet memories came flooding back to the summer when she'd first met Ian. He had been formidable even then, but also tender and kind, tilting her world off its axis in the span of a summer. Crazy in love, they began a passionate, long distance relationship that culminated in Ian proposing marriage and Natasha impulsively accepting.

But then reality had set in when she got word she'd landed her first adult role on Broadway. As a child, she'd starred in *Annie*, but right afterward, Anitra had plucked her out of show business proclaiming that Natasha couldn't audition until she completed a formal education, classically trained in music, dance and acting at Juilliard. Sheltered from the outside world and immersed in her craft, Natasha had worked diligently because nothing brought her more pleasure than singing and using her talent to make others happy. Before meeting Ian, her whole world had consisted of music and performing.

When she fell in love with him, she fell hard. She hadn't known how to balance their love with her commitment to her career. Sadly, neither had Ian.

Maggie gently squeezed Natasha's hand. "I remember everything you wrote me following the break-up. I'm glad you kept in touch with us over the years."

Natasha hugged her. "How could I not? I love you and Ranald. And I *loved* Ian, with all my heart. I never meant to hurt him, but he wasn't able to compromise."

Maggie nodded. "Time has passed and he's older and wiser. Perhaps his heart has changed."

"I doubt it. He was eager to be rid of me at Inverness."

Maggie waved her hand in dismissal. "Och. The stubborn lad hasn't gotten over you." "It's not like that. We hadn't spent ten minutes together in his New York office before we argued," Natasha said, rolling her eyes.

Maggie grinned. "It's good to have a little conflict now and then. Ranald says he looks forward to little fights with me so he can enjoy makin' up. You ken?"

"Aye, Maggie, I ken," Natasha said. "But what about Danielle?"

"Who told you about Danielle?" Maggie asked, surprised. She looked heavenward. "Never mind, I'm sure it was chatty Ranald."

"Are Ian and Danielle a couple?"

Maggie hitched a shoulder in a half-shrug as if she didn't give it much importance. "Last I heard, he wasn't dating her anymore."

"But aren't they collaborating on Ian's clinic?" If so, Ian had to have close contact with Danielle, girlfriend or not.

"I'm not sure. I wouldn't worry about that, luv. On another note...your mother called earlier," she said, changing the subject before Natasha could ask more questions.

Natasha's eyes shot open. "Oh no. What did she say?"

"She asked if I knew where you were, but I didn't say anything about you coming here."

"Good!" She touched Maggie's hand. "Thank you. I wasn't able to reach Anitra before I left, so I left a message that I'd be out of the show on a temporary leave of absence. I don't want her to know I'm at Glenhaven, considering how she feels about Ian."

"It's a shame those two never got along," Maggie said, her mouth making a tsking sound.

"I've never understood how Daddy likes Ian so much, yet Anitra hated him from the start."

Maggie looked mystified as she sipped her tea. "I dunno. Different personalities, I guess," she said after a pause. "Just like Ian and his father. As different as night and day, those two."

"What was Malcolm like? Ian never said much about his father."

"Malcolm was Ranald's older brother, ye know. He was verra successful and ambitious, but also callous—in business and with women. Ian's mum, Fiona, had a gentle spirit, but Malcolm was a notorious ladies' man."

"Really?" This was the first Natasha had heard of it.

"Aye, but Fiona looked the other way. She wanted Ian to have a normal childhood and not be sent to boarding school. She was devoted to Ian and loved his company. Fiona knew how much Ian loved animals and they spent most of their afternoons outdoors, hiking and fishing." She shook her head in bewilderment and shrugged. "Fiona loved Malcolm, in spite of his faults, and he had many."

"Oh." Natasha didn't know how to respond.

Maggie's mouth tightened. "God rest his departed soul, but the man was imposing and dictatorial. He didn't relate to Ian and for some odd reason, it seemed to annoy him that the lad was verra smart and mature for his age.

Even as a *bairn*, Ian had astute vision and a huge heart. Malcolm never appreciated that Ian was born to be a doctor. He wanted his only son to be a ruthless businessman like himself. Selfish. That's what he was!" she spat out.

Natasha was floored by Maggie's outpouring of emotion. It was as if she was unloading years of pent-up frustration. "I had no idea it was like that. Ian is brilliant and formidable, and I just assumed that he took after his father since Malcolm was so successful."

Maggie shook her head. "They weren't close."

"No wonder. After the funeral, any time I brought up his father, Ian shut down the conversation. I thought it was because his loss was too recent and raw."

"Ian is nothing like Malcolm. He doesn't even look like him. Straight from the womb, Ian was a brilliant *bairn*. He excelled in all areas, especially maths and science. As a teenager, he spent more time in the science lab and learning to heal animals than at social functions. He was so handsome, the girls swarmed to get his attention. He dated a lot, but never fell in love." She paused and gazed at Natasha. "Until he met you."

"Oh," Natasha said in a small voice, trying not to feel even worse.

"Chin up, lass. All will be resolved soon enough," Maggie said cheerfully as she rose from the bench. "Will you listen to me ramblin' on? I'm going inside to check on dinner. Stay awhile and enjoy the fresh air."

"I think I will." When Maggie left, Natasha's gaze followed the stone path to the roses named after her. Ian had probably renamed them "heartbreaker" by now. She rubbed her arms as the temperature plummeted along with her heart. Drawing in a shivery breath, she rose from the bench and headed inside.

Back in the bedroom, she hung her clothes in the armoire and neatly arranged her toiletries in the bathroom. Lifting the lid off the glass jar of her perfumed body cream, she inhaled deeply and closed her eyes. The rose fragrance sent tingles through her when she remembered Ian used to tell her, "your rose scent intoxicates me."

With a sigh, Natasha closed the lid and turned her attention to the empty suitcases. Where to put them? She closed the smaller one and put it on the bench in front of the bed. When she tried to close the larger one, she noticed the inside lining close to the handle was frayed. She tucked the loose threads inside the seam and her hand touched something hard under the lining. She slipped her hand through the seam and retrieved a small, rectangular object.

Her stomach did a nosedive when she realized she was holding a flash drive.

*The missing flash drive!*

Stunned, Natasha's heart lodged like a fist in her throat. When and how on earth had Tony put the flash drive in her suitcase? He'd only been to her apartment a few times! Her pulse pounded a warning beat in her eardrums. Things just got very complicated and she hadn't even spent one day in Ian's Highland refuge. She sat on the bed and bent her head forward, gulping deep breaths to calm herself.

Should she tell Maggie and Ranald straight away, or wait and contact Ian first? Or should she call the police? She'd wait until tomorrow to contact the detectives. She ran to her laptop and opened it, hoping she still had battery left. She plugged the flash drive into the side of her laptop and waited for it to load up. *Damn!* It wasn't working. She took the flash drive out and slid it back into the suitcase lining where she'd found it.

Natasha shoved the suitcase in the armoire and locked it. Forcing strength in her wobbly limbs, she changed into a scoop-necked, ivory angora sweater and a long black tulip skirt with high-heeled lace-up booties. Knowing Maggie and Ranald, they would be dressed nicely for her welcome dinner tonight. She put extra effort in her appearance, fluffing her hair, adding her pearl earrings and a swipe of apricot lip gloss. Somehow, she'd have to get through the evening in a cheerful mood without letting on that she had just found the damned flash drive.

Tonight her acting would be tested to the limit.

# CHAPTER SIX

Natasha entered the grand dining room with her arms linked through Maggie's and Ranald's. Just as she'd imagined, they were decked in finery with Ranald in a tartan kilt and starched white dress shirt and Maggie wearing a hunter green wool dress. They were in a festive mood and it was contagious. Natasha felt like an honored guest when she saw the gleaming mahogany table set with Wedgwood china and sparkling crystal. Sleek alabaster tapers glowed in silver candelabras in various sizes along the center of the table.

The cook stood next to it with a silver breadbasket in her hands. Rosy-cheeked and with a head full of cropped white curls, Dugie, short for Dora MacDougal, greeted Natasha with a warm smile. "Welcome, Miss."

Natasha smiled. "Thanks, Dugie. It's good to see you again."

"Four settings? Are we expecting someone else, Dugie?" Maggie asked.

"The fourth setting is for Dr. Ian." Dugie's gap-toothed grin widened as she set the basket on the table and rushed out of the room as if she'd just spilled a secret.

"I thought he wasn't coming," Natasha said, trying to calm the wild flurry in her stomach. "You thought wrong." Ian's voice boomed from the doorway.

They turned and stared at Ian as he strode into the room in a black leather bomber jacket and snug jeans with a dark red and blue MacGregor tartan wool scarf streaming behind him. Looking like a hunter come in from the wild Highlands, Ian's urbane celebrity surgeon persona in America contrasted sharply to the untamed laird he became in Scotland. In his homeland, he was a man's man who enjoyed the outdoors with gusto.

Natasha's breath caught in her throat when his silver-green eyes zeroed in on her. She met his nod with a smile and was surprised to see a flicker of uncertainty in his keen eyes. The candlelit room did nothing to soften his austere features or the tautness of his jaw, sharp as a Highland peak.

The moment Maggie rushed toward him with outstretched arms, his eyes softened. "Welcome home, my lad," she said, giddily kissing both his cheeks.

Ian lifted her and swung her around in an arc, laughing at her protests. Natasha couldn't help smiling as she watched him twirl his plump little aunt in the air.

"Put me down, naughty pup," Maggie admonished, wiping happy tears from her face. "I'm an old woman."

"Rubbish, you're not old. Why the tears, daft auntie? I haven't been away that long."

Maggie wagged her finger at him. "Too long for sure!" She smoothed her wool dress in place and patted her errant curls. "I'm glad you came in time for dinner."

"Welcome, lad," Ranald said, clapping him on the back. "Dugie has prepared a feast for our Natasha."

Ian's eyes gravitated to Natasha and a jolt of desire held him captive. Her lustrous copper hair fell in soft waves framing a glowing face and sparkling blue eyes. A soft sweater molded her high, round breasts and her narrow skirt hugged her shapely dancer's hips and long legs. She stood at the sideboard watching him curiously.

Natasha's sultry dimple deepened at the corner of her lush mouth as she raised an eyebrow. "Long time no see, Dr. Who," she drawled, her melodious voice vibrating through the dining room.

Maggie looked surprised. "Dr. Who? I don't miss an episode! Is that what you call Ian?"

"Yes, and he used to like it," Natasha said mildly.

Ian barely managed a smile. He was still irritable after his meetings in London. He took Natasha's arm above her elbow and led her toward the high-backed chair. "Natasha?" he said, seating her cordially.

Natasha glanced at him just as his gaze slid down her spine. The delectable curve of her heart-shaped bottom taunted him as she leaned forward to sit down.

"Thanks," she murmured with a smile.

"You're welcome," he said, rounding the corner of the table to sit across from her.

Dugie carried in a tray of poached salmon steaks topped with béarnaise sauce and capers, accompanied by tiny red potatoes and garden peas. Her daughter, Emma, helped Dugie serve the meal, while Gerald, Dugie's husband, poured a small amount of wine for Ian. He stood by while Ian swirled the wine before tasting it. At his nod of approval, Gerald poured wine for everyone.

Natasha lifted the Baccarat goblet in a toast. "May the roof above never fall in; may we below never fall out," she said in a saucy Scottish accent, eliciting chuckles from Maggie and Ranald.

"Hear, hear." Ranald lifted his glass and clinked it with Natasha's.

"Where did you learn that? From one of your plays?" Ian asked, spearing a potato.

"Maybe," Natasha said lightly.

"How did your trip to London go?" Maggie asked Ian.

"Not very well. I had to cut it short before I murdered someone," Ian said.

Maggie's eyes popped open. "Murder! Such tough talk." She patted his hand. "Have some wine, luv, and forget about it for now."

"I'll probably have to return to London next week." He tasted the salmon. "Ahh, there's nothing like our Scottish salmon. Dugie outdid herself tonight."

"Indeed," Maggie said, glowing.

"I thought you were going back to New York," Natasha said.

"Not yet," Ian replied cryptically. His plans had changed, but he saw no need to explain. He only wanted to enjoy Dugie's excellent meal and not think about the witch in London standing in the way of his plans.

Maggie kept the conversation light, while Ranald talked about their upcoming trip to Ayr Racecourse in November.

When they finished eating, Maggie told Dugie, "Ranald and I will take our dessert in the library."

Dugie nodded and left the room.

"I'd rather eat it here," Ranald said.

Maggie squinted at Ranald and gave him a meaningful look. "Ian and Natasha have much to discuss. And so do we," she said, taking his elbow when he stood.

Ranald threw his hands in the air and left with a hangdog expression.

Dugie returned and served a golden apple tart and cinnamon ice cream. "Will you be taking whiskey with your coffee, sir?"

"No, thanks. I'll have some in my room later."

Dugie nodded and glanced at Natasha. "Would you like one of my special toddies, lass?"

"I'd love one of your special toddies," Natasha said with an eager smile. "Thank you."

"No whiskey," Ian said firmly.

"Yes, whiskey," Natasha countered, bristling.

Dugie cleared her throat. "Shall I bring out the boxing gloves, then?" she said, glancing from Natasha to Ian with a raised brow.

"That'll be all, Dugie," Ian said.

Natasha frowned at him. "Why can't I have whiskey?" she asked when Dugie was out of earshot.

"I'm looking out for you. Liquor and antibiotics don't mix well," Ian said, noting her disgruntled look. "You'll survive."

Natasha patted her lips with her napkin and set it down on the table. "I think I'll join Maggie and Ranald in the library," she said, rising from the table.

Ian's hand closed over her wrist, noting how delicate it felt in his grip. "Don't go."

She stood before him with her hand on her hip and her head tilted to the side. "Why should I stay? I don't want to argue. Your mood hasn't exactly been light this evening."

"I want you to stay, Tasha," he said inflexibly.

His iPhone buzzed with a text message and he released his grip on her. He read the text and seethed at what he read. "What the fuck," he said, staring at the phone before he shoved it in his pocket.

"What's wrong?" Natasha asked, shocked at his sudden outburst.

"Bloody hell." He slapped his palm on the table. "I'm going to throttle the conniving bitch!"

Natasha sank down on the chair and stared at Ian. She could feel his simmering rage from across the table, in his severe eyes and the harsh set of his jaw.

"Who sent you the text?" she asked softly.

"The woman claiming half of my rightful inheritance," Ian grated through clamped teeth.

"Who is she?"

Ian's mouth formed a grim line as he struggled to contain his temper. "My father's mistress." The veins in his neck stood out as he knocked back the rest of his wine. "I inherited the bulk of Dad's estate, but he left half of Glenhaven castle and the surrounding land to her."

According to Maggie, since his father's death, Ian had purchased a Kensington Garden flat and a New York penthouse in Central Park West. But none of those properties held the strings to his heart as his family estate. No wonder he was livid that he had to share it with his father's mistress.

"If your dad was already a widower, why didn't he marry her?"

"Because she was married to another man," Ian said scathingly. "She and Dad had a clandestine affair for over a dozen years."

Natasha's jaw dropped. The whole thing sounded like a soap opera. "What are you going to do?"

"I'm contesting the will. Dad signed it on his deathbed, probably delirious from morphine. His mistress kept his illness a secret and had her lawyer draw up a new will when she knew he was close to dying."

"That's so evil. Are you sure your father was in love with her?"

Ian snorted. "She has the galling nerve to claim she was the love of his life," he said roughly, his face flushed dark red. "It's a lie. Dad adored Mum to her dying day. They were childhood sweethearts."

The way Maggie had stated things, it hadn't sounded as if Ian's parents had had such a loving relationship. Of course, Fiona died when Ian was only eight, so he had seen it through a child's eyes.

"You never suspected anything?" Natasha asked, even though Ian's face had become shuttered. She didn't want to end it there, not when he was finally opening up.

"No." Ian poured another glass of wine and drank deeply. He raked a hand through his thick hair and met her questioning gaze with a half-hearted smile. "Let's change the subject. No use letting her ruin the evening."

"Okay," Natasha said, bolstered by his smile. Whether she liked it or not, she had to tell him about the flash drive right away. The timing was unfortunate, especially after the recent text, but she couldn't wait any longer if she was going to alert the detectives tomorrow.

With Ian's full attention on her, she took a fortifying breath. "Promise me you're not going to go ballistic when I tell you…"

"What is it?" Ian's dark brows drew together over narrowed eyes as he watched her.

"You know the flash drive the mob is looking for?" At his nod, she said, "It incriminates the whole Capelli crime syndicate."

"And?" He drummed his fingers on the table top, his sharp gaze steady on her.

Natasha drew in a tremulous breath. "It's upstairs."

Ian's eyebrows shot up. "What? Where the hell is it?"

"In the lining of my suitcase. I found it when I unpacked before coming down to dinner."

A muscle in Ian's jaw ticked as he went very still. "Bloody hell," he said, the guttural sound deep in his throat.

"Can you help me get it to Detective Carson in New York? I don't trust the regular mail," she said in a rush, her heart thumping.

Ian's hands formed a steeple, his fingertips grazing the cleft in his chin as he considered what she'd just said. "Did you see what was on the flash drive?"

"No. It wouldn't open for me."

He slanted a look at her. "It might be encrypted."

"I don't think Tony was enough of a techie to know how to do that."

"Don't be too sure.

"How can we find out?" she asked anxiously.

"I'll take care of that. Tomorrow I have an appointment to visit a wee patient in Edinburgh. You can come along. We'll go to Edinburgh University. Maggie's cousin, Connor, is an internet technology whiz. He'll know what to do."

"Oh good. I'd love to come along. Thank you," she said, relieved he was being helpful and understanding.

"Connor is closer to my age than Maggie. We grew up spending many summers together." Ian rose from the table. "Let's join Maggie and Ranald in the library."

On the way there, Gerald informed Ian that his aunt and uncle had already retired for the evening, and that they insisted on keeping Evita with them.

Natasha shook her head with amusement. "If Evita was pampered before arriving here, she'll be spoiled rotten by the time she leaves," she said, following him into high-beamed, oak-paneled library. Looking around, she luxuriated in being surrounded by so many rare, valuable books. "I swear, Ian, your assortment of first edition medical books would make any book collector green with envy."

"I've tracked another one in Oxford that I'm keen on buying." He placed his hand in the small of Natasha's back, sending shivers skittering up her spine. "

"How is your injury?" He motioned toward the cognac-colored leather couch in front of the large stone fireplace. "Sit there and I'll take a look."

Natasha's breath caught in her throat and her pulse tripped up. "Here?"

"Sure, why not?" he asked as it were nothing out of the ordinary.

"It feels awkward here. I mean, outside of your office," she said, her cheeks heating up.

"Rubbish. Let's have a look."

She sat down and Ian hunkered down in front of her.

"Turn a bit to your side. That's it," he said as she leaned sideways to rest on her left hip.

A shaky sigh escaped her when Ian's long fingers lifted the hem of her skirt high enough to check her thigh. Unhinged by the sudden intimacy of his touch, she wondered if he could see the pulse leaping at her throat. His warm hand on her bare thigh left a trail of gooseflesh everywhere it touched. Holding her breath, she stared at the top of Ian's dark head bent forward, precariously near her breasts. Her pulse fluttered like a hummingbird's wings as she remembering the velvet softness of his lips kissing her breasts and nipples. He used to love to bury his face in her breasts and inhale her scent. She drew air into her lungs and tried to calm her racing heart.

"Does it hurt?" he asked, jarring her back to the present. His voice sounded hoarse as he gently touched the area around her wound, his face bent forward in concentration.

"No. Not anymore," she said in a strangled voice. Ian's dark hair tumbled over his forehead, glinting like flint in the light of the chandelier. She ached to smooth it back and kiss the faint furrow between his brows. His closeness made her burn with desire, and when he finally lowered her skirt, she felt a stab of disappointment.

"It's healing nicely. Be sure to finish the antibiotic just in case," he said briskly, reverting to his medical persona.

"I will." She inhaled a shaky breath and licked her dry lips.

"Are you staying in the blue room?" he asked.

"No. I'm sleeping in the hidden chamber tonight."

Ian froze and a disapproving look in his eyes shot into her like lasers. "Who gave you permission to sleep in my hidden chamber?" he asked in a quiet tone.

"You sound like one of the three grumpy bears chastising Goldilocks," she scoffed. When he remained silent, she lifted her chin. "Maggie thought it was best for me to stay there. We didn't think you were going to be here."

"It wasn't a good choice. The blue room is on the bottom level. Climbing so many stairs puts a strain on your wound."

"Oh well. There's not much we can do about it now," she said with a shrug.

"Yes, there is." Bending, he lifted her in his arms and carried her toward the staircase.

"Put me down," she protested like a hypocrite. "I can make it upstairs on my own." Held this close to his solid chest, she could hear his solid heartbeat and feel the heat emanating from his strong body. She suddenly wanted him so badly it *hurt.*

Ian ignored her protests and climbed the stairs.

"I think you just wanted an excuse to hold me," she teased softly.

His face boarded up at her harmless taunt and she regretted it. "Ian, I never meant for things to end the way they did between us. You must believe me. On the flight over, I wanted to—"

"Not now, Natasha," he cut in tersely. The dark look in his silver-green eyes silenced her.

Ian was back to calling her Natasha and with not an ounce of warmth. Her spirits deflated. She much preferred hearing him call her Tasha in his rich Scottish burr. She would have loved hearing him call her "angel" as he once had, but one look at his distant eyes told her she was being delusional.

He set her on her feet when they reached the second floor. Sliding open the door to the hidden passageway, he said, "Get some rest. I plan on getting an early start tomorrow morning. Be downstairs at seven. Sharp."

So he was back to being curt and bossy. He sure was moody tonight! Frowning at his back, Natasha saluted him when he closed the connecting door to his quarters.

# CHAPTER SEVEN

Ian crossed to the fireplace in the master bedroom and kindled it, then sat in his favorite Moroccan leather armchair before the fire. He kicked off his loafers and propped his feet on the matching ottoman. He poured two fingers of whiskey into the crystal cut glass on the silver tray left by Dugie and noted with disgust that his hands were shaking.

He stared at the blaze. The flames flickered golden orange, reminding him of Natasha's glossy curls. His grip tightened on the glass as he downed the whiskey in two gulps. He shouldn't have invited her to go with him to Edinburgh, but he'd had no other choice. He couldn't exactly leave her there to figure things out, and he didn't want to cancel the appointment in Edinburgh. He felt compelled to protect Tasha, but he didn't want the type of involvement that would bring. She would distract him from the reason he'd returned to Scotland—to open his clinic and reclaim Glenhaven.

Unfortunately, she had an uncanny ability to get under his skin and land in his heart like a precise bullet. His body had reacted strongly to merely touching her bare thigh. What the bloody hell was wrong with him? When he'd carried her in his arms tonight, he'd had to fight the urge to take her straight to bed and make love to her until she couldn't walk.

For the past seven years, he had told himself she wasn't the girl he'd thought she was, that she was just like her mother, self-centered, vain and ruthlessly ambitious, with an outsized ego that craved constant stroking. But deep in his gut he knew it wasn't true. Tasha was still the radiant girl who wore her heart on her sleeve, constantly giving and caring about others. *Others*, but not him, he reminded himself derisively.

She had tossed him aside once and she would do it again just as easily. He'd be a fool not to remember that. Acting was in her blood, just as healing was in his.

His insides churned at the memory of how soft she'd felt in his arms when he'd carried her upstairs. Her rose scent had ignited long ago memories of her fragrant body clinging to his, her pale, round breasts rising and falling with each shivering breath, her naked limbs entwined with his. The last image he wanted to conjure was of Tasha lying in his bed, beautiful and naked, lazily smiling at him with a satiated smile.

Raw primal desire reared up in him. So forceful it bordered on savage. He had claimed her as his own a long time ago. He wanted her under him, writhing in ecstasy, welcoming his hot length inside her with wild abandon.

Ian's member engorged to the point of pain as he stalked to his bed and stripped. He yanked the coverlet down and sprawled on the mattress. Breathing heavily, he willed his roused body to settle down as he braced his arms behind his head and stared at the crackling flames. He finally drifted into fitful slumber with erotic visions of Natasha, gorgeously naked with nothing on but his pearls in her earlobes.

Natasha struggled between the labyrinth of deep slumber and the urgent need to wake up. Her skin prickled with a sensation of imminent danger that forced her eyes to open. A startling flash of lightning entered through the narrow, slotted window in the stone wall, illuminating the room and jolting her awake. Her heart buffeted her ribs when the explosive crack of thunder followed.

She relived the awful dream again. But it wasn't a dream; it was a living nightmare. At seven she had gotten lost in the woods in a blinding rainstorm, paralyzed with terror every time lightning had struck the earth. Her friends had gone on ahead of her while she'd stayed behind to practice a song she would sing at the end-of-summer party at Camp Merry Cascades. The trees looked like gargoyles, frightening her as bone-jarring thunder resounded in her ears repeatedly. Lightning struck the tree beside her, knocking it to the ground. A sharp branch ripped through her T-shirt and sliced her arm. She could hear her high-pitched child's voice screaming "Help!" repeatedly until her throat was raw, but nobody came to her aid.

Tears streamed down her face and clogged her throat as the spurting blood mixed with the pelting rain. She passed out and woke up in the hospital emergency room asking for her mommy, but she never came. Daddy was the one who brought her home from camp. The incident happened twenty-three years ago, but the nightmare always felt agonizingly real.

Reeling from the dream, Natasha's pulse galloped out of control. *Calm down. Breathe. You're awake now. It was just a dream.* She groped in the dark, switched on the wall sconce and ran to the window. Lightning struck again, followed instantly by deafening thunder signaling the electrical storm was directly above the castle. The sconce light flickered and went out.

*Ian.* Going to him was all Natasha could think of as she made her way to his room, her hands using the wall as a blueprint. She reached the connecting door, slid it open and pushed the tapestry aside.

Her heart almost stopped when she saw him sprawled on his back, asleep in the center of the bed—naked. Taking measured steps she reached his side and gazed at him, mesmerized by his raw male beauty in repose. Ian's strong arms and legs were outspread, his handsome face turned to the side as his muscled chest rose with each deep breath. His sex nestling quietly between his lean hip bones was deceptive—she knew the powerful engine it became when aroused. Paralyzed with mind-numbing fear and dizzying desire, she stared at him, willing him to wake up and take her in his arms. Lightning struck again, followed immediately by a thundering boom.

Natasha shivered and clutched the sides of her nightgown. "Wake up, Highlander," she implored, her heart leaping in her throat.

Ian's eyes opened at the sound of Natasha's voice. Illuminated by white lightning, she stood before him like a primeval goddess, fiery curls forming a halo around her pale face. The light outlined her body, rendering her nightgown transparent. Spellbound, he caught a glimpse of round breasts and the outline of her supple thighs and mons, bare beneath the gossamer fabric. Hardening instantly, he pulled the sheet over his groin.

A loud crash of thunder struck with ear-splitting force. Natasha catapulted into Ian's arms, clinging to him as her pliant body molded to his hard length.

"Still scared of a wee storm, Tasha?" he murmured gruffly. He smoothed her hair from her face and gently tugged one of her curls.

"I had that awful nightmare again. The one where I got hurt in the woods," she said, passing her palm over the hard planes of his chest. She turned her face and nuzzled the crook of his neck, her soft nose tickling his skin. "Let me stay here with you. Please. Just for a little while," she pleaded as if he were heartless enough to kick her out of his bed.

Ian struggled to control his body's treacherous reaction to her as he nodded silently and Tasha kissed his jaw.

"Thank you," she whispered hoarsely, her lips moving hesitantly toward his mouth.

The silky softness of her lips so close to his shredded the last remnant of restraint. Hot blood roared in his ears, bringing his body close to boiling. He began a slow and steady exploration of her sweet mouth as he maneuvered her onto her back and underneath him. Like a starved man, his tongue mimicked what he wanted to do to her. *Damn the consequences.* He had to have her one last time before letting her go.

He held her beautiful face in his hands and looked deep into her wide eyes. "Do you want me to continue?"

"Yes. Please," Natasha breathed into his mouth, winding her arms around his neck.

Ian slid her nightgown up and over her arms until it tangled about her wrists, anchoring them above her head. His eyes roved over every inch of her bare skin as she lay trapped in his web of desire. She moaned low in her throat, a faint, raw sound when he kissed the rapid pulse at her slim wrists and inside her elbows. Ian's hands trembled with need as they caressed her satiny skin from her shoulders to her firm thighs. Natasha rained kisses on his face and neck when his hands closed over her round buttocks and pulled her close. Palming their supple firmness, he pressed his swollen erection against the silken cradle of her womb.

His lips nipped her fragrant neck and trailed across her graceful collarbone, tasting every delectable inch of her skin. Gathering her breasts in his hands, he savored their cool plumpness and the way her nipples pebbled in his palms. He lowered his mouth and laved the honeyed tips while his fingertips strummed the moist bud of her sex.

"Make love to me," she said between breathless pants. She untangled her hands from the confines of her nightgown and lowered her arms. Her soft hands caressed the length of his spine and clasped his buttocks, coaxing him with hot urgency. "I want all of you. Take me," she said, her husky voice bewitching.

On the brink of madness, Ian's biceps bulged as he braced his weight above her. He hungered to dominate and possess her, to conquer her and make her beg for him. *To tame her and be tamed by her.* Beads of sweat dampened his forehead, tortured by the reckless need to have her and the fear of letting her snare his heart again.

He cursed the hold she had on him. It was madness that defied logic.

*Logic be damned!* he thought with a lusty groan. He positioned himself between her waiting thighs and eased inside her tight, liquid sheath. Natasha arched her body upwards and opened to him, welcoming his slow and purposeful thrusts. She gazed into his eyes with a look of profound trust and love, one he'd never forget.

"I'm where I want to be, Ian," she said, moaning raggedly. "In your arms and close to your heart."

Her words were Ian's undoing as he lost all control, plunging inside her over and over again until she came with wild, explosive cries. Tears rolled down the sides of her face when Ian stiffened and came almost simultaneously with a hoarse shout. He gathered her in his arms and held her until the aftershocks of their fevered lovemaking quieted.

The next morning Natasha rolled over in bed with a dreamy smile. She snuggled her face in the pillow, her eyes closed as she relived the previous night when Ian had reverted to the man she adored—primal, dominant and exquisitely tender. She felt deliciously achy all over. After their first urgent coupling, he'd made love to her again taking his time as he wrung the last drop of pleasure from her. She sighed at the memory of his face ravaged with lust while he brought her to ecstasy. Her startling climax had unleashed tears as the blissful, mounting spiral of sensations unleashed an explosive release. Afterwards, Ian had cradled her close to his body. Hugging him tightly, she'd listened to his steady heartbeat and silently vowed to never let him go.

Natasha stretched languidly and opened her eyes. She blinked and looked around, confounded when she realized she wasn't in Ian's bed, but hers. She had fallen asleep in Ian's warm embrace; she knew that much for sure. When had he carried her back to the hidden chamber—and why?

*Never mind. You know why.* Her heart ached with bitter disappointment. Ian's separation from her spoke volumes—he hadn't wanted her in his bed after they'd made love. She wondered if he even considered it making love or simply sexual release. Had he wanted to purge his desire for her once and for all? Natasha swallowed against the lump in her throat, her pride smarting with humiliation and hurt.

How would she face him this morning? With a stab of despair, she glanced at her watch. 6:30 a.m. Last night, Ian had told her to be downstairs by seven in the morning sharp so they could leave for Edinburgh. Why hadn't he awakened her, knowing she was still on New York time? He'd gotten rid of her quickly last night after their impulsive lovemaking. Was he planning to leave her behind too?

Natasha swung her legs over the side of the bed and got ready as fast as she could. There was no way she was going to be left behind. Not if she could help it!

She took a five minute shower, gasping and squealing as the icy water pelted her. By the time she shut off the faucet, the warm water had kicked in. She finger-combed her curls, put on dark brown mascara, apricot blush and lip gloss and got dressed in a soft, long-sleeved royal blue T shirt, skinny indigo jeans and ankle boots. She grabbed her leather jacket and looped a rust and royal blue knitted scarf around her neck. With her shoulder bag slung across her body, she ran downstairs to join Ian.

# CHAPTER EIGHT

"Good morning," Natasha said to Ian's back as she entered the kitchen.

Seated at the table, he turned to look at her. Dressed in jeans and a black button down shirt with sleeves rolled up his strong forearms, he looked alpha and urbane at once. His thick, dark hair was slightly damp from the shower and his clean-shaven jaw glistened in the morning light.

"Morning, Tasha," Ian said, the clipped Scottish burr rolling off his tongue. "Dugie is in the garden collecting herbs for dinner. She left a plate of food warming in the oven for you. And there's coffee already brewed if you want a cuppa," he said, indicating the coffeemaker on the navy and white tile counter.

"Thanks." She hung her shoulder bag on the back of a chair and willed strength into her legs as she walked to the stove and retrieved the plate from the oven. She could feel Ian's gaze boring into her back as she poured herself a cup of coffee. She turned to him, holding the decanter. "Can I freshen your coffee?"

"No, thanks."

Natasha sat down and placed the plate of scrambled eggs, broiled tomato, and sausage before her. She unfolded her cloth napkin and carefully spread it on her lap. Her stomach was tied up in knots at the silent tension in the room.

Ian looked up from buttering his toast. "Better eat something. We have a long drive ahead of us. Edinburgh's not too far, but most of the drive will be on a two lane highway."

Natasha pushed her fork against the scrambled eggs, then the sausage and back again. "It looks delicious, but I'm not very hungry." She paused, warmth flooding her face and neck as she looked into his eyes. "How did you sleep last night?"

"Like a rock. You?" he asked with a raised brow.

"No more nightmares. I slept deeply," she said, disgruntled that he was acting like nothing had happened between them.

His silver-green gaze held hers with bemusement. Natasha glanced at his lips, remembering all the places they'd been last night. *The devil*, he might be acting nonchalant now, but last night he'd been unhinged. Wild and untamed—almost savage with desire. The erotic memory made her sweet spot pulse with pleasure as she squirmed on the wooden seat. She had to look away from his keen eyes to collect her wits and to eat a few bites, even though she had no appetite.

When the silence between them became unbearable, Natasha said, "Did you move me to the hidden chamber? Or did I sleep walk there?"

Ian pushed back from the table and observed her with wry detachment. "I carried you there. You were sleeping like a drugged woman."

She smiled. "I was." *Drugged by you.*

He remained silent as he ate his breakfast.

Natasha moved her plate away and huffed air into her lungs. "Why did you take me out of your bed? I don't understand," she said meeting his gaze squarely. Last night's intimate lovemaking had pushed them beyond the threshold of formality. She didn't know how much time they had left together in Glenhaven, and she wasn't going to waste it on small talk.

Ian gazed at her with earnest eyes. "I'm sorry for that, Tasha. But what did you expect from me? Last night was out of control."

"Yes, and I enjoyed it. We both did." That was an understatement, she thought hiding a smile as she took a sip of coffee. Her body still hummed with pleasure. "So why the distance now?"

Two grooves formed between his dark brows as he regarded her. "We need emotional distance to survive the next few days together."

"I don't," she said, issuing a challenging look.

Ian sighed heavily. "I do. From the moment you fainted in my office, you became my responsibility. Now, I have to keep you safe."

Natasha stared at him, her heart aching. "Have to? I'm not forcing you."

His eyes looked burdened. "I know. It's my choice."

"Can't we try again now that we've reconnected?" she dared to ask.

He leaned forward, his forearms braced on the wooden table as he stared at her intently. "That would only work with mutual trust."

Indignation swelled inside her. "And you can't bring yourself to trust me? Are you going to punish me forever for a decision I made seven years ago?"

"This isn't the time or place to discuss the past," he said, tight-lipped.

"Breaking our engagement was the most painful decision I ever made. But maybe it was the right decision after all," she said, hurt and anger fueling her.

Ian's features hardened to granite as he pushed away from the table and got up. "Then there's nothing more for us to discuss."

"There's plenty to discuss. You need to hear me out."

Ian's face remained stubborn and closed to communication. "Why? Your goals are the same as they were seven years ago, and they don't include me."

He set the mug down and turned to leave. Natasha shot up from the table and grabbed his arm. The heat of his skin scalded her icy hand. Suddenly, mere breathing became a chore. "Listen to me. Give me a chance to explain."

Ian's unwavering eyes met hers, and then glanced at his watch. "Go ahead. We have five minutes to spare."

Natasha ignored his arrogance and pressed on. "When you tended my wound so kindly in your office, I hoped that the past seven years had mellowed you." She exhaled a frustrated breath. "But I can see you're still bitter."

His jaw tightened. "I'm not bitter. I am focused on two goals here, and I don't want or need any distractions."

"I want peace between us once and for all," she said firmly. "The reason I broke off our engagement was because I wanted to perform on Broadway and you didn't understand how important that was to me—even though I had worked toward that goal all my life."

Standing ramrod stiff, Ian's hands gripped the back of the chair. "I told you I was willing to compromise so you could get the stars out of your eyes. I had planned to stay in New York and complete my Ph. D. You could have performed all you liked during that time."

"Ian, there are no guarantees in the theatre. One day you're at the top, and the other your understudy is screwing the director and you're out of a job," she said, hoping that wouldn't be the case with Lisette, but those things happened in the business all the time.

"What does that have to do with me?" he said roughly.

"My career wasn't the only thing holding me back. I loved you with all my heart, but I was scared of moving to Scotland permanently."

"That's right. I would have kept you as a prisoner in my castle. The beast to your beauty," he said sarcastically. "I promised you paradise, not a life of misery."

"Yes, but you never understood my dreams. The theatre is in my blood as much as Glenhaven is in yours."

"I'm not standing in your way anymore." His silver-green eyes skewered her with scorn. "Enjoy your career and your controlling mum's approval."

Natasha groaned. "I don't deny Anitra played a huge part in my decision. When I met you, I was naïve and inexperienced. It might sound ridiculous, but I'd never even had a boyfriend. My whole life was performing. Anitra convinced me that you wouldn't let me perform after we were married. She said you had a possessive, domineering streak like your father did."

"When did she say that to you?" Ian blazed.

A miserable knot formed in Natasha's belly. "I told her you weren't like him, but she insisted you were. She said she had known your father since college when she was dating Daddy."

Ian gripped the chair with white-knuckled fists. "Damn her. Only a cruel, selfish bitch would destroy her daughter's engagement!"

"Anitra may not be perfect, but she's still my mother," Natasha pointed out, flinching at the loathing in his eyes.

"Perfect? She's anything but," he grated.

Anger surged through Natasha like an electrical shock. "That's right, and neither are you. Stop scowling down your arrogant nose at me. I'm tired of hearing you blame me for the past. Grow up!"

"You grow up!" Ian reached out and pulled her toward him. Coiling his hand in her hair, he kissed her hard. She struggled against him, but as anger turned to hot passion, she gave in to the wild sensation. Her tender breasts swelled against his chest and pebbled instantly. One big hand cupped her bottom, while the other wound in her hair, holding her still. Pressed against his aroused body, Natasha's insides melted like warm molasses. She clung to him, returning his fierce kisses with her own.

Ian loosened his grip on her hair and his hands caressed the length of her spine, exploring, molding, palming her buttocks. Her pelvis tilted upward as she moaned into his mouth, her insides tingling and her heartbeat running amok.

Natasha pushed her fingers through the thick strands of his hair, stroking and clutching, as his lips and tongue plowed her swollen mouth with deep, slow kisses.

"Aye, they're a lovely couple of lovebirds again, aren't they Ranald?" Maggie exclaimed as she walked into the kitchen, chuckling when they jumped apart.

"That they are," Ranald said merrily.

Startled, Natasha drew in a sharp breath and stared at them ruefully. Her heart pounded like a tap dancer's feet inside her chest as she waited for Ian to do something.

Natasha's face flamed at the twinkle in Maggie and Ranald's discerning eyes. Evita's yelps drew attention away from Natasha's predicament as the puppy leaped from Ranald's arms into hers.

"It's—it's not what you think," Natasha said lamely when she caught her breath.

Maggie raised her brows at Ranald. They grinned and exchanged a private look. Natasha looked at Ian for support, but he remained silent and his ironic half-smile did nothing to ease her embarrassment.

"Ian can't seem to control the impulse to kiss me," she said after a pause, returning his smug smile. That wiped away any semblance of amusement from his face.

Coughing as if to clear his throat, Ian turned to Maggie and Ranald, who were still grinning broadly. "We'll be leaving now. If things take longer than I expect, we'll return tomorrow," he said.

"You didn't say anything about spending the night in Edinburgh," Natasha said. "I haven't packed an overnight bag." The word overnight elicited a flutter of excitement as she realized they'd be staying in a hotel together.

"We don't have time for you to go upstairs and pack. Did you take your antibiotic already?" he said briskly.

"I took the last pill early this morning."

Ian gave a short nod. "Good. If we stay over, I'll pick up what we need in Edinburgh."

"What about Evita?" Natasha said, hugging her close. She had missed her puppy last night, but in retrospect it was a good thing she hadn't been in the room with them.

"We'll watch her," Ranald and Maggie said in unison. They laughed heartily and shook their heads at their identical responses.

"Be on your way, then," Maggie said. "The sky is clear and the air is lovely out."

"Thank you for watching Evita," Natasha said, smiling at Maggie. She kissed Evita's cute little face. "Be a good girl. Mommy will be back soon, and I'll bring you a present."

Ian rolled his eyes and placed a hand on the small of Natasha's back, nudging her toward the door. "Time to go," he said.

Natasha wished she knew what he was thinking, but his face was an inscrutable mask. She warmly hugged Maggie and Ranald goodbye and promised to phone them if they decided to stay overnight in Edinburgh.

On the way to Edinburgh, Ian drove past the moors and craggy mountains with the windows down. He breathed in deeply of the fresh Highland air and enjoyed the simple pleasure of it. After the storm last night, the air had cleared to a crisp coolness and the blue sky was littered with white clouds frayed at the edges.

They drove in silence while Ian considered his recent flare-up in the kitchen. How like Natasha to wring out the last drop of his self-control. They hadn't been together more than ten minutes this morning and they were fighting and lusting for each other simultaneously. He shook his head when he remembered what had goaded him into kissing her. She had yelled, "Grow up!" No one he knew would have had the nerve say that to him—no one but Tasha.

She was right, though. He was a respected, successful physician, yet for seven years he had held on to the pain and resentment their breakup had caused him. He had dated many women afterward, but no one had ever filled the bleak emptiness left by Tasha. It was time to put the past behind where it belonged and forge ahead. It amazed him that her insult to "Grow up!" suddenly put everything into perspective.

Tasha was in danger and he would protect her regardless of their past. But there remained a major hurdle. She drove him wild and he couldn't seem to keep his hands off her. She was still a thistle in his heart, more now as a confident woman.

After what seemed like an interminable hour of stony silence, Natasha couldn't take it any longer. She had tried to take a nap, but she was too wired up. She had counted hearty hikers walking with their dogs and sheep grazing on the blue-green mountain sides. If they didn't talk soon, she'd burst from the restless energy inside her.

The friction between them in the kitchen had lit her up like a match. Now that it had been ignited, the dousing was near impossible. She glanced at Ian's granite jaw and his straight, bladelike nose. His gaze was focused directly ahead, absorbed in his thoughts while he listened to the strains of Irish rock violin.

"Ian," Natasha said.

Ian turned to her, silver-green eyes brooding. Refusing to be dissuaded by his mood, she flashed a friendly smile.

"Tell me about this patient you'll be seeing at the orphanage," she said.

He turned his attention back to the road. "Arthur is a wee lad of six. His mum is a poor, ignorant woman who had five children already. When she widowed suddenly, she gave Arthur up for adoption, blaming him for her husband's death."

"Why?" Natasha asked, startled.

"She had some odd religious belief that Arthur's scarred face was the curse of the devil."

"What's wrong with his face?"

"The left side is covered by a dark port wine stain." He glanced at her. "The head of the orphanage, Mrs. Byrne, called it grotesque," he said in a disgusted tone. "She said the other *bairns* ostracize wee Arthur because of it."

"That's so sad. How old was he when his mother gave him up for adoption?"

"I don't know for sure, but he was still an infant."

"So the only home he's ever known is the orphanage? That's tragic. Can you help him?" she said anxiously.

"I'll do my best to remove it. That type of port stain could get worse as Arthur grows older. In time it could become raised." He shook his head ruefully. "Mrs. Byrne told me he's been praying every night that I'll come to see him soon."

"Aw, you have a kind heart, Ian. I admire that," she said with all sincerity, wishing they hadn't quarreled earlier.

He glanced at her, his eyes sharp. "Do you know that in the short time we've been together, I've been tempted on too many occasions to wring your neck?"

"You're not the only one," she replied smartly. "I don't enjoy arguing with you."

"I don't either, but the mere mention of Anitra makes my blood boil."

"Then we won't mention her. Don't you think I always wished for a different type of mother? Someone who would hug and kiss me and tell me how much she loved me? I've had to come to terms with her type of parenting...or lack of it." She touched his forearm hesitantly. "Let's call a truce. We won't talk about my mother. Or the past. No more arguing. Agreed?"

Ian grunted. "I don't know if it's possible to spend time with you without arguing, but I'll do my bloody damnedest."

"Good. I'll hold you to it, Dr. Who."

He grabbed her hand and held it firmly. "If you rile me again, we'll argue."

"If you don't want me to rile you, then don't provoke me," she said pleasantly. "I'll only be here a few days, Ian. Let's enjoy each other's company. As soon as the flash drive is resolved, I'll leave," she said, her heart hurting at the finality of it.

# CHAPTER NINE

Ian's look of disappointment caught Natasha by surprise. "I'm not kicking you out of my home. You can stay as long as necessary," he said. It sounded as if he didn't want her to leave yet. He slanted a rueful glance at her. "I might have been a bit hard on you these past days. But the way you resurfaced out of the blue stunned me."

Ian apologizing? His softening toward her made her heart lift. "*Dinna fash*," she said in a lighthearted tone. "I forgive you. You made up for it last night in more ways than one." She flashed a saucy grin and was rewarded by Ian's incredibly appealing robust chuckle. It felt wonderful to hear him laugh.

"Damn right I did, wench. The well isn't dry yet."

She gave a mock gasp. "Ian! Are you referring to mine?" she said, having fun turning it with innuendo. "I'd say it's definitely wet, but not bottomless."

"I don't know about your well, Tasha, but your figure is not bottom-*less*," he said with a roguish smile, his eyes crinkling at the corners. "I'd say that part of you is nicely rounded. And firm."

"How do you know?" She smiled impishly. "Oh that's right, you have first-*hand* knowledge, Dr. Who."

Ian's silver-green eyes darkened a shade as his mouth eased into a slow smile filled with wicked intent.

Sensual heat rose from her neck to color her cheeks and her belly did crazy flips as the possibility of Ian making love to her again became more than a hot fantasy. She loved the way he was flirting with her and she didn't want him to stop. The tension between them was scorching; she could feel the sexual heat radiating from his strong body as he drove. Hopefully, they would run late and spend the night in Edinburgh. The prospect made her giddy with anticipation.

When they neared the site of infamous Rob Roy MacGregor's tomb, Natasha turned to him with a teasing grin. "Do you have any honest, law-abiding relatives who might still live in the Trossachs?"

Ian arched a brow. "Taunting me about Rob Roy again?"

She shook her head. "Gotta watch out for those MacGregors. Your clan seems to be—" She was stopped in mid-sentence when the Rover hit something on the road. The jeep lurched to the side as one of the tires blew out.

Ian pulled over to the side and got out. "Bloody hell! The tire's flat."

Natasha joined him at the side of the car. "Do you have a spare?"

He looked at her incredulously. "Of course I have a spare. I just can't *spare* the time to change it. I was planning on getting to Edinburgh with plenty of time to go to the University before I see Arthur."

"Oh. What can I do to help?" Natasha said cheerfully. "Not that I know what to do, but I'm willing to learn. My friend Ronnie is another story. She can change a flat in two shakes of a lamb's tail."

"I don't need help. Stand on the other side and don't distract me," he said rolling up his sleeves.

"Why so grumpy all of a sudden? It's not my fault we got a flat. *Men* and their cars," she grumbled, turning away in a huff. Five minutes later, she returned to his side. "Have you finished yet?"

Ian's head shot up and banged against the wheel wall. He muttered an expletive and rubbed the offended part. Ignoring her question, he removed the lug nuts from the tire.

"By the way, did you tell Maggie and Ranald about the flash drive? I'm worried about them."

"Aye, I've already alerted them to be extra careful."

Natasha breathed a sigh of relief. She squatted beside him and placed her hand on his hunched shoulder. "Do they know we have it here?"

"I told them about it this morning before they took Evita for a walk. They understand." He dropped the wrench on his toe. "Damn it. Stop distracting me or we'll be here all afternoon," he said, retrieving the wrench.

She straightened and walked away muttering *dunderheid* loud enough for him to hear.

"I heard that."

"Good."

Ian turned his attention to changing the tire and in no time they were on the road again. "Sorry I snapped at you back there, but your chattering was slowing things down," he said.

"I don't chatter, I speak. I sing too." She gave him a saccharine smile. "Would you like me to sing an aria?" she asked knowing he hated opera.

"No thanks," he said, his dry tone eliciting a dainty snort from Natasha.

As they neared Edinburgh, rays of sunshine bathed the city in a glow so brilliant, Natasha blinked to make sure it wasn't a mirage. It was the first time she had seen Edinburgh Castle on a sunny day. Regally situated over the massive dead volcano, Castle Rock, the castle glistened in the golden sunlight.

"It's breathtaking," she said, turning to see Ian's reaction.

Ian nodded. "I remember the first time I visited with my father when I was a wee lad. I stood there with my mouth hanging open." He glanced at his watch. "We need to go straight to the University and then stop for lunch. I called Connor and he'll be pleased to help you with the flash drive."

"That's great. But what about Arthur? When are you going to see him?"

"We'll take him to lunch with us. How's that?"

Natasha smiled. "Perfect."

"The business school building was recently completed in 2010," Ian said. "All the equipment and rooms are state of the art."

"Is it far from here?"

"Not at all. It's in the core of the University's central campus."

When they arrived and parked near the business school complex, a feeling of trepidation plagued Natasha.

She hesitated and slowed her steps as they walked toward it.

Ian rested his large hand on the small of her back and leaned toward her. "What's wrong?"

"Nothing," she said, wishing she could sound more convincing.

"You look pale. Are you all right? "

"Yes," she said, willing her overactive imagination to turn off.

"Don't be concerned about Connor. He's trustworthy. I say it with complete confidence."

"Good to hear." Natasha took a deep breath and straightened her spine, determined to walk into the office calmly, even if the thought of seeing what was on the flash drive gave her the willies.

Connor McKinney was indeed much younger than Maggie. He was tall, lean and handsome in a nerdy way, with rumpled auburn hair, horn-rim glasses, warm brown eyes and a ready smile. He welcomed them and led them to his computer.

"Natasha tried opening the flash drive, but it wouldn't on her laptop. It's a highly confidential and sensitive matter. One for the police," Ian said, handing him the flash drive.

"I understand." Connor inserted the flash drive in the computer. His thick brows knitted as he squinted at the screen. "Hmmm. It might take a few minutes, but we'll get it to open."

"Thanks, I hope so," Natasha said, sending Ian a hopeful look.

Connor typed in several commands and shook his head. "It looks like it's either damaged or something else is going on."

"Damaged?" A chill snaked up Natasha's spine. "How is that possible?"

"Flash drives take a lot of wear and tear," Ian said. "It could have been tinkered with. Or maybe just knocking around in your suitcase did it. Who knows?"

"Can it be fixed?" Natasha asked.

Connor nodded. "Probably. Let me try something else. The USB connector seems to be intact, so that's a good thing."

Natasha's mind raced with all kinds of questions. What if the mob caught up with her and demanded the flash drive? What would happen to her if they couldn't access the information? She didn't even want to think about it. She glanced at Ian to gauge his mood. He stood rigidly behind Connor, his eyes glued to the screen.

After several minutes, Connor leaned back in his chair. "Done," he said with an air of triumph. "All the files are accessible now." He got up and rolled another chair beside the one he'd been sitting in. "You can sit here and read them."

"I'd rather not," Natasha said nervously. "Would you take a look, Ian?" She walked away from the desk and let Ian sit beside Connor.

Ian clicked on several files and gave them a quick glance. "Some of these have names, addresses and dates. And events." He turned to look at Natasha, his expression dire. "Looks like we have a directory and timeline of Mafia activity here."

Natasha returned to his side and peered at the screen as he clicked on a few files. "Wait a minute. I think I see someone I recognize here," she said, shocked. "Doesn't *gamberi* mean shrimp in Italian?"

"Yes, why?"

She pointed to the screen. "Look, it says Rico the shrimp here. That has to be him!"

"Who the hell is Rico the shrimp?" Ian demanded.

"He used to own the jazz club with Tony. The irony is that Rico isn't a shrimp, he's pretty tall," Natasha said. "Now I'm wondering whether it was Rico or one of the mob guys who were in my apartment."

"Do you want me to take it to the police?" Connor asked. "I have a friend who's a detective—"

"No," Ian cut in. "Thanks for the offer, but I'd rather not involve Interpol. We need to get this back to the detectives in the States so they can put the word out that Natasha doesn't have it. Her life is in danger until they do."

The walls of the small office seemed to close in on her as icy terror crawled up Natasha's spine and spread over her suddenly chilled flesh. Ian was right about everything, especially the part about her life being in danger.

# CHAPTER TEN

Back in the car, Natasha's hands shook as she stared at the flash drive. "To think this tiny object holds information that's already gotten one person killed."

"Tell me about this Rico guy," Ian said, eyes on the two lane road.

Natasha shuddered. "He's scary. The morning after my place was ransacked he ambushed me outside my building and demanded that I give him the flash drive."

Ian's eyebrows shot up and he turned to her with an exasperated look. "Why didn't you tell me the *scunner* showed up at your building?" he demanded, his voice deepening with each word.

"Hey, don't get mad at me. There was so much going on, I forgot to mention it."

His eyes narrowed suspiciously. "What else did you forget to mention?" he growled.

"Nothing. I was in a state of shock…and injured, remember?" she said defensively.

Ian shook his head and muttered a string of expletives.

Natasha touched his biceps, the tension steely beneath her hand. "What do we do now?" she asked cautiously.

"We can't go to Interpol because you'll be detained forever as they try to sort it out." He thought for a moment. "Do you have a lawyer you trust?"

"Yes. Her name is Saundra Armstrong. She handles all my contracts."

"Good. Call her first tomorrow and fill her in on everything. She can contact the detectives on your behalf. In the meantime, I'll arrange for Ron, my pilot, to hand over the flash drive to one of the detectives."

"That would be great." She stared at him in awe. "When did you come up with this?"

His gaze flicked over her with concern. "It occurred to me while we were looking at the files. Anything to keep you safe," he said resolutely. "Once the police have the flash drive, they'll have to move quickly to put the word out so the mob knows you don't have it."

She nodded. "I just want all of this to be over with. I wonder if Detective Carson was able to identify the fingerprints of whoever ransacked my apartment." She paused and considered it. "I guess it's doubtful they got any prints if they were wearing gloves."

"Don't be too sure. Certain types of plastic gloves aren't thick enough to conceal fingerprints, especially if the fingers are deeply ridged like a man's."

"Really? Are you certain?"

He slanted a look that said are you kidding me? "I'm a dermatologist, I know about skin."

"True. You know about a lot of things. I don't know what I would have done without you."

"I won't let any harm come to you. And you're not going back to New York until it's safe for you to return," he said, turning his attention back to the road.

She kissed his lean jaw. "Thank you, Ian. I so appreciate your help," she said, touched he wanted to protect her, but disappointed he was already mentioning her going back to New York. She looked out the window, lost in thought as Ian drove to the orphanage.

They arrived at the Old Edinburgh Orphanage after a short drive and entered the old stone building to find Mrs. Byrne waiting for them outside her office door. Ian introduced Natasha to the middle-aged headmistress. Mrs. Byrne wore her steel gray hair in a no-nonsense pixie cut and was dressed in a perfectly pressed, but faded blue shirtwaist dress.

She greeted them courteously. "Wee Arthur will be verra pleased to see you, Dr. MacGregor. He has high hopes that you'll be able to help him."

"I'd like to meet him. Where is he?" Ian asked.

"Outside, playing. I'll take you there."

They followed the tall, athletic headmistress to a birch tree-lined playground filled with run-down wooden swings and one old metal climbing gym showing signs of erosion and peeling paint. She pointed where a skinny pint-sized boy sat, tracing circles in the sand. Small shoulders slumped and dark head bent, he was alone, away from the other children his age playing and shouting happily.

Mrs. Byrne clapped her hands briskly. "Arthur!" she called, "Dr. MacGregor is here to see you. Come quick, laddie."

Natasha was struck by the stark loneliness in Arthur's eyes when he glanced up. When he saw Ian, his face blossomed with hope. He jumped up and brushed the sand from the seat of his worn, oversized jeans and ran toward them. Natasha's heart clenched with despair when she saw the vivid purple blotch that started at the boy's left temple and swept down the whole side of his face to just below his chin. Thankfully, it didn't cover his eye. How on earth was Ian going to be able to erase it? It would take a miracle. Adding to the tragedy, the other half of his face was beautiful, almost poetic. The boy's fair complexion and deep blue eyes contrasted vibrantly to his dark, close-cropped hair.

Ian smiled at Arthur who stood before him, thick-lashed eyes downcast. He tilted Arthur's chin up with a gentle hand and looked into his eyes. Natasha watched them quietly, captivated by Ian's tender expression as he gazed at Arthur's face.

"Hello, Arthur, I'm Dr. Ian." His big hand engulfed Arthur's tiny one in a man-to-man handshake. "Come with me and I'll examine your face. Then I'll explain how I'm going to erase the mark. Would you like that?" he said kindly.

Arthur nodded, his grave face transformed by an eager grin. Natasha's heart melted as she watched Ian hold Arthur's small hand in his on the walk back to Mrs. Byrne's office. Ian would make an amazing father one day, she thought, her heart melting.

Natasha waited beside Mrs. Byrne outside the office, while Ian examined Arthur's face. Moments later they emerged laughing together.

"Mrs. Byrne, I've invited wee Arthur to lunch with us. Does he have your permission to join Miss White and me?" Ian said.

"Aye, Dr. MacGregor," Mrs. Byrne said with a courteous smile. "He'll miss spelling, but he can make it up tomorrow." She turned to Arthur and fussed over him, tucking in his shirt and smoothing his hair. "Mind your manners, laddie. Remember what you've been taught here."

"Aye, Mrs. Byrne." Arthur looked up at Natasha and smiled shyly.

Natasha couldn't resist taking Arthur's little hand in hers as they walked to the car.

They stopped at a store near the park. When they entered, the room grew hushed. The patrons stopped talking and stared at Arthur with perverse curiosity. The mother lioness in Natasha emerged as she leveled a deadly stare at them until they averted their eyes and minded their own business. Why did strangers have to be so cruel? Through no fault of his own, Arthur was born with a defect, yet they thought nothing of staring at him as if he were a freak. Her heart went out to him, and she wished she could protect him from similar episodes in the future.

Natasha took Arthur outside while Ian bought a picnic lunch of sandwiches, fruit and cookies, and a soccer ball to play with. After lunch, Ian played soccer—or football as they called it in Europe—with Arthur at a playground off Bruntsfield Links. She was anxious to find out Ian's diagnosis for Arthur's face, but she would have to wait. They were having too much fun playing and she knew Ian was doing it to make Arthur relax and trust him.

When they rejoined her, out of breath and ready for a sweet treat, they stopped at S. Luca, an ice cream shop on Morningside Road. Ian bought them "cheeky chocolate" ice cream, as Arthur had requested, and they went outside to eat it. The afternoon sun tinged the clouds a salmon color. Natasha slowly inhaled the cool, damp air, enjoying the aroma of distant bonfires. She and Ian walked down the cobblestone street with Arthur happily ensconced between them.

"Do you like school?" Natasha asked Arthur.

He shrugged and tilted his head to one side as he regarded her pensively. His clear, somber eyes had the astuteness of an adult's, yet his face was that of a child. "Sort of," he said at last.

"What's your favorite subject?" she asked.

"Art. I like to draw pictures."

"I love art too," Natasha said. "What do you like to draw?"

"Faces. Bonnie ones like yours," he said ducking his head as his cheeks bloomed hot pink.

"Why, thank you, Arthur." Natasha smiled at his bashful admission. "Do you like Mrs. Byrne?"

"Aye. She treats me like the other kids, even though my face looks like the devil himself," he said, nodding emphatically.

With a sinking heart, Natasha realized he was repeating what others had told him. All because his mother had gotten it in her head that he was the devil's son. So bizarre. "You don't look like a devil, Arthur. Quite the contrary! You have handsome eyes and a wonderful smile."

Arthur's face lit up and he flashed a surprised smile as his dark blue eyes regarded her curiously. "I do?"

"Yes, you do." Natasha's throat clogged with emotion at his look of relief. She winked at him. "I can tell you're smart too."

"And brave," Ian added with a kind smile. "We'll be starting the treatments soon. Your scar will improve and I may be able to erase it completely."

"Will it hurt?" Arthur asked, round-eyed.

"No, not too much. Maybe a twinge or two. Laser treatments are a bit like magic," Ian said.

"They are? Are you sure it won't hurt?" Arthur's eyes narrowed with suspicion. "Don't you have to stick me with needles?"

Ian shook his head. "No. Lasers aren't like shots at all," he assured him. "I'll explain each step of the treatment before we start. Do you trust me?"

Arthur nodded vigorously and took a large spoonful of the chocolate ice cream. The ice cream missed his mouth and landed on his blue shirt. He nervously clutched his cloth napkin and dabbed at the spot, making it worse. "Oh, no! Tis my Sunday shirt," he wailed anxiously. "Mrs. Byrne will be mad that I spoiled it." He looked like he was about to cry and Natasha wondered if he was afraid of being punished by Mrs. Byrne.

"Don't worry, sweetie. I'll get the stain out for you," Natasha said quickly. She ordered a club soda and when it arrived, she saturated her napkin with it and worked the stain out of his shirt.

Arthur glanced at her with grateful eyes. "Thank you, Miss."

"You're very welcome. And you may call me Natasha," she said giving him a hug. She exchanged a look with Ian before releasing him.

"I wish I could change my name," Arthur mumbled.

"Why would you want to?"

Arthur shrugged. "The kids make fun of it."

"Don't pay attention to them. Arthur is a very noble name. Don't you think so, Ian?" Natasha said, glancing at him.

Ian nodded sagely. "Arthur is a grand name for a brave lad like you. Do you know the story of King Arthur and his knights of the round table?"

"No," Arthur replied in a small voice.

"Arthur was a smart and noble king who ruled over a perfect land called Camelot. When he was a wee lad," Ian paused and smiled at Arthur, who was listening raptly. "Around your age, I believe ..."

By the time Ian finished the story, Arthur was beaming. "I think I'll keep my name. Arthur's a name to be proud of, eh?" he asked Natasha.

"It is," Natasha agreed with a warm hug.

When they returned Arthur to the orphanage and Mrs. Byrne's care, Ian stood with him just outside the headmistress's office. He was so much taller than Arthur, he had to squat down before him to look directly in his eyes. "As soon as my laser equipment arrives, we'll start your treatments. Until then, if you need anything, you can call me."

Ian retrieved a small calling card with his cell phone number on it. "Here is the phone number where you can reach me. Can you read it?"

"Yes, sir. I know my numbers and my letters," Arthur said earnestly.

"Good. If you have more questions about the treatment, you may call me and I'll explain."

Mrs. Byrne's lips pressed together in a thin line as she reached for the card. "I'll hold on to that for safekeeping."

Ian stayed her hand. "That's all right. I'm sure Arthur will find a safe place to keep it." He gave Arthur an encouraging pat on the shoulder. "Won't you?"

Clutching Ian's card in his hand, Arthur nodded solemnly. "Aye."

"I'll be waiting for your call tomorrow morning before I leave," Ian said.

Arthur's face brightened. "I promise I'll call you, Dr. Ian."

Mrs. Byrne nodded. "Verra well." She bent down and whispered in Arthur's ear. "Don't forget to thank the kind doctor."

Arthur extended his hand to Ian and shook it. "Thank you, Dr. Ian."

"You're very welcome, Arthur," Ian said, smiling warmly.

Natasha pulled Arthur's slight frame into her arms for a hug. His torso felt bony as she wrapped her arms around him, all ribs and very little flesh. "Good-bye, sweetie. It was nice to meet you. Dr. Ian will take good care of you when he comes back."

Arthur nodded and trudged away.

"Arthur, please don't drag your feet," Mrs. Byrne chided.

He turned around, his eyes anxious as he stared at her. "I'm sorry, Mrs. Byrne."

"It's all right," she replied with a long suffering sigh.

When Arthur left the room, Ian turned to Mrs. Byrne. "Arthur seems overly cautious for a six year old lad. It's as if he's afraid to make a mistake."

Mrs. Byrne's mouth tightened. "He's a bright wee lad, but many of the children shun him because of his scar. They've heard his mum left him here because she thought he was the devil's *bairn*." Her eyes narrowed to slits. "I have forbidden them to call him that. The wee lad keeps to himself most of the time. I don't coddle him so that he will grow up to be strong enough to handle the outside world and its cruelties."

Giving Arthur love and compassion wasn't coddling in Natasha's opinion. He was only six! The poor little guy needed a lot of nurturing and social interaction to grow up strong. She was sad to say good-bye to him so soon.

"Mrs. Byrne, I would like to get started on Arthur's face as soon as possible," Ian said. "It will take many treatments. All of them free of charge."

"That is most generous of you, Dr. MacGregor! Thank you," Mrs. Byrne said, looking very pleased. "When can you start?"

"Could be in a few months," he said. "After I meet with my partner, I'll have a better answer for you. Good bye," Ian said, shaking her hand.

Her heart sank. *His partner. Dr. Danielle Parkhurst.* Natasha had been so caught up in her feelings for Ian and everything else going on, she hadn't thought about Danielle.

# CHAPTER ELEVEN

Back in the car, Natasha watched Ian as he started the ignition. "You said you were going to start Arthur's treatments in a few months. When will the clinic be ready?"

"Soon. It's close to completion. I said a few months to buy time in case something goes awry. I don't want to raise the lad's hopes and then disappoint him. " He frowned as he backed the car out of the space.

"I can't stop thinking about him. His eyes haunt me. They were filled with pain and insecurity. And his posture was so hunched over and humble. It broke my heart," she said, remembering Arthur's drooping shoulders and bent head.

Ian glanced at her and nodded gravely. "I know what you mean. I want to help him as soon as I can."

"What's holding you back? Does the clinic have to be completely finished before you start treating him?"

"The equipment is set up. I just have to strong arm a certain person to make things move faster." His hand tightened on the steering wheel.

"Your partner?" From the way Ian was acting, it didn't seem as if he was in love with another woman. Still, she was dying to hear what he would say about Danielle.

"Not my partner. I meant the witch who's claiming half of Glenhaven," Ian said with disgust.

"Oh." So much for learning about Danielle.

Ian drove in deep thought, his eyes focused on the road and his body on edge.

"Where are we going?" Natasha asked.

"It's a bit late to drive back and I have some things to take care of. There's a hotel not far from here where we can stay the night."

"Sounds good to me," Natasha said, happy to spend more time together.

Moments later, he parked the car at Princes Street. "We're here."

A sign that said The Gable Hotel in shiny brass letters hung above a charming, arched entryway leading to a courtyard garden. The three story building was painted pale gray and trimmed in white; its high gables reached toward the sky. Clouds shifted over the sun as the wind rustled through the trees and ushered in cold air.

"The sky is turning purple. I hope we're not in for another storm," Natasha said.

"You'll be safe in the hotel." Ian's hand descended and settled on the small of her back, eliciting tingles. "With me," he added, his voice smooth as the finest Scottish malt whiskey.

A shiver of pleasure flitted through Natasha as they locked eyes. He kissed her temple and led her into the grand, wood-paneled entrance hall that resembled an elegant hunting lodge. It had a high, peaked ceiling and the walls held an assortment of taxidermy. The room smelled manly of leather and spice, making Natasha swoon with anticipation of the night ahead.

Ian approached the reception desk and requested a room.

The young clerk scratched his head. "I'm sorry, sir. I can only offer you the V.I.P. suite."

"Perfect. We'll take it," Ian said right away.

Moments later they entered a light-filled, spacious suite. Natasha was immediately drawn to the pale pastel Edwardian décor and floor to ceiling windows. She stood at the bay window opposite the rose marble fireplace and marveled at the extraordinary view of Edinburgh Castle in the horizon.

Ian came up and silently stood behind her. Every nerve in her body leaped to attention. She shivered and rubbed her arms as she turned to face him. "Yes?"

"I'm going out. I'll be back in a few hours." His dark brows drew together as he looked her up and down. "What size are you?"

"I'm a four. I'm not sure what that would be in Scotland."

He rubbed his chin. "Hmmm." His hands touched her shoulders, then lowered to her hips and lingered there for a moment. She held her breath, wondering if he was planning on kissing her, but he lightly squeezed the indentation of her waist instead.

She yelped. "That tickles. What are you doing?"

"Checking your size."

"Ah, so that's how it's done. Now my turn," she said, mischievously reaching for him.

His finger tapped her nose while his other hand tapped her bottom. "Not now," he said, heading toward the door.

Natasha chuckled. "You don't know what you're missing." When he didn't respond, she said, "All right. I'll call Maggie and tell her where we're staying if she needs to get in touch."

"Good idea," he said and left.

She phoned Maggie, but Dugie answered and said Maggie and Ranald had gone to Fort William on an errand. Natasha left a message for them and hung up, eager to soak in the tub.

Humming to herself, she went into the bathroom and drew a hot bath. She poured scented bath gel in the steaming water before stepping in. After a soothing soak, she wrapped herself in the fluffy white robe provided by the hotel and made her way to the bedroom. She turned down the covers and reclined on the Edwardian style bed, basking in the softness of the sheets on her skin.

She opened the *Hello* magazine she purchased at the market and leafed through it. A picture of hotel heiress Theodora Behr, known to everyone as Teddy, made her smile with fondness. Over the years, Natasha had stayed in touch with Teddy and Ronnie, her two Heart sisters from summer camp and they were close friends. She loved the picture of Teddy, dressed to the nines in a slinky black sequined gown with a black feather head dress. With her long blond hair slicked back and obscured by black swan feathers that curled over her head in a small cap and framed her face dramatically, she looked stunning. Her gold-flecked chocolate eyes peered from beneath long, curly lashes as she flashed a playful scarlet grin. Natasha smiled and shook her head. Leave it to Teddy to dress like a vamp and grin like a scamp.

Teddy managed several charitable endeavors and stayed away from Miami where her evil stepmother controlled everything, including Teddy's father, The Riviera Hotel magnate, Theodore Behr. "The inimitable Teddy Behr takes Paris by storm at the *Fête d'automne* charitable ball," the caption beneath the picture read. Natasha slid under the covers and enjoyed the rest of the article until she dozed off.

A few hours later, the door swung open and a gust of cool air woke Natasha up. A tremor of excitement coursed through her at the sight of Ian, his dark, wavy hair windswept and the peaks of his hollowed cheeks flushed from the afternoon wind. Her pulse accelerated. His mouth looked sensuous, warm and inviting. Her hand automatically went to her lips recalling his hard, passionate kiss that morning. She dropped her hand as delicious heat rose to every pore of her skin and spread over her body warming her from her face to the tips of her toes.

"Get up, angel. I have good news, and I brought a surprise." Ian's voice rumbled out of his chest, gravelly and sexy.

*He called her angel, just like old times.* Her heart did a giddy leap and her knees turned to jelly as she neared his side.

"What's the good news?"

"I gave Ron the flash drive. He'll fly out with it tomorrow."

"So soon? That's wonderful!" She let out a whoop and did a high five with him. "I'm so relieved. Thank you!"

"You're welcome. Call your lawyer first thing tomorrow morning so she can alert the police that Ron will deliver the flash drive at the airport. He should arrive around 1:00 in the afternoon."

"Okay."

"Here. These are for you." He handed her the packages he was holding and walked to the nightstand where he placed a small bag. Returning to the sofa, he sat down and contemplated her with his arms crossed behind his head and his long legs sprawled out in a V.

Ian enjoyed watching Natasha's enthusiasm as she peeked in the bags. He usually didn't like to shop for himself, but he'd enjoyed shopping for her. She looked adorable in the oversized hotel robe, her shiny copper hair tousled from sleep and her cheeks pink with excitement. He glanced at her kissable rosebud mouth and looked forward to the night ahead.

"Thanks, I love it." She held up the sky blue cashmere mini dress to her figure, pinning it against her slender waist.

"Same color as your eyes. Looks like it'll fit," he said, pleased with his choice. The mini dress would showcase her stunning dancer's legs, and that wasn't all. The cashmere would cling nicely to her full breasts and high, round bum, he thought, admiring her curves.

Natasha blew him a kiss. She opened another package and retrieved a pair of buttery soft knee high boots. "Ooh, I love these too!"

Ian's eyes connected with hers. "You know how I feel about you in boots." He was tempted to say "and nothing else" but refrained.

She blushed, her soft cheeks rosy and appealing as she nodded. "What's in the small package?"

"Open it."

Natasha pulled out blush pink panties edged in black lace and a matching bra. She lifted a delicate brow. "Knickers? Smart thinking, Dr. Who. You already melted mine," she said with a smile that lit up her face.

"Oh?" He crooked a finger at her. "Come and show me."

"I would if I were wearing them," she taunted.

Ian instantly rose and brought her back to the couch. Settling her on his lap, he grew hard at the delicious feel of her firm buttocks resting on him. He parted the top of her robe and kissed her bare breasts, inhaling deeply of her clean, feminine scent. Natasha threw her head back and arched when he took her the pink bud of her breast between his lips and sucked gently. Her fingers wound in his hair, keeping his mouth anchored on her breasts as she moaned with pleasure. When he got his fill of her creamy breasts, he pulled back and gazed into her eyes as he stroked her supple legs.

Tasha's soft hand caressed the stubble on his jawline. "I want to feel this on my skin," she said huskily.

Ian parted her robe and ran his cheek along the silky skin of her belly. Natasha squeezed her thighs together and drew in a shuddering breath. "Yes, like that," she murmured, her voice sweet and hoarse.

A knock at the door interrupted him and he closed her robe quickly.

"Oh no," Natasha groaned. "Are you expecting someone?"

Ian frowned. "No, it must be the blasted room service. Ignore it." He was too thickly aroused to think of food. All he wanted was Tasha and the banging on the door was irksome.

Natasha made a disappointed face. "Better answer it. I don't think they're going away any time soon." She got up and ran into the bathroom.

Annoyed by the untimely disruption, Ian opened the door and the waiter rolled the serving cart into the room and lit the candles. He uncorked the wine and poured two glasses. "Shall I serve you, Dr. MacGregor?" he asked.

"No thank you, that will be all," Ian replied, giving him a generous tip. When the waiter left, Ian called out. "Tasha, you can come out now. The coast is clear."

She joined him at the table and raised the silver domes off of two platters. "What a banquet! Goose liver and wild mushroom pate. Roast pheasant with wild rice and beef scotch olives." Her eyes met his with tenderness. "Thank you." She lifted another dome. Her pink tongue darted out and wet her glistening lips, igniting his blood. "Mmm, fresh raspberries in meringue glace for dessert," she said with an appreciative sigh.

As they ate, Ian sipped wine and watched Tasha. Her luminous blue eyes held him captive and her creamy skin, glowing in the candle light, made him want to open her robe and feast on her, not the food. He wanted her breasts in his hands and the sweet curves of her buttocks and thighs nestled against him. An insatiable hunger to taste her and make her moan with pleasure made him put his fork down and push the plate away.

"I called Maggie, but she wasn't home, so I left a message with Dugie," Natasha said.

Ian barely heard what she said. All he wanted to do was take her there, on the floor in front of the blazing fire.

Natasha cleared her throat. "Did you hear what I just said?"

"Aye," he said hoarsely. He glanced at the tiny pulse leaping in the hollow of her throat above her cleavage and couldn't think of anything but having her—now.

Natasha seemed to go boneless before him. Her lips parted and she drew in shallow breaths as a rosy flush crept up her neck and flooded her cheeks. "Do you want more wine?" she asked softly, her tongue wetting her lips.

"No. I want you." He rose from the table and pulled her up, coiling his hands in her glossy hair and holding her still as he kissed her slowly, deeply. Tasting of crisp white wine and heady desire, she clung to him, her arms locked around his back, her lush breasts pressed against his chest. Not taking his gaze from her heated eyes, he led her to the bed and sat her on the edge. He untied her sash and opened her robe, revealing her beautiful body to his fiery gaze.

"Gorgeous," he breathed, tracing a finger down her neck and across her graceful collarbone. He cupped her breasts and kissed each pink tip, reveling in their velvety softness. Kneeling before her, his hands slid under her bottom as he kissed her belly and sweet inner thighs.

"Ohhh," she moaned, inhaling sharply when his thumb stroked her wet heat. Her nostrils flared as his breath fanned her pulsing feminine core and he kissed her there, his lips feather light.Seconds later, Natasha quivered violently and clutched his hair as the building crescendo overtook her and she shattered with keening moans. Ian held her in his arms, gentling her with Scottish endearments until she calmed. He undressed quickly, his trousers joining his shirt and socks on the floor. Not taking his eyes off her lush body, Ian reached for the box of condoms in the bag he'd left beside the bed. He tore open a foil packet and pulled on a condom before joining her.

"Come here, angel," he murmured huskily, pressing her back into the mattress as he began a kissing celebration of her fevered body.

Natasha's nails lightly raked down his back before her soft hands curved over his hips. Braced above her, Ian fitted himself between her thighs and lifted her buttocks to meet his first thrust. Joined together, he surged inside, over and over, his breath hot on her neck as he nipped it.

"So beautiful," he whispered hoarsely between thrusts. "I can't get enough of you."

Her face tightened with sweet agony. "Take me. I'm yours," she cried eagerly. "All yours." She came with shuddering sobs and Ian groaned savagely, hugging her tightly as he climaxed with powerful, shuddering force.

Later, they lay fused together and drained of strength, cozy in bed. Ian held Natasha close to his heart and kissed the top of her head as he caressed her smooth back. After a while, she pulled away and ambled to the table. Placing two pillows behind his neck, Ian sat up and watched the provocative play of muscles in her shapely buttocks and long legs.

Natasha returned with the bowl of raspberries and fresh whipped cream in a meringue shell and two spoons. He was already hard when she balanced the bowl on his chest and climbed on top of him, her lithe thighs straddling his hips. They ate dessert feeding each other between kisses. Natasha put the bowl on the nightstand and leaned forward, kissing him with a mouthful of whipped cream. Ian licked the cream from her lips and swallowed the sweetness.

"Now it's my turn to pleasure you," she murmured, her glistening mouth erotic and inviting.

And pleasure him she did until he came with such force the bed shook.

Natasha collapsed against him and buried her face in his hot neck. "You are so delicious, Ian. I can't get enough of you either."

"You might have gotten too much of me last night." He slid his hand up and down her spine, enjoying the suppleness of her skin.

She lifted her head and stared at him with questioning eyes. "What do you mean?"

"We didn't use a condom. It was reckless and impulsive." He didn't want to consider the consequences.

"I'm only reckless and impulsive when it comes to you," she said.

He stiffened, remembering she'd just come off a relationship with Tony. That had been reckless. Jealousy and raw distrust surfaced. "The idea of you sleeping with that *scunner* Tony makes me sick…or anyone else for that matter," he grated.

"I never slept with anyone but you," she said, rubbing her cheek against his chest with a ragged sigh.

He pulled back to stare at her. "Are you telling me the truth?"

She sat up. "Of course. Why would I lie? "

"You've lied to me before," he said, watching her face crumble.

"I didn't lie about loving you or wanting to be your wife," she said with a catch in her voice. "If this is about when we broke up, you never let me explain, Ian. I wanted a chance to perform on Broadway before settling down. It was always my lifelong dream."

He didn't feel like hashing it out. They would only be talking in circles. Ian ran a rough hand through his hair. "Tonight was a mistake," he said flatly.

Natasha yanked the sheet and wrapped it around her with shaky hands, shielding her naked body from his eyes. "Why?" she asked, red-faced and blinking back tears.

"Because you're a drug to me and I won't get addicted again." He got up from the bed. "Are you ready to tell me anything has changed in seven years?"

Natasha gnawed her lower lip, her soft blue eyes anguished as she silently stared at him.

"I thought so." He drew in a harsh breath. "No one, not even you, Tasha, will stand in the way of my dream of returning to Scotland," he said and walked to the bathroom.

When he returned, she was on her side on the bed, turned away from him. Ian sank down on the sofa and rubbed a rough hand over his face as he eyed Natasha with deep regret. Hot passion scorched between every breathing moment she was near. His libido had ruled over rationality tonight, hoping she would remain emotionally detached as they enjoyed a night of hot sex. But who was he fooling; *he* wasn't detached. It was impossible to be when it came to Tasha. When they made love, the raw beauty of her soul shined in her eyes and held him spellbound.

*I never slept with anyone but you.* Her admission invaded his peace of mind, haunting him, stripping all defenses and leaving him vulnerable. It shook him to the core and made him want to pull her in for a long bout of lovemaking and mark her as his. But he couldn't.

Ever since she'd snaked back into his life, Tasha had acted as if everything was the way it had been before their break-up. It annoyed him that she could be so naïve, and it annoyed the hell out of him that he didn't have control when it came to her. She'd only been in Scotland two days and he was supposed to be protecting her, but he couldn't keep his hands off her. Like a siren luring a drunk sailor, she aroused erotic feelings he couldn't resist.

*Damn her,* she was a thistle in his heart, pricking him with her magnetism and luring him with tenderness. By coming back into his life, she had decimated his hard won control and filled his heart with joy…and false expectations. But he wouldn't let her cripple his defenses again. He had to keep a distance and a level head. If he let her back into his heart, he wouldn't let her go. Not now. Not ever. And sooner or later, she'd choose New York again.

If he allowed their intimacy to deepen, his plans for the clinic would be sidelined.

He'd let his guard down twice now. He'd be damned if he'd do it again.

# CHAPTER TWELVE

The sound of a ringing phone jarred Natasha awake, and the gloomy reminder of how last night had ended enveloped her. She tried to focus her vision in the hotel room, still dark from the drawn curtains. A glance at her watch told her it was only 7:00 a.m., early for a phone call. Ian was in the shower; she could hear the water running.

The phone rang again. In the dark room, she groped the nightstand and realized it was Ian's smartphone ringing. When she answered, a child's quivery voice said, "May I speak to Dr. Ian, please?"

Surprised to hear from him so early in the morning, Natasha said, "Arthur, is that you?"

"Yes, ma'am," he replied softly.

"Hi, sweetie. Hold the line. I'll run and get Dr. Ian for you." Natasha raced to the bathroom door and knocked several times, worried that Arthur might be crying.

Moments later, Ian opened the door with a towel wrapped around his lean waist. He looked like a sleek wolf, his dark hair rumpled and wet. Too bad he hadn't come back to bed last night, instead sleeping on the couch like a disgruntled lover.

"Arthur's on the line. He sounds upset," she said, tearing her gaze from his hot torso.

Ian reached the telephone in seconds. When he hung up, his eyes were sharp with concern.

"What's wrong with Arthur? He sounded like he was crying," Natasha said.

Ian nodded grimly. "The lad begged me to start the treatments as soon as possible. He wants to get away from the orphanage."

"What happened?"

"A group of kids got the card I gave him and tore it up last night."

"That's mean. How did he call you then?"

"He had written down my number thinking Mrs. Byrne might take the card from him. They beat him up too." Ian's jaw clenched and his eyes glittered ferociously. "I'm taking him out of there," Ian said, pulling on jeans and sliding his arms into a slate blue shirt.

"Good!" she said, her heart expanding with love as she watched him.

Ian used the discarded towel to dry off his hair and ran his fingers through the thick waves. "I'll take him to Glenhaven," he said. "Maggie and Ranald can care for him while I start the treatments."

"Oh, that's wonderful of you!" She wished she could fling her arms around him and hug him with all her might. "Arthur will love Glenhaven. I'm going with you to the orphanage," she said, reaching for the bag with the cashmere dress.

Ian shrugged into his black leather jacket. "No, you'll take too long to get ready."

She grabbed the other bag that had the boots he'd given her. "No, I won't. Give me fifteen minutes," she said, heading toward the bathroom.

"Be quick about it," he said briskly. "I'm going to make a few phone calls to check on the legalities of taking Arthur out of the orphanage. If you're not down in fifteen, I'm leaving without you."

On the way to the orphanage, Natasha called Saundra, her lawyer, and filled her in on everything. Saundra offered to contact Detective Carson with the drop-off details and also to make sure that the word was put out that the police had the flash drive, not Natasha.

"I'll handle it from here," Saundra said.

"You will?"

"Yes, it's best for you to go through me from now on."

Natasha breathed a sigh of relief. "Okay, but this might put you in danger too."

"I'm not worried about that," Saundra said confidently. "I'll contact you as soon as I have an update from Detective Carson that she has the flash drive."

"There's spotty reception in some areas here. If you can't reach me by phone, please email me. Or leave a message with my friends, Maggie or Ranald Duncan in Scotland. I'll email you their contact information."

"Will do. Be safe."

"You too. Thanks for everything."

Natasha hung up and turned to Ian. "Wow, she's fearless. I'm glad Saundra wants to manage it, but I don't want her to be in danger. She said she's not worried about it, but I am—for both of us."

"Don't be. She knows what she's doing." He squeezed her hand lightly. "Nothing is going to happen to you. You're safe with me."

Hearing Ian say that made Natasha feel better. So he did care about her. The memory of his touch last night made her ache for more. Hopefully, he'd come to his senses and give them a second chance.

When they arrived at the orphanage parking lot, Natasha turned to Ian. "Do you think Mrs. Byrne will let him leave with us?"

"It might take some convincing. I'll sweeten the offer by making a donation to the orphanage. I was planning to anyway."

"Good idea." Natasha wrung her hands. "I've been praying all the way here that you would take him out of this bleak place."

A fleeting glance of tenderness passed over Ian's face. "Keep praying, we might need it," he said, taking the key out of the ignition.

"Are you talking about the legal implications?"

"No, I spoke to my lawyer. It shouldn't be too complicated as long as Mrs. Byrne cooperates. Come on. Let's go," he said, opening the car door.

Inside the orphanage, Mrs. Byrne ushered them to her office. She seemed surprised that they were there so early. Motioning to the chairs before her desk, she said, "Please sit down. What brings you here this morning?"

"I want to make a donation to the orphanage so you can buy new playground equipment and whatever else the children might need for entertainment."

Her eyes widened. "Thank you, Dr. MacGregor. How generous of you."

"You're welcome." Ian leaned forward in the wooden armchair and braced his elbows on his knees. "Mrs. Byrne, I just received word that my laser equipment will be arriving sooner than expected. I'll need to do medical tests on Arthur right away."

"Right away? What does that entail?" she asked, gazing at him with a furrowed brow.

"He'll have to travel with us to Glenhaven today." When Mrs. Byrne's mouth dropped open, he added, "Would you prepare the papers we need to complete before he can leave?"

"Today?" Mrs. Byrne's astonished gaze traveled from Ian to Natasha, then back to Ian. "I suppose I can," she said hesitantly. "How long will he need to stay at Glenhaven?"

"I can't say for sure. The treatments should be completed within a year," Ian said in a noncommittal tone.

"A year? Are you sure you want to take him with you? Wee lads of six can be a handful!" She drew her jaw back rigidly, causing several chins to crease her neck.

"Arthur won't be a problem. He behaved perfectly yesterday. We'd love to have him stay at Glenhaven estate," Natasha said.

Turning to Natasha, Mrs. Byrne looked her curiously. "Do you live at Glenhaven?"

"No. I'm a close friend of the family visiting from the States. I live in New York."

"I see," Mrs. Byrne murmured.

"In my foster care, wee Arthur will be well taken care of," Ian assured her. "Where is he? I'd like to see him," Ian said.

Mrs. Byrne swallowed nervously and folded her hands on the desk. "I'm afraid that won't be possible until much later."

"How much later?" Ian asked, impatience lacing his tone.

"Not until this evening." Mrs. Byrne fidgeted with the droopy neck bow of her white blouse, not meeting Ian's eyes. "He had an unfortunate incident yesterday."

"What kind of an incident, Mrs. Byrne?" Ian asked, leveling a grave look at her.

Mrs. Byrne's eyes met his with trepidation as she released a drawn-out sigh. "Some of the children picked on him and roughed him up a bit."

"How badly was he hurt?" Ian asked in a chilling tone.

"He didn't break anything. He got bruised a wee bit, mostly his feelings. But rest assured, the mischief-makers have been sternly disciplined," she said, her mouth tight with displeasure.

"More reason for him to leave with us today." Ian stood and glanced at his watch. "We must leave Edinburgh by early afternoon. Would you kindly expedite the arrangements?"

Mrs. Byrne gave a brisk nod. "I suppose I can." She rose from her chair decisively. "Indeed, return at noon. By then I'll have the necessary papers drawn up to place Arthur in your care temporarily. You'll need to sign them before leaving."

"Please see that all of Arthur's belongings are packed for him, including a special teddy bear or stuffed animal," Natasha said.

"Arthur is six now. He stopped sleeping with stuffed animals long ago," Mrs. Byrne said starchily.

Natasha glanced at Mrs. Byrne with mild reproach. "A stuffed animal to hold at night drives away the loneliness, and the boogeyman. I used to love my—"

Before Natasha could continue, Ian quickly said good-bye and ushered her out the room.

"Why did you cut me off?" she said the minute they were outdoors.

"So Mrs. Byrne would hurry up and get everything ready for Arthur," he said.

"But I wanted to make a point with her. I know she's trying to toughen Arthur up, but he could use a lot more affection."

"There isn't a warm bone in that woman's body," Ian said. "Most likely she doesn't want to get emotionally invested with her charges."

Natasha sighed heavily. "Could be."

They drove to Princes Street in search of a restaurant to eat breakfast. "Where's a good bagel place when you need it?" Natasha quipped in a New York accent.

Ian chuckled. "You won't find bagels here. Most of the pubs don't open until noon, so we'll stop at a bakery."

They chose one with a small table near the window and ordered Selkirk bannocks and strong coffee. Ian bit into the rich, fruity bannock and chewed pensively. He shook his head. "For a moment there, I thought Mrs. Byrne wouldn't let Arthur leave. Especially at such short notice."

"Good thing she agreed. It's wonderful you're taking him out of there, but how is he going to feel when you have to return him?"

"I'll cross that bridge when I get there. First I'll work on his face and then I'll find a suitable home for him," Ian replied.

Natasha's heart constricted over Arthur's depressing circumstances. "He is the sweetest little boy. I wish people weren't cruel to him."

"Many people can't see beyond the mark on his face."

"Wouldn't it be great if they could?" she mused. "What are we going to do until it's time to pick him up? Can we go shopping?"

Ian groaned and looked heavenward. "More shopping? What else do you need?"

"Nothing for me. I want to buy a few things for Arthur."

His expression lightened. "Sure, we can do that."

"Can you tell me about the woman who holds part of your inheritance?" she said as they walked down the sidewalk.

"I'd rather not." Ian stopped and stared at her. "What made you think of her?"

Natasha shrugged. "You've said she's a witch, but nothing else. I'm trying to understand what's going on."

"I don't want to discuss it," Ian said bluntly.

"Fine, then we won't," she replied. She didn't want to pry, but she wished he felt comfortable enough to confide in her. Leaving his side, she contented herself with buying new clothes for Arthur, some toys, books, and a fluffy teddy bear.

"Time to go back," Ian said as they left the shop. "Arthur should be ready by now." He called and alerted Mrs. Byrne that they were coming.

When they drove up to the orphanage, Mrs. Byrne was waiting outside at the entrance with Arthur standing beside her. A brown, battered suitcase rested on the floor next him.

Ian and Natasha greeted them.

"Is that all he's bringing?" Ian said, indicating the small suitcase.

Mrs. Byrne gave him a raised eyebrow look. "Wee Arthur doesn't have much." She patted Arthur's shoulder—not giving him a hug, just a perfunctory pat. "Be a good lad now."

"Aye, Mrs. Byrne," Arthur said, looking up at her wide-eyed.

"I'll miss you, but you'll be happy in Glenhaven. Dr. Ian is kind and generous," Mrs. Byrne said.

Arthur's face scrunched up. "I'll miss you too, Mrs. Byrne."

Ian smiled at him. "Are you ready then, Arthur?"

Arthur nodded eagerly.

After they said good-bye to Mrs. Byrne, Ian took Arthur's hand and led him to the car. "You're limping," Ian said, glancing at Arthur's legs. "Does it hurt anywhere?"

"Aye," Arthur said quietly.

"Where?" Ian asked.

"Here." Arthur raised his trousers' leg and showed him a bluish purple bruise that covered his shin from his knobby knee to his scrawny ankle.

Natasha flinched and closed her eyes, feeling his pain as if it were her own.

Ian knelt and gently touched the tissue surrounding the bruise, his dark brows creased over sympathetic eyes. "How did that happen?"

"The lads kicked me," Arthur said. "I kicked them back, but it didn't help. When I yelled, Mrs. Byrne came and stopped them."

Ian shook his head. "Sorry to hear they did that to you." He gave the boy's back a comforting pat. "You're going to be okay. It won't happen again," he assured him.

"Arthur, there's someone here who needs a friend," Natasha said, pointing to the teddy bear in the back seat.

Arthur's eyes brightened. "Is that for me?"

Ian ruffled his hair. "Yes."

"Can I hold him?"

"Of course. You can hold him and cuddle him at night," Natasha said smiling at Arthur.

Arthur's cheery grin warmed her heart. He rose on his tiptoes and motioned for her to lean down. Depositing a kiss on her cheek, he said, "Thank you, Natasha. And thank you, Dr. Ian."

"You're welcome, honey," Natasha replied, hugging his thin frame and helping him in the car.

They stopped for lunch before heading back to Glenhaven. The drive was glorious. A cool mist enveloped the varied landscape of the Highlands providing an enchanted background as Ian described his castle and estate to Arthur. He told him he would let him stay in the room he grew up in. Arthur's eyes lit up like sparklers when Ian promised to show him his collection of medieval swords.

Listening to them talking filled Natasha with happiness. Arthur already seemed less timid and less afraid, and Ian was enjoying his company.

When they arrived at Glenhaven in the early evening, Maggie, Ranald and Dugie beamed at them as Ian carried Arthur and his teddy bear inside. He had dozed off with it in his arms during the drive. Ian had called ahead and let them know he was bringing Arthur.

Signaling to Maggie and Ranald that they would talk later, Natasha followed Ian into the castle. Once upstairs, she helped tuck Arthur in bed. She ran her hand softly over his fuzzy, dark hair and leaned down to kiss his scarred cheek. A surge of affection and maternal feelings surfaced as she gazed down at his sleeping face. She desperately wanted to see self-confidence there, not fear or inferiority. To see him strong and robust, running and laughing like a normal child with other children.

A lump lodged in her throat as she watched Arthur's face in repose. Nobody should ever have to experience the dejection he had already had in his young life. Ian removed the boy's worn shoes and his threadbare socks and skinny little ankles were revealed. At that moment, she met Ian's gaze and knew he was feeling as badly as she. He took her hand and kissed the back of it tenderly, exchanging a look of compassion that warmed her heart more than any words he might have said. His eyes mirrored what was in his heart—a longing to make Arthur's life better. Natasha wanted that too, more than anything she had wanted in a long time.

Leaving Arthur sound asleep in the room, Natasha stepped into the hall with Ian and turned to him, concerned. "Arthur is painfully skinny. I know it can't be helped, but he's going to bed without dinner."

"Let him sleep. We'll check on him in a little while." Ian smiled reassuringly. "I'll have Dugie save dinner for him in case he wakes up."

When they reached downstairs, Maggie and Ranald were waiting for them in the front hall. Ian told them about the flash drive and filled them in on the details of Arthur's temporary residence.

Maggie turned to Natasha. "You had a phone call today from a Detective Carson."

Natasha's heartbeat quickened. "What did she say? I wonder why she didn't call my cell phone."

"She did but you must not have had service where you were. You're to call her back as soon as possible."

"Okay, thanks. I'll call my lawyer first thing tomorrow," Natasha said, glancing at Ian.

Maggie's eyes widened. "Oh, my! With all the excitement about wee Arthur's arrival, I almost forgot to tell you about your visitor this morning."

"My visitor?" Natasha's palms grew cold and clammy.

"Who was it?" Ian asked, his brows snapping together as he stared at Maggie.

"It was Natasha's agent. Marty Cranshaw."

Natasha blinked. "Marty?" she said, astonished. "That can't be. Why would he come here?"

Maggie shrugged. "He said he had important things to discuss with you about a contract."

"That's odd. He could have just called me." A wave of apprehension crept over Natasha. Something was way off.

"He wouldn't come in when I invited him to," Maggie said. "He said he'd be back to speak to you in person."

"Did he say where he's staying?" Natasha asked.

"No, but he said he'd return tomorrow."

Natasha frowned at Ian. "That's weird. What else did he say, Maggie?"

"That was all." Maggie darted a look at Ranald. "When he turned to leave, I couldn't help noticing how fine-looking he was."

"You think he's fine-looking?" Natasha asked, bewildered at her choice of words. Marty was short and wiry, with close-set eyes, a hook nose and a balding head.

"Aye. He was tall and strong, yet slim with black hair and dark eyes." Maggie nodded thoughtfully. "Looked like a verra handsome Italian."

Natasha's heart rose to her throat. "Maggie, that man wasn't Marty!"

# CHAPTER THIRTEEN

Maggie stared at her with mystified eyes. "What do you mean it wasn't Marty?"

"It doesn't fit his description at all." Natasha turned to Ian, her pulse beating rapidly. "It had to be one of Tony's friends. Maybe Rico."

Maggie glanced from Natasha to Ian. "Who are Tony and Rico?"

Ian's gaze zeroed in on Maggie. "Can you give us a better description?" he asked, deflecting her question.

Maggie pursed her lips. "Well, let's see." She pondered a moment. "As I said, he was handsome. In his early thirties, I'd say. Wearing a fine suit."

"I wonder who he was," Natasha said, suspicion crawling under her skin like a snake.

"Call New York and alert them. It doesn't matter what time it is," Ian said. "Whoever's on duty can help you, even if it isn't Detective Carson."

"Okay," Natasha said, reeling from the news.

"Do you think he's dangerous, then?" Maggie asked, her gaze darting from Natasha to Ian.

"Aye," Ian said tightly.

Maggie gasped and rubbed her arms. "Och, I just got a chill in my bones."

"Aunt Maggie, until all of this is resolved, don't open the door to anyone without knowing who they are."

"I told you not to answer the door so quickly, woman," Ranald chastised Maggie. He wagged his finger at her. "When are you going to learn to listen to me, Mrs. Duncan?"

Maggie lifted her chin and ignored him. She turned to Natasha. "You must be hungry. I'll see about heating dinner."

"Where's Evita?" Natasha asked.

"Wee Evita is asleep in her little bed," Maggie said smiling. "Do you want me to bring her to you?"

"No, don't disturb her. I'll see her in the morning," Natasha said absently.

When Maggie and Ranald left, she and Ian went into the study where Natasha made the call. Thankfully, Detective Carson answered. After speaking with her briefly, Natasha hung up, feeling unhinged.

"What's wrong? What did she say?" Ian asked right away.

Natasha's eyes welled up and her lips quivered as she struggled to speak. "Marty's in the hospital with fractured ribs and two broken legs. Somebody wearing a ski mask broke into his house in Connecticut. He beat Marty up and left him for dead."

"The bloody bastard," Ian said contemptuously. He pulled Natasha in his arms. "Sorry to hear it," he said, rubbing her back consolingly.

She swallowed hard and squeezed her eyes to block out the horrific image as she leaned her forehead on Ian's chest. "Marty would have died if he hadn't gained consciousness and called for help. He told the police his passport was missing along with my personal file of contracts and headshots."

Ian swore savagely. "Damn it. What a convoluted mess."

"I know," she said, heartsick about her poor agent. "When I told Detective Carson that someone showed up here pretending to be Marty, she told me to go into hiding."

"Are you all right?" he asked, his concerned eyes roving her face.

"I've been better, but I'm not going to let this destroy me," Natasha said, straightening her spine and lifting her chin. "I hope they're getting ready to close Rico's club and arrest everyone using the evidence. But who knows? There's nothing I can do but wait."

Ian released her and began to pace like a lion, every muscle in his body twitching for action. "Now that they've tracked you here, you must leave first thing tomorrow morning."

"I know," she replied, miserable at having to leave so soon. "My good friend, Teddy, is in Paris. I'll go there."

"You're not leaving alone." Ian clasped her shoulders and stared into her eyes with a look that said *you're mine and no one is going to harm you*. It warmed her heart and gave her hope. "I know the perfect place where you can hide out safely," he said.

"Where?" Natasha asked, touched by his protectiveness.

"The Isle of Skye. It's far from here and you have to cross over by ferry. There are some very desolate areas, but I know it like the back of my hand."

"I can't drag you into this mess any further, Ian. You'd be risking your life for me."

Ian stared at her, his silver-green eyes hot and unblinking. "I won't have it any other way."

"But what about Arthur? He's only just arrived. We can't abandon him so soon," Natasha fretted.

"He'll be fine. Maggie and Ranald can take him on holiday. He'll be well taken care of. They helped raise me and look how well I turned out," he said with a wry smile.

"Ha, quite the humble Highlander," she said, smiling slightly.

"We need to get you to a safe place. I'll be damned if anyone's going to hurt you," he said, pulling her into a hug. Resting his chin against her forehead, he held her firmly and she could hear his strong heartbeat beneath her cheek.

Dugie entered the room and cleared her throat. "Dinner is served," she announced and left discreetly.

Natasha pulled away from Ian and followed him into the dining room. They ate in silence, immersed in thought. When they finished, she followed him upstairs as he carried a tray of food for Arthur. She turned on the light and searched for him, but couldn't find him in the large room.

"Arthur," she called out. "Where are you?"

A tremulous voice answered, "I'm here. Under the bed."

Exchanging a surprised look with Ian, Natasha got down on her hands and knees and peered under the bed.

"So this is where you were hiding," she said in a light voice. "What are you doing under there?"

"I was scared," Arthur admitted sheepishly, clutching the teddy bear.

Natasha pulled his skinny body out and hugged him. "Why didn't you call us or come downstairs?"

"I couldn't see anything but monsters," Arthur confided in a whisper.

Natasha's tipped his little face up and saw his eyes were swollen from crying. "Oh, sweetie, there are no monsters here. If you're ever scared just call and we'll come to you. Everyone here is kind."

"I wanted to call you, but no sound came out when I tried," Arthur replied.

She hugged him again. "I know exactly how you felt. When I was little, I used to be scared of a lot of things, but you know what helped me?"

"What?"

"I would sing a song." She smiled. "Let's get you back in bed so you can eat the yummy dinner we brought you."

Ian set the tray down on the nightstand beside the mahogany, four-poster bed. "Are you all right now?" he asked, helping Arthur into bed.

Arthur nodded. He sniffled and looked around. "Can I keep a light on while I sleep? I don't like the dark."

"Of course," Ian said readily. He handed Arthur a tissue from a box on the nightstand. "Here, blow your nose and dry your eyes."

Natasha silently berated herself for not realizing that Arthur would wake up to an unfamiliar, dark room that might seem spooky. He looked adorable, perched in the center of the four poster bed like a little prince. She smiled and laid a hand on his shoulder. "I understand how you feel about not liking the dark, Arthur. I don't like thunderstorms myself. But I know you're going to love it here. Glenhaven is a safe and happy place. In fact, it's a lot like Camelot."

Arthur's blue eyes shined like midnight stars. "It is?"

Ian's eyes crinkled at the corners as he regarded Arthur. "Glenhaven isn't Camelot, but it will be your home while you're here. And this will be your room. Do you like it?"

Arthur looked around him, wide-eyed with delight. "Oh, yes! It's grand. When can I see your sword collection?"

"Tomorrow morning," Ian said. "It's in the great hall. I'll show you the banners with the crests of both sides of my family, the MacGregors and the Farquharsons."

"I can't wait!" Arthur cried eagerly.

"Cook sent this up for you," Natasha said, reaching for the dinner tray. She fluffed the pillows behind Arthur and tucked a napkin under his chin. "Are you hungry?" she asked, handing him a fork.

Arthur nodded. "And thirsty," he chirped, taking a large swig of milk. He tilted his head and gave her a milk-moustache grin.

Smiling at the cute picture he made, Natasha handed him a napkin. "Here, dry your whiskers."

Arthur wolfed down the meal of roasted chicken, mashed potatoes and green peas. When he finished, Natasha checked inside his suitcase for his pajamas and toothbrush, and then handed them to Ian.

Ian placed his arm around Arthur's narrow shoulders and led him out the door. "Come, I'll show you to the bathroom," he said.

Natasha ran to her room and retrieved a tube of arnica cream for Arthur's bruise. As a dancer, arnica was her constant companion for aches and bruises.

When they returned to the bedroom, Ian carefully rubbed the arnica on Arthur's bruise. "There," he said tucking him in. "That should help your leg feel better. Tomorrow morning I'll give you a grand tour of the grounds. My bedroom door will be open tonight so I can hear if you need anything."

Natasha sat beside Arthur on the bed. "You were a good boy to eat all your peas. Now you have to go to sleep."

"Would you sing me a song?" Arthur asked.

"Sure, which one do you want me to sing?"

He thought for a moment and then grimaced. "I don't know any songs," he said softly. "That's stupid, eh?"

"Stupid?" Natasha said, distressed that he didn't know any songs. "Nah. Don't say that again or I'll tickle you. Like this," she said, running he fingers up and down his sides until he squealed and wriggled away.

"Okay, okay," he said, giggling. "What song are you going to sing for me?"

"I have the perfect one," Natasha said, smiling at him tenderly. "Camelot."

Ian leaned against the doorway and watched them together, fascinated by how effortlessly Natasha related to Arthur, and he to her. It was as if he'd known her forever. She got in bed and lay beside him and began to sing.

Gooseflesh formed on Ian's forearms when he heard the first notes of Natasha's clear soprano as she sang the moving lyrics. He stood rooted to the spot, hypnotized by the magic of her singing. Her face glowed and her blue eyes shimmered. The sheer emotion and radiance in her voice gripped Ian, bringing him back to the night he'd gone to see her on Broadway. The critics were calling it her breakout role and he was curious to see what the buzz was about. He also wanted to see firsthand why she would reject everything he'd offered her to live like a gypsy, going from show to show and city to city while performing and touring.

It had been three years since they had broken up, but he still hadn't been able to get her out of his mind...and heart. He had sat in the audience, center orchestra, his heart hammering when she stepped on stage. When she finished singing the first song, he'd felt sucker punched. She had owned that song, nailing it with so much heart, the audience clapped riotously. When she hit the final soaring note, he felt petty for expecting her to consider another lifestyle. He'd never realized how exceptionally talented she was. He'd been too caught up in his feelings for her, in wanting her all to himself. Witnessing her transform into the character she passionately portrayed had held him and the audience in thrall.

That night he left at intermission, more determined than ever to forget her.

It was difficult to watch Natasha and Arthur together now. She was warm and affectionate, her maternal instincts coaxing the lad out of his shyness with ease. In the short time she'd spent with Arthur, he'd evolved from being a forlorn *bairn* to a happy one.

Ian didn't remember Tasha ever mentioning wanting to have children, but she was a natural. She would make a wonderful mother someday. She had once told him she was afraid she wouldn't be a good mother because she'd never had a good role model. He couldn't blame her for feeling that way with a mum like Anitra.

But it didn't really matter. Natasha had never said she was interested in a conventional life. Her career came first, before anything else. She was a dazzling triple threat of song, dance and acting. It was a natural gift, just as his healing hands were a gift he couldn't imagine not using.

What a muddle they'd landed in, he thought, turning away with profound regret.

## CHAPTER FOURTEEN

The following morning, Natasha got out of bed with a start when she saw it was already 8:00 a.m. She had tossed and turned most of the night, getting up several times to check on Arthur, who had slept soundly with his teddy bear tucked in beside him. Every time she'd tiptoed past Ian's bed, she'd been tempted to dive into his arms. But that wasn't going to happen, especially after the way their last night had ended.

She showered and dressed quickly in skinny jeans, a faux fur collared chocolate brown sweater and the boots Ian had given her. When she went to check in on Arthur, she didn't find him in the room and figured he must be with Ian.

On the way downstairs, she reflected on Ian's somber mood after they had put Arthur to bed. She had wanted to spend time with him in the study, but he wasn't in a talkative mood. Something had made him clam up after they left Arthur's room. With nothing more to do, she'd said good-night and retired to the lonesome hidden chamber.

Natasha yearned for the banter and the intimate closeness they'd shared the past two days. Ian had been warm and sexy, and they'd had fun together in Edinburgh. But their argument had left her feeling despondent. The worst part was that she'd been rendered speechless when he'd asked, *Are you ready to tell me anything has changed in seven years?* Reflecting on it, she couldn't blame him for shutting down after she wasn't able to answer a simple question. But it hadn't been simple. Had anything changed in seven years? *Hell yes.* She had grown, matured, become more independent. And she'd been able to distance herself from Anitra's constant meddling. But her love of singing hadn't changed. It was ingrained in her.

With a sigh, she headed to the kitchen and found Maggie, Ian and Arthur seated at a table with Dugie standing nearby.

"Good morning, everyone. I can't believe I slept in so late." Natasha walked to the table and kissed the top of Arthur's head.

"Morning, luv," Maggie said. "Hungry?"

"A bit," Natasha said, smiling at her.

One glance at Ian's handsome, recently shaved face made Natasha want to plant a kiss on the cleft of his firm chin and burrow her face in his warm, masculine neck. He looked up at that moment, his silver-green eyes giving her a once over. Natasha's heartbeat sped up and she smiled at him.

"Good morning, Miss," Dugie called out cheerfully. She placed plate of fried eggs, ham and a broiled tomato before Arthur. "Eat up, laddie," she said, fussing affectionately.

Arthur's cheeks puffed up as he grinned at her impishly.

"Will ye be having a cooked breakfast, Miss?" Dugie asked.

"No, thank you," Natasha replied. "It looks delicious, but I'll just have corn flakes and milk."

Dugie clucked her teeth. "You're not dieting are you, lass?" She wiped her plump hands on a clean linen dish towel and filled a bowl with corn flakes. "You must eat hearty in the morning to be healthy."

"You're right, but I haven't been exercising or dancing." She gave a short laugh. "I have to fit into my costumes when I return to New York."

"They must be awfully small costumes," Dugie said, shaking her head. She poured milk into the corn flakes and placed the bowl in front of Natasha.

Natasha kept silent. One of those "small" costumes was a short satin teddy she wore in her key dance number. Ian watched her beneath hooded lids. He hadn't said a word since she had entered and now his brooding gaze unnerved her. She swallowed hard and said, "How did you sleep last night?"

"Well enough," he replied. "You?"

"The same," she said, not wanting to say that she hadn't slept well at all.

"Where's Evita?" Natasha asked Maggie.

"Ranald took her for a walk."

"That's nice. Has she behaved?"

"Perfectly. We've enjoyed having her, luv," Maggie said.

"Oh good." While Dugie fussed over her newest charge, Natasha ate her cereal. She enjoyed hearing Arthur and Ian talk about fishing in nearby lochs.

"Dr. Ian is going to show me the great hall this morning after we finish breakfast!" Arthur said, hopping up and down in his seat with excitement.

"I want to see it too," Natasha said, smiling at Arthur's puppy-like eagerness.

"Haven't you ever seen it?" Arthur asked, tilting his head at her.

"Yes, a long time ago," she said.

His face glowing with excitement, Arthur said, "Can we go now?"

"We can," Ian replied, rising from the table.

"Are you coming too, Auntie Maggie?" Arthur asked Maggie.

"No, lovey. I'm going to check on Evita and Ranald." She turned to Ian. "Please bring wee Arthur to the stable when you're finished."

Ian nodded. "Will do." After she left, he led Arthur and Natasha into the great hall, which was unchanged from the last time she'd been there. Majestic and grand, the large rectangular-shaped room had a wood-beamed, high ceiling and colorful banners hanging from the side stone walls. An open stone fireplace, large enough to roast a whole side of beef, stood impressively on the far wall.

"This is the only room that was left exactly as it was when it was built hundreds of years ago. Clan Farquharson would gather here every night for entertainment and food," Ian said.

"Which one is the MacGregor banner?" Arthur asked.

"Isn't it the one with the fallen tree on a white background?" Natasha said.

"Aye. There's a sword driven through the tree trunk." Ian pointed to another banner. "That one belongs to my mother's family, Clan Farquharson. Mum inherited this castle from her father, Ian. It was her wish that I live here with my future family," he said, glancing at Natasha.

She watched Ian, awestruck by how noble he looked in the great hall. Her heart clenched as full realization hit—there were hundreds of years of history here he couldn't turn his back on. His roots were firmly planted where his mother's wish had been for him to remain. Ian felt honor bound to fulfill his legacy at Glenhaven. He had a magnificent plan to build a charitable clinic in Scotland, one that would change many lives for the better. The enormity of his life's goals was staggering and brilliant.

"Can I see the swords?" Arthur asked.

"Of course." Ian led him to the west wing of the room where there was an impressive collection of large, engraved swords. "This claymore is very old. During the Middle Ages, it belonged to my ancestor, Angus Farquharson." Ian touched the hilt of a large two-handed sword. "He fought a mighty battle with it to rescue my great-grandmother, Katrine, when an enemy tried to kidnap her from Glenhaven Castle."

Arthur's eyes widened as he stared at him gape-mouthed. "Was it a bloody battle?" he asked.

"Aye. During the Middle Ages the battles were brutal. Angus Farquharson was a fierce warrior and he would have done anything to save his lady love."

Natasha smiled at Arthur's worshipful expression. "What do you think of all that, Arthur?"

"It's awesome!" He ran up to a large tapestry that covered an entire wall and pointed at it. "Why are those people running to the hills?"

"It's the story of Clan MacGregor. We've been known through time as the Children of the Mist."

Arthur scrunched up his face and stared at Ian. "Why?"

"Because even though my father's clan was considered of royal descent from King Alpin, they lost most of their lands and were outlawed twice. They were hunted like animals."

"Like animals?" Arthur repeated, puzzled.

"Aye, and they couldn't admit to the MacGregor name without fearing for their lives."

"Do you fear for your life?" Arthur asked in a hushed tone.

Ian chuckled. "No. In 1775, King George III and an Act of Parliament restored our name."

"That's brilliant. Your clan is famous!" Arthur skipped back to the swords.

Ian turned to Natasha. "I'm going to take him to Maggie and Ranald. Do you want to come?"

"No, I better not. I need to call and check on Marty."

Ian nodded. "I'll be back shortly. Stay here until I return."

"I will. Don't worry."

Arthur hopped up and down. "Are we going to see the puppy? What's its name?"

"Her name is Evita and she loves to play," Natasha said, thinking Arthur was a puppy too.

"Can we go now?" Arthur asked eagerly. "Can we, Dr. Ian?"

"Aye, I'll take you there," Ian said.

"Wait. I want a hug from Arthur first." Natasha crouched beside Arthur and enveloped him in a tight hug. "Have fun and be a good boy," she said, kissing his cheek.

Arthur nodded and kissed her cheek, a wet, little boy's kiss that she cherished.

When they left, Natasha went to the hidden chamber and tried to call Marty at the hospital, but the operator said he wasn't taking calls. Frustrated she couldn't speak to him, she set about organizing her things. She pulled her large suitcase out of the armoire and took things out for her trip to Skye. But she couldn't concentrate; she felt too restless. She was about to call Saundra and tell her lawyer the latest when her phone rang in her hand, startling her.

"Hello?" she said, wondering at the foreign number.

"Tashie! I'm so glad I caught you," Teddy crowed happily. "I thought you might be in rehearsal or something."

"Hey, Teddy! Do you have a new number?"

"No, I'm calling from my flat in Paris."

"Oh. I saw your fabulous picture in *Hello* magazine. How are you? I miss you."

"Aw, I miss you too. What would we do without our Heart Sisters?"

"I know, right?" Natasha, Ronnie and Teddy, her Heart Sister, were different from each other in personality, but loyal to the bone. Ronnie was assertive and plainspoken, whereas Teddy was happy go lucky and well-intentioned, but often landing in one jam or another.

"I can't wait all the way to Christmas to see you. Why don't you come to Paris next month? I'm throwing a Thanksgiving bash for my expat friends. A friend of mine just opened an American bistro here and I want give it a boost."

Natasha smiled and looked heavenward. Teddy collected friends like a pied piper. None were as close as her Heart Sisters, but she had many acquaintances. Natasha could just imagine her flitting around, planning a huge party to help her friend's restaurant. She was generous to a fault, and unfortunately, many took advantage of her generosity.

"I wish I could come to Paris, Teddy, but my life has gotten very complicated."

"Then I'll come to New York. How about next week? I'd *love* to see Legs LaRue on her opening night." Teddy's warm, husky voice enveloped Natasha in a cocoon of friendship.

"I'd love that, but I'm not in New York," Natasha said.

"You're not? Where are you?"

Natasha drew in a deep breath and let it out slowly as she collected her thoughts. She didn't want to lie to Teddy, but she couldn't get into details either. "I'm in Scotland. With Ian. At Glenhaven."

"*Shut up*," Teddy said in a shocked voice. "Ian MacGregor? Your ex-fiancé?"

"Yes," Natasha said, not quite believing it herself. Her life was in turmoil, between the danger she was in and her love for Ian.

"Wow. What have I missed?"

"A lot. Listen, Teddy, I have to swear you to secrecy. Nobody can know I'm here," Natasha said emphatically.

"Okay, I won't tell anyone. Cross my heart and hope to die," she said quickly. "Now tell me what's going on."

"I'm hiding out with Ian until it's safe to go back to the States."

"What? You're hiding out until it's safe? What kind of trouble are you in?"

Natasha groaned. "Don't kill me, but I can't tell you anymore."

"Wait a minute. You can't stop there! Tell me about Ian. Are you two back together?"

"Well…kind of, but with no future plans—or commitments," Natasha said with a pang.

"Oh, gosh, I remember how long it took you to get over him," Teddy said gently.

"I don't think I ever got over him, and now after just a few days with him, I'm so in love, I don't know what to do," Natasha admitted mournfully.

"What about Ian? How does he feel about it?"

Natasha sighed. "I don't know. He's trying to be detached, but it's not working. He's my self-appointed protector and like a stick of dynamite when we're together. It's pretty hot."

"Ooh, sounds amazing," Teddy said with a throaty chuckle. "So what's the problem?"

"The same issues as before. He's close to moving to Scotland permanently and I landed a dream role in 'The Bee's Knees'. The more I think about it, the more unlikely it seems we'll—"

"Stop over analyzing everything, Tash!" Teddy said, cutting her off in mid-sentence. "All your life you've done nothing but plan, plan, plan. Don't you think it's time to stop planning your career and start living your life?" Teddy was an expert at living in the moment, and it stemmed from suddenly losing her mother at a very young age. After her mother died, she was sent to a Swiss boarding school and stayed in Europe through college and afterwards.

"It's easier said than done, Teddy. I don't want to get hurt again. Neither does Ian."

"Oh, come on! I don't mean to be dramatic, but what if one of you died tomorrow?"

Natasha gulped at her ominous worlds. *If Teddy only knew!* "Hopefully, that won't happen anytime soon," she said with a shaky laugh.

"Well, what if it did?" Teddy persisted. "Wouldn't you regret not enjoying every moment you have now? If I had that kind of love, I'd never let go," she said fervently. "You and Ian were meant to be together. I'm sure you can work something out."

"I'm glad one of us is sure," Natasha said wryly.

"Who are you talking to?" Ian said, entering the room.

Natasha jumped at the sound of his deep voice. "Teddy, I have to go now. Sorry," she said into the receiver.

Teddy groaned loudly. "I can't believe you're hanging up in the middle of this conversation, Tash! Please take care of yourself and call me when you can," she said in an urgent tone.

"I will. I promise. Bye."

She hung up and looked at Ian. "I was talking to my friend, Teddy," she said, mortified when her voice came out in a splutter. How much of her conversation had he heard?

"You weren't making plans to meet her in Paris, were you?" he asked, scrutinizing her face."No, I already agreed to go with you to Skye." She eyed him curiously. "Did you hear any of my conversation with her?"

"No. I'm not in the habit of eavesdropping," he said dryly.

The concentrated look in Ian's silver-green eyes gave her pause. His body was tightly coiled from the rigid set of his shoulders to his muscular legs. "How is your agent?" he asked.

"I don't know. I wasn't able to get through." Natasha flushed. She'd been so caught up talking about her love life, she hadn't gotten around to calling Saundra either. "I was about to call my lawyer when Teddy called. I'll call her now," she said.

Ian paced the room while Natasha talked to Saundra, getting more agitated by the moment as she listened to the latest from her. When she finished, her stomach was in a jumble as she put the phone on the nightstand and sank down on the edge of the bed.

"Ugh, more bad news," she said, gazing at him anxiously.

"What is it?" Ian asked, his eyes fixed on her as he stood before her with hands braced on hips.

Natasha took a calming breath and forced herself to get a grip on her jittery nerves. Times like these called for Ronnie's bravery. She could just imagine how fired up Ronnie would be in a similar situation.

"Saundra said that Detective Carson told her Rico Gamberi has vanished. She suspects he's the one who beat Marty up." She shook her head in disgust. "Rico is in trouble with the IRS too."

Ian grunted. "He's probably up to his neck in debt with the syndicate."

"Maybe." Natasha grimaced. "When I told Rico I didn't know where the flash drive was, he said the mob wouldn't mind roughing me up to find it. Look what they did to poor Marty."

Ian's face darkened. "I won't let them harm you. They'll have to go through me first."

"Thanks. I thought I was safe here, but now someone has followed me." She clutched his arm. "What if it was Rico? I'm terrified he might harm somebody here."

"We're leaving for Skye today and I'm closing up Glenhaven. Everyone is on holiday as of now," Ian said, tension lining his shoulders and neck.

"Where will they go?" Natasha asked.

"They'll stay at Maggie's widowed sister's home. She has a large estate near Pitlochry. Dugie and her family will stay there too."

Natasha gave a sigh of relief. "That makes me feel a lot better. I'm glad I got a tight hug from Arthur. Is he okay with us leaving?"

"Aye, he's fine. Maggie and Ranald will spoil him rotten and he's already crazy about Evita."

"Oh good. Did you tell them about Arthur's fear of the dark?"

"No, you can call them from the car and tell them. I'm going to alert the police about Rico and give them a description. Hurry up and finish packing," he said, motioning to the items on the bed. "Bring warm, comfortable clothes and sturdy boots. It's rugged territory. I'm going down to make arrangements and get what we need."

"Like what?"

"Canned food, blankets, a kerosene lamp, a battery-operated radio, candles and matches..." Ian ticked off.

"Sounds like we're going camping." Natasha's eyes widened. "How primitive is the Isle of Skye?"

"Where I'm taking you, it's no frills," Ian said, the corners of his mouth lifting slightly.

## CHAPTER FIFTEEN

"You can come up front now," Ian said, peering in the back seat of the Rover.

"Finally!" Natasha tossed aside the blankets and clambered into the front seat. She'd been riding in the back, covered by stifling blankets since they'd left the castle in case someone was watching. Itchy from all that wool, she blew a stray tendril from her face and sneezed.

"Good thing I brought my allergy pills," she muttered, rummaging in her shoulder bag. She pulled out a plastic pill container and popped a tablet in her mouth, downing it with half a bottle of mineral water. "Now I can enjoy the view of the Highlands. They're so beautiful in the fall."

Ian nodded, but didn't respond and his silence unsettled her. He'd been quiet since they'd left. Deep in thought, his mouth was set, his jaw tense and his silver-green eyes motionless on the road ahead.

"Do you have friends in Skye?" she asked, hoping to draw him into conversation.

"Aye, a few. As a lad, I spent many summers there with friends who were like family. One of them is a private investigator."

"Oh, that's good. Hopefully, we won't need his services."

He slanted a thoughtful look at her. "Agreed."

They lapsed into silence and Natasha couldn't stop thinking about what Teddy had said earlier. *What if one of you died tomorrow? Wouldn't you regret not enjoying every moment you have now? If I had that kind of love, I'd never let go.* Teddy could be so astute sometimes. Most people saw her as a party girl with no roots, but she was that way because she didn't have a home.

*Home.* Natasha didn't feel like she had one either at the moment. The prospect of going back to her New York apartment was unnerving, especially since she'd had to leave it in shambles. She felt violated whenever she thought of how her place had been ruthlessly ransacked. Her life was in danger and she had no idea what tomorrow would bring or how Ian felt about her. Sometimes, she felt like chucking everything and starting all over again. Letting out a mournful sigh, she gazed at Ian wistfully.

He turned to her with furrowed brows. "What's wrong?"

"Nothing," she said with a despondent sigh.

"I'll tell you what's wrong," Ian said after a moment, his voice brusque. "You're stressed, and I'm furious. Not with you," he assured her quickly, "but with whoever's after you." He rubbed his face with an impatient hand. "I'm frustrated because I don't know how much time we have left together" he said, making her want to cry at the reality of it.

"I know, and I'm dreading going back to New York. But I have to," she said, her heart aching over how much she would miss him.

Ian sucked in a rough breath and exhaled it heavily. "I can't keep you here, but I'll be damned if I'll let anyone harm you. While you're in Scotland, you're mine," he said, his tone darkening with ferocity. He glanced at her, his hot, unblinking gaze making her heart feel close to bursting. "I won't have it any other way, Tasha."

"I *am* yours," she said, placing her hand on his tightly clenched jaw. "I've *always* been yours."

"Good. It's settled then," he said with gruff male satisfaction. His hand curled around her nape and pulled her in for a brief kiss, his mouth crushing hers with possessiveness.

He released her just as quickly as he'd grabbed her and turned his attention to the road. Natasha smiled as happiness surged inside her. *While you're in Scotland, you're mine.* Ian's words—punctuated by a fierce kiss— would forever be etched in her heart. When he set his mind to something, he was a force to be reckoned with and she was thrilled to be the object of his focus.

"We're approaching Mallaig," he said a few moments later. "Get in the back before we get on the ferry."

"Again?" she groaned.

"Aye. We need to get to Skye without anyone noticing you in the car."

"All right." She tossed her shoulder bag in the back and got on her knees, inching between the passenger seat and the driver's. Leaning forward with her head down and her butt up, she steadied her hands on the back seat cushion.

Ian swatted her bottom. "Hurry up, we're almost there."

"Hey!" she said, giggling.

"I couldn't resist."

Once she was settled under the covers, she asked, "Where are we staying in Skye?"

"There's an abandoned stone house in Portree. People don't go near it because they think it's spooked by the spirits of Flora MacDonald and Bonnie Prince Charlie."

"Are you kidding?" she said, her voice muffled by the covers.

"No."

"Great. I'm normally not superstitious, but staying in a haunted house in the wilderness gives me the willies. Especially at night."

"Don't worry. I'll be with you."

"That's not comforting, unless you're an exorcist," she retorted, her nose twitching from the wool fibers. A sneeze punctuated her words.

Ian snorted. "Can't help you there. Better toughen up. The cottage is ancient and there's no electrical heating."

"No wonder you brought so many blankets. We're going to freeze our buns off!"

"Not if I can help it."

*Ooh, can't wait,* she thought, her belly fluttering wildly.

When they arrived at the harbor at Mallaig, Ian drove aboard the Armadale ferry. The ferry ride across the Sound of Sleat took approximately ten minutes, but it seemed like forever as Natasha's nose and eyes twitched from the effort not to sneeze.

When Ian disembarked the car, she said, "Where are we? Can I get up now?"

"Not yet. We're in Portree. Stay underneath the blankets until I say you can get up."

"B a a a a ah!" she bleated. "Now I know what a sheep feels like."

Ian gave a short laugh. When they were a safe distance from the Armadale harbor, he said, "Climb up here, sassy lassie."

She gladly obliged. "The sky looks so serene. I love the way the stars glow through the mist."

Ian looked at the stars above and nodded. "It is a nice evening. Another few minutes and we'll be there," he said, maneuvering the car up the dirt road.

"Is that the cottage?" Natasha asked as the headlights shone on a stone house at a short distance. It was a small dwelling, surrounded by an unkempt garden, giving it a wild, primitive appearance.

"Yes." Ian parked the car and lit a kerosene lamp. Holding the lamp, he led Natasha up the winding gravel road.

"How are you going to get in?" she whispered, gesturing toward the heavy, wooden front door.

"It's not locked," Ian said, turning the latch and opening the door.

"Well then how are we going to feel safe here?" She stalled at the doorway.

He pulled her along. "Don't worry about it. Come on. We'll bolt it from the inside."

The moment they entered, Ian set the kerosene lamp on a wooden table in the center of the room, illuminating it in a golden glow.

"Good thing there's a broom," Natasha said, eyeing the large broom beside the stone fireplace. "This place needs a good sweeping."

"You sweep, I'll unload the supplies," he said.

"But the dust will make me sneeze, even with the allergy pill I took. How about I unload the car and you sweep?" she said, knowing he wouldn't agree.

"Right." He shot her a cynical look. "*You* unload the car? That would take all night." He walked to the hearth and returned with the broom. "Start sweeping, Cinderella. There's a lot of work to be done so we can sleep comfortably tonight." He handed her his muffler. "Tie this over your nose and mouth. It'll keep the dust out."

Natasha wrinkled her nose in response, and he tweaked it while he held the broom out to her.

"All right, but don't overdo your position as protector. You might be the laird of Glenhaven estate, but I'm not your minion."

He looked down his aristocratic nose at her with amusement. "Get to work."

Making a face, she wound her hair up at the crown of her head as best she could. Several tendrils escaped as she began to clean.

Ian brought in a hunting rifle and propped it next to the cot.

"Where did that come from?" Natasha said.

"My father's hunting collection. Here's another one for you," Ian said, taking a smaller gun out of a holster on his side.

"Me? No way," Natasha said, backing away from it.

"We'll store it in a special hiding place in the floor. Come I'll show you."

Natasha watched Ian lift a wooden plank underneath the bed. "I have to hand it to you Scots. Pretty crafty. Secret chambers in castles, hiding places in the floor...cool," she said, staring at him as he placed the gun on its side and covered it with the wood board. "Is it loaded?"

The look Ian gave her said she was daft for asking. "Of course. Now back to work," he said with an infuriating grin.

He went outside and made several trips back and forth, carrying everything inside they'd need for at least a week. By the time he finished, Natasha had swept out the cottage, dusted every surface and made up the cot with the clean sheets he'd brought.

"Great job, minion," he said.

"Thank you, my lord," she said, rolling her eyes.

"You look adorable with your hair up like that," he teased, kissing the tip of her pink nose. "I'm hungry. Let's have the picnic Dugie prepared."

Natasha rubbed her arms. "Can you start the fire first? I'm freezing."

"Sure." Ian gathered several pieces of wood he had brought inside and ignited the fire.

"I'll light some candles, so we can shut off the kerosene lamp. It's cozier that way," Natasha said.

Moments later, they sat at the round wooden table that she covered with a blue and white checkered tablecloth from the hamper. She set two places with paper plates and plastic utensils in front of the containers of food.

"I noticed you moved the car. Where is it?" she said, handing Ian a drumstick of cold roast chicken.

"Down the road a bit, hidden behind a cluster of trees."

"Is that necessary? This place is so desolate."

"I'm not taking chances," he said, tearing a chunk of chicken with gleaming white teeth.

Natasha bit into a chicken breast and chewed appreciatively. "This is probably the best meal we'll have while we're here."

"You're probably right. Here you go," Ian said, relaxing as he handed her a bottle of ale.

She took a sip of the dark ale. "How did you know about this place?"

"I used to play here as a lad. Once when I was thirteen, I ran away from home during the school year. This is where I spent the night."

She set the chicken down and wiped her mouth with the napkin. "Why did you run away?"

Ian chugged down several gulps of ale. "I was sick of the pressure Dad was putting on me to study business and finance. When he found out where I was, he wouldn't let anyone come and get me until I had spent the night here alone."

Natasha studied the chiseled planes of Ian's face, thinking how handsome he looked in the firelight. "What happened?"

He shrugged. "I realized I could survive on my instincts. That gave me a lot of self-confidence at thirteen."

"I'll bet." Natasha took his hand and turned it palm up. She kissed the inside of his palm, her lips lingering at the center. "I love your confidence...and your hands. So healing and strong," she murmured, filled with longing to have those masterful hands stroking her again.

The blatant eroticism of Natasha's whisper-soft kiss in the center of his palm sent hot lust coursing through Ian and all he could think of was covering her pliant body with his. Her face glowed in the candlelight, her wide blue eyes clear and luminous. She was breathtaking—an incandescent, copper-haired angel sharing a simple meal with him in an ancient stone house.

Fascinated, he stared at the rapid pulse beating in the hollow of her throat above the downy fur collar of her sweater. Her high breasts rose and fell as her nostrils flared slightly and her mouth parted. Her tongue swept over her lips, turning them the same delicate pink staining her cheeks. Yearning shimmered in the depths of her dreamy eyes as their gazes met and held. She was as deeply aroused as he; it radiated from her in powerful waves, seductively luring him.

He pulled her from the table and within seconds, they were pulling each other's clothes off. Kissing madly, they fell onto the cot in front of the fireplace. The cabin was still cool inside, but the kindling fire scorched Ian's back as he leaned over Natasha and covered her satiny skin with hot kisses. Holding her in his arms, he turned on his back and anchored her on top of him. Soft moans escaped her throat, encouraging him to continue. She nipped and kissed his taut chest, licking his flat nipples from one hard tip to the other, before her sweet tongue dipped into his navel. Ian almost lurched from the bed when her lips inched across his taut midsection. He clutched her long hair and groaned in sweet agony.

Natasha smoothed her silken hands up and down his thighs. "I love your Highlander legs. So solid and powerful," she whispered huskily, her mouth trailing kisses along his inner thighs. Close to bursting, he grabbed her shoulders and pulled her up, desperate to bury himself inside her.

A loud knock at the door jolted them apart. Ian's eyes formed aggressive slits as he motioned for Natasha to be quiet. He pulled his jeans on and retrieved the rifle next to the cot. The loud banging suddenly stopped, replaced by the crunching sound of shoes on gravel and twigs.

Ian glanced at Natasha and saw her sitting upright with the blankets clutched under her chin, her blue eyes as wide as her shocked mouth. Spurred by an overwhelming need to protect her, Ian catapulted into action.

# CHAPTER SIXTEEN

Ian ran to the window and peered through the slats of the wooden shutters to see where the crackling sound was coming from. He could barely see anything in the darkness, but detected a large body looming beside the window. Suddenly, a loud bang preceded a force that flung the shutters open to reveal a man's head and torso. As he climbed forward, Ian cracked the butt of the rifle over the guy's head, knocking him out. The incoming air blew out the candles and Natasha let out a frightened gasp.

"Light the lamp and bring it here," Ian said as he grabbed the intruder's shoulders and heaved him inside. The man landed face down on the stone floor.

Wrapped in the blanket, Natasha joined his side and held the lamp up to illuminate his body. Ian turned the man over and snorted. "Well, I'll be damned. It's Alec MacLeod. What in bloody hell was he doing breaking in here?"

Natasha held the lamp to the man's face and saw he was good-looking with dark hair and thick eyebrows. His broad, rugged face was punctuated by a high-bridged nose and a strong jaw. She clutched Ian's arm and whispered loudly. "Who is he?"

"A good friend of mine."

Natasha made a scoffing sound. "Not anymore. You just knocked him out."

Ian put the gun down and lifted the man's brawny torso up, slapping his face a few times. "Alec, wake up!"

Alec stirred and when he opened his eyes, they gazed directly at Natasha. "Who are you, *a bhean àlainn*?" he murmured with a Scottish burr.

Natasha turned to Ian and whispered, "What did he say?"

Ian rolled his eyes. "He's showing off. He called you beautiful woman in Gaelic." Ian shook Alec when he closed his eyes again. "Alec. Wake up!"

Alec scowled at him. "Why'd you have to ruin my dream?"

"It's no dream. This is Natasha White and she's off-limits," he added for good measure. Alec looked too charmed by Natasha's state of undress.

Alec extended his hand to her. "A pleasure to meet you, Natasha." He attempted to get up, but sank back down, clutching his head as he moaned.

"Stay put for a few minutes," Ian advised.

Alec glowered at Ian. "You didn't have to clobber me like that. I wouldn't steal your girl, bonnie as she is," he said with a rakish smile.

"Why were you breaking in here?" Ian asked, rocking back on his heels.

"The door was bolted from the inside," Alec retorted. "What are you doing here? Not that I mind you using the place, but I would've liked to know before so as not to think it's a burglar."

Ian raised his brows and gestured to the sparse surroundings. "You don't have to worry about anything getting stolen," he observed dryly.

Alec chuckled, and then sobered when he saw the rifle. "Good thing you didn't shoot."

"I was planning to until I saw it was you," Ian returned, rising to his feet. He picked up the rifle and placed it beside the fireplace.

Alec rubbed his aching head. "Well, it's good to see you too."

Ian pulled Alec to his feet and hugged him, clapping his back enthusiastically. His childhood friend had grown into a big bear of a man, several inches taller than Ian who was six foot two.

"How long are you staying on?" Alec asked, looking from Ian to Natasha.

"I'm not sure. How did you know we were here?" Ian asked.

"I didn't know it. I just got into town myself and wanted to check on the old place," Alec replied.

A strong gust of air rattled the open shutters and Natasha hurried to the window. Rising on her tiptoes, she leaned forward to close the shutters while struggling to keep the blanket secured around her.

Ian bolted forward and was at her side in an instant. "I'll do that. Get dressed. You almost mooned Alec," he whispered, raising the blanket from where it had slid down to reveal a bare expanse of Natasha's lithe back and shapely hips.

Natasha's face reddened as she clutched the blanket in front of her. She rushed to the bed and retrieved her clothes. Holding them against her chest, she faced the men. "I'd like a little privacy to get dressed."

"It's too late for modesty, lassie," Alec pointed out with a hearty chuckle. "But if you insist, we'll turn our backs."

Ian grabbed Alec's arm and led him to the door. "We're going outside while Tasha gets dressed."

"Ah, Tasha is it?" Alec said with a mild lift of his brows.

Ian shot him a meaningful look. "Tasha to me." He walked to the door and opened it. "Let's go."

Alec didn't move a muscle. "Ordinarily, I'd agree to go outside, but it's cozy in here."

"Outside," Ian said, nudging him out the door.

When he closed the door with a thump, Natasha got dressed quickly, then walked to the door and called out, "You can come in now."

Ian's gaze swept over her as he entered with Alec, his close inspection making sure she was decent before they entered further. Natasha smiled, amused by his show of propriety.

"Oh dear, I have a pissy headache," Alec droned in an imitation of an old lady's voice, making Natasha grin and Ian choke on a laugh. "Have you got a wee dram to fix me up?"

"Aye there's plenty," Ian said. He crossed over to a rustic oak sideboard and poured two shots of whiskey for them.

"Ahhh, that's good stuff," Alec said, taking a long pull. He seated himself at the table across from Natasha and Ian, watching them with a smile.

"How do you know Ian?" Natasha said, noting how at ease Alec looked leaning back with his shoulders relaxed and his big hands on his muscular thighs.

"Him?" Alec said, indicating Ian with his chin. "Your man and I practically grew up together."

Ian nodded. "We've known each other for years." His face sobered as he looked at Alec kindly. "Aunt Maggie told me about Bessie's passing. I'm sorry, Alec."

"Aye, well she was getting on in years. Would have been ninety this December," Alec said fondly.

"Who's Bessie?" Natasha asked.

"My granny. The dear wee tyrant," Alec said, his robust voice softening. "Kept me in line, that one."

"Oh, I'm sorry for your loss," Natasha said, enjoying Alec's charm.

Alec downed his glass of whiskey in one neat gulp. His eyes, the color of golden sherry, twinkled devilishly at Natasha. "What about you, luv? Won't you drink with us?"

"Yes, I think I will. A shot of whiskey is just what I need to warm up," she said, hugging herself.

"Oh? Ian's not doing his job then," Alec teased, hiking his bushy brows.

Ian didn't rise to the bait as he got up and poured a glass for Natasha and refilled his and Alec's glasses.

Natasha took a sip and coughed slightly as the pungent liquid seared her throat. She pointed to the whiskey and shot glasses. "When did you pack those?" she asked Ian.

"Dugie packed it up for us. No Scotsman is ever without his fine malt whiskey," Ian said with a cocky grin.

"Amen!" Alec clapped Ian's back. "What brings you here, MacGregor?"

"I'm keeping Natasha out of harm's way," he said in a level tone.

Alec's eyebrows knotted over curious eyes. "What do you mean?"

Ian told Alec about the flash drive and Natasha being in danger. When he was finished, Natasha added a detailed description of Rico. By the time they filled him in on everything, Alec's jovial face had turned solemn.

"Stay here as long as you need. I'll help any way I can," he said gravely.

"Thanks. Alec is the private investigator I mentioned earlier," Ian said to Natasha.

"I used to work for Scotland Yard, but I'm on my own now," Alec said.

There had to be two sides to Alec's personality. He was a real lady killer with a ready grin and twinkling eyes. Natasha couldn't imagine him in Scotland Yard on a case, but he had to be a good investigator if he had worked there.

"Alec's a regular Sherlock Holmes. He also owns this house," Ian said.

"I figured as much," Natasha said, "about the house that is." She leaned back and regarded Alec with interest. "Ian told me this cottage was abandoned because it's haunted by the ghosts of Flora MacDonald and Bonnie Prince Charlie."

Alec rocked back in his chair and threw his head back. Laughter rumbled from his chest. "Ian's been teasing you, lassie."

"I thought so," she said, shaking a fist at Ian.

Ian gave a humorous lift of his brows, but didn't say anything.

"He's partially right about it being abandoned. Nobody has used it since I moved to London," Alec said.

"Were you planning on staying here tonight?" Natasha asked.

Alec shook his head. "No, I'm staying with my sister, Eileen. Our family house is two miles down the road." He gingerly rubbed his head where Ian had clubbed him. "I'm going to have a goose-size egg on my head tomorrow."

"Sorry about that. Your face will look like a skelped arse from the way you landed on it." Ian grinned. "Who knows? It might improve your appearance."

"Get it up ye, MacGregor. Too bad it wasn't yours," Alec replied good-naturedly. He eyed the rumpled cot and his wry expression showed he realized he'd interrupted an intimate moment. "I'll be leaving now. Thanks for the whiskey. It helped clear my head."

Ian jotted numbers on a napkin and handed it to Alec. "Here's my cell number in case you need to reach us. Or if you have information on Rico."

"Good. Let me give you mine," Alec said, reciting numbers. Ian programmed it on his phone as they walked with Alec to the door.

"Sleep well and don't let any ghosts in," Alec said, smiling. "Nice meeting you, Natasha."

Natasha smiled back. "You too, Alec."

After Alec left, Ian lay on the bed with his hands folded behind his head. Natasha turned her back and pulled her sweater off, giving him a glimpse of her bare back before she dropped a flannel nightgown over her head and was instantly engulfed in yards of fabric. The nightgown was wide and short on her, barely reaching her legs mid-calf.

"What the hell is that?" Ian asked, sounding alarmed.

With her back still turned, Natasha stifled a giggle as she reached under the gown's hem and pulled off her jeans and panties. "It's my sexy nightie. Where's the bathroom?"

"The only loo is outside, behind the bushes," he said in a voice laden with irony.

Natasha whirled around and stared at him. "You're kidding. Please say you're kidding."

"Sorry. Can't help you there, angel. I told you the facilities were primitive."

"But you didn't mention there wasn't a bathroom," she said, willing one to miraculously appear.

Ian shook his head in disbelief. "Didn't you realize that when you walked in here? Where did you think it was?" he asked, regarding her with an arched brow.

"I don't know. Attached to the side somewhere? I hate having to go out there at night," she wailed. "There could be coyotes or snakes lurking around."

"More likely a sheep is what you'll encounter," he said calmly.

"I'm scared of them too," she said. "I'm sorry about making a fuss, but I can't help it."

He gave her shoulder a reassuring pat. "You'll be fine. Just be quick about it. I'll stand guard nearby."

"No thanks. Stay at a distance." A hot flush rose to her cheeks as she reached for her bag of toiletries. "What wild animals should I watch out for?"

"Only this one when we get back," he said baring strong, white teeth in a wolfish grin.

"I'll keep that in mind." She sighed and straightened her shoulders. "Okay, time to suck it up," she muttered. Pulling a sweater over her nightgown, she shoved her feet into her boots and grabbed a flashlight.

Still wearing his jeans, Ian shrugged into his leather jacket—without a shirt. The sight of his muscular chest beneath the leather made Natasha stop and stare, but this wasn't the time to admire him. Forcing steel into her backbone, she cautiously ventured outside in search of a secluded area with enough foliage to give her privacy to relieve her bladder. Holding a lantern, Ian followed behind and waited at a distance.

"I'll be taking a piss, so don't return too soon," he called out chuckling.

Several moments later when Natasha returned to his side, her teeth were chattering. "Brrr. Is it always this cold in the fall?"

"It's not Baltic. The wind makes it feel colder than it is," Ian said, putting his arm around her shoulders as they walked back.

The minute Natasha entered the cottage, she removed her boots with icy fingers and crawled into bed. Keeping the sweater over her nightgown, she pulled the covers up to her chin, wishing it could warm her frozen nose.

"Where did you get the sexy nightie?" Ian asked, lips twitching.

"Very funny. It's your Aunt Maggie's. She left it in the guest room for me."

Ian's face eased into a slow smile. "Come here, angel. I'll warm you up." His rich, seductive voice turned Natasha's insides to mush.

"I wish I could, but I'm chilled from head to toe. I can barely move," she said, watching him undress. "You are a true Highlander. I can't believe you're not cold."

"I'm far from cold," he said, grabbing a condom and advancing on her. He nudged Natasha on her side away from him and spooned her body with his as he wrapped her in a warm embrace Natasha's chilled skin began to thaw at the feel of his hot, muscular length engulfing her. She moaned with pleasure when his firm hands eased her nightgown up and began to knead and massage her all over until she was sizzling and panting with need.

"I want you. Now," he growled in her ear, causing gooseflesh along her spine as his warm, big hands cupped her breasts and tweaked her nipples.

"Take me," she urged, rubbing against his rigid member.

Ian's arm held her back anchored against his chest as he burrowed his face in her neck and slid into her throbbing feminine core. His fingers skillfully stroked the slick nub of her arousal, pleasuring her until she came with a scorching orgasm, followed by his explosive one.

"Warmer now?" he rasped, his breath tickling her ear.

"On fire," she said, barely catching her breath.

Hours later, they fell asleep listening to the wind rustling through the trees outside.

The following morning, Natasha awoke to the glorious sight of a Celtic mist hovering over the black Cuillin Mountains. Ian stood by the open shutters and smiled at her. "Wake up, angel."

"Good morning," Natasha said, smiling back. Memories of how he'd pleasured her last night over and over again, making her body burst into flames, made her pulse quicken. Ian looked more relaxed than he had in the past week. The open smile on his face reminded her of how he'd been many years ago. "It's nice to see you looking cheerful," she said.

"Holding you captive in a haunted house does wonders for my mood," he teased, silvery eyes twinkling. His lighthearted mood was infectious and Natasha marveled at how gorgeous he looked against the backdrop of the mountains.

The sky was a misty pewter color and the cool morning air entered the room filling it with the sweet smell of peat bogs drifting in from the coast. She pulled a sweater over her nightgown, wishing there was an indoor bathroom to bathe and groom in.

"I'll be right back," she mumbled as she stepped into her boots and zipped them up.

The moment she stepped outside, cold air seeped into her bones as the wind swept under the hem of her nightgown just above the edge of her boots. But every inconvenience was erased by the glorious sight of leaves turned to gold. She paused to breathe in deeply, filling her expanded lungs with fresh mountain air as she took in the trees ablaze with autumn colors.

When she returned to the cottage, Ian had made coffee and was setting out rolls and cheese. Natasha placed a sprig of wild flowers she'd picked on the way back in a whiskey shot glass and set it on the table as she joined him.

"Looks lovely. Thanks," she said, biting into one of the yeast rolls. She took a sip of the steaming coffee. "I wonder how Arthur is doing. I hope my smartphone works here in the wilderness."

"Try it now. I want to know too."

She dialed Maggie to let her know they'd made it safely to Skye. Relieved and happy to hear that Arthur was doing fine and enjoying his time with Evita, Natasha made the bed after breakfast and straightened the cottage. Ian went outside to bathe and returned with his dark hair damp and curling slightly at the neck. A towel was wrapped around his waist, leaving his muscled torso bare as his broad shoulders filled the doorway. Natasha's heart skipped a beat when she saw the heat in his eyes.

"The sun is out and the stream isn't too cold once you get inside." His smile held an open invitation. "If you want to bathe, I'll rub you down when you come out."

She was tempted by the prospect of being rubbed down by Ian's strong hands, but she couldn't imagine jumping into an icy stream. "No way. I'll turn blue in that water."

Ian came up to her and shook his head, sprinkling her face with cool droplets of water. "What a diva," he scoffed. "There was a time when you would have jumped in beside me. Your cushy life in New York has spoiled you."

"No, it hasn't," she said, rising to the challenge. "Where's the damn stream?"

"Come with me," Ian said, grabbing towels from the suitcase. He led Natasha to a gurgling silver stream at a short distance, but when she saw the trout inside, she recoiled instantly.

"I changed my mind. There are big fish in there," she said backing away.

No sooner had she blurted that out, than Ian threw off his towel and lifted her up. Holding her tight, he jumped in the stream with a shout of laughter. The oversized nightgown billowed around Natasha like a parachute, revealing her naked body as she came up to the surface, gasping.

"You beast! If I get bitten by a trout, it'll be your fault!" she yelled, adding every obscenity she knew. Laughing wickedly, Ian grabbed her squirming waist and pulled her in for a kiss. He devoured her chilled lips and tasted deep inside her mouth. When he pulled the nightgown over her head and off, Natasha pushed at his chest and managed to break away. Filling her mouth with water she spewed it in his face. While he sputtered, she turned abruptly and neatly dived away from him. Ian growled and chased her. He reached her in seconds and they wrestled playfully. Laughing and out of breath, she finally went limp in his arms and tried to slip away, but Ian didn't relax his grip. He tickled her until she was giggling helplessly. He finally let go and she splashed water in his face.

When she reached the shore, she climbed out with Ian right behind her. He wrapped her slippery body in a towel and tossed her over his shoulder. Running naked into the cottage, Ian burst inside and tossed Natasha in the middle of the bed. He briskly rubbed every inch of her damp skin until it glowed, then descended upon her, tasting her with gentle love bites.

His smartphone rang and they jumped apart. "Ignore it," Ian said in a strangled voice as he resumed nibbling on her.

Natasha pushed away from him. "I can't. It might be Arthur." Out of breath, she answered the phone. "Alec, how nice to hear from you," she said between panting breaths, trying to sound composed.

Ian punched the bed and signaled for her to hang up.

"Dinner at seven?" She glanced at Ian and he nodded. "Yes, that would be lovely. Thank you."

She had scarcely hung up, when Ian crooked a finger at her. "Come here, angel," he said, his voice dark and seductive.

Natasha's breath caught in her throat at the ravenous look in his silver green wolf eyes. On wobbly legs, she reached his side and he instantly hauled her on top of him, his strong arms holding her body in a vise. He kissed her hard, his lips demanding and hungry.

"No more interruptions," he growled, rolling on his side and taking her with him. He kissed her breasts, tasting the buds with a swirl of his tongue as his hands skimmed over her shoulders and down her sides, from breasts to waist, then smoothed over her belly, triggering tremors along the way. He stroked her into a frenzied, greedy chaos of needing, craving, *aching* to have him inside her. No matter how many times Ian made love to her, it only made her want him more.

He turned her over and kissed the indentation of her spine all the way down, lingering at her buttocks and thighs. She moaned at the sensual assault when his teeth grazed one cheek, making her skin prickle where he'd nipped her.

"Now you have my mark," he murmured huskily.

He turned her over and looked in her eyes, his face dark with arousal as his hands palmed her buttocks and he slid inside her moist passage in one strong stroke. Moaning and pleading for more, she dug her nails into his taut buttocks and bucked upward, meeting him stroke for stroke. Ian thrust inside her repeatedly, taking her on a wild, riveting ride, heating her blood to flames. Fused together, they breathed the same tortured air and reached their climax together.

Holding her in a tight embrace, Ian stroked her spine and rested his hand on her bottom. "I hope I wasn't too hard on you," he murmured, kissing her temple. "Did I hurt you?" He pulled back to look in her eyes.

Natasha melted under his direct gaze, full of tenderness and warmth. "No, not at all," she said, throbbing with pleasurable aftershocks. "You were hot and wild. That's how I love you." Her last three words lingered in the air.

With a profound sigh, Ian held her tightly. "And I love you," he said, making her heart soar with bittersweet happiness. Natasha laid her head on his solid chest and listened to his steady heartbeat, feeling like the luckiest girl in the world.

An hour later when she woke up, Ian was outside chopping wood for the fireplace. Wrapped in a blanket, she stood at the window and watched him swing the axe in powerful strokes against the backdrop of the black mountains. Framing anyone else, the towering peaks flanked by scarred ravines might have looked desolate and foreboding, but behind Ian they created a mystical panorama and he looked like he belonged there.

The temperature was quickly dropping now that the clouds covered the sun. Natasha shivered, but not from the cold. What would her life be like when the danger was over and she would return to New York? Performing on stage filled her spirit with joy, but she couldn't imagine being separated from Ian again.

Tears gathered in her eyes as she closed the window and pulled the blanket tightly around her. She would remain in the present, savoring each moment with Ian. Despite his fiercely possessive lovemaking, he hadn't once told her he wanted to keep her in Scotland. But he had said, *And I love you.*

She'd hold on to that forever.

## CHAPTER SEVENTEEN

Ian whacked his axe against the wood and tried to clear his head after another bout of lovemaking that left him craving Natasha more. Each tough stroke of his axe pounded with impatience to replace their temporary arrangement with something permanent. *You were hot and wild. That's just how I love you.* Natasha's words wrapped themselves around his heart and squeezed. He wanted to marry her, give her *bairns* and grow old with her with such ferocity it made his head spin.

His axe powerfully sliced through the wood as reality crashed in. He couldn't coerce Tasha to stay in Scotland any more than she could convince him to leave his homeland. Releasing pent-up frustration, he chopped wood until sweat poured down his face and his muscles fatigued. He cleaned up in the stream and headed back to Natasha, determined to find a solution to their dilemma.

When he entered the cottage, her back was turned as she heated a can of soup on the kerosene burner and stirred. Ian walked up and kissed the back of her satiny neck. He inhaled deeply. "Why do you always smell so good and taste delicious?" he mused huskily.

She leaned back and sighed. "Ooh, you just sent millions of little goose bumps down my spine."

Ian nibbled her earlobe and murmured, "Lucky goose bumps."

Natasha turned and smiled coyly, the tiny dimple beside her mouth charming him. Scrubbed free of make-up, her face was happy and relaxed. Her eyes sparkled and her lips looked rosy and plump, ripe for kissing.

"Lunch is ready," she said cheerfully. She portioned out soup and served sandwiches she'd made with the cheese and smoked sausage. Shiny red apples and Dugie's shortbread biscuits completed their lunch.

After they ate, Ian said, "Let's go for a walk."

"Okay, let me grab my jacket first."

They hiked for a good hour before he stopped and indicated a grassy area. "Let's sit here."

Natasha joined him on the grass. "Hey," she said, regarding him with a lift of her brows. "Why so serious? What are you thinking about?"

"You." His voice sounded brusquer than he'd intended and he regretted the flash of uncertainty on her face.

"Me?" she asked lightly, leaning back and gazing at him expectantly.

"Yes, you." His gaze held hers uncompromisingly. "I can't live in limbo when it comes to you anymore. I hate the uncertainty."

"I don't like it either," she said, tormented. "So where are we, Ian?" Her big blue eyes searched his face.

"Where do you want to be?"

"Here. With you," she said instantly. "But I don't have the freedom to make decisions right now…because of my circumstances."

*Was she referring to her career or the danger she was in?* Natasha looked burdened and he wanted to hear her out, so he kept silent.

"I'm holding onto our time together for dear life. I love you, Ian. I never stopped loving you." She took his hand in hers and kissed it. "It's selfish, I know," she said looking down, "but I don't want to ruin what we have thinking about the danger I'm in. Or the danger I've put you in."

"You haven't put me in danger." He lifted her chin and met her gaze intently, fiercely. "I'm here to protect you."

"Thank you," she whispered, her eyes filling with tears. "So many things can happen in the next few days. Please." She drew in a shaky breath and released it slowly. "Can we just take one day at a time? I'll always treasure these memories."

Hot blood surged to his head, making it pound with despair. "Don't say that. I don't want only memories," he said tersely. "I want *you*, dammit." It was all he could do not to grab her and take her on the ground like the untamed savage he became at the thought of losing her. He let out an exasperated breath. "Yesterday I said while you're here, you're mine. But that was an understatement. You're mine—no matter where you are. No ocean can separate our love." He entwined his hand in her hair and kissed her hard, hammering the message home.

She went pliant beneath the onslaught of his kiss, and when she finally pulled back, her chest rose and fell with shallow pants. "I *am* yours, Ian. I love you, and I desperately want things to work for us, but—" Natasha's voice caught and she swallowed hard. She blinked back tears and shook her head helplessly, clutching handfuls of his shirt in her fists as if she never wanted to let go.

Ian pulled her in his arms and kissed her temple. "Hush. I know you're stressed about everything. We'll take it a day at a time...for now," he said, his jaw clamping down in resignation.

That evening, Ian's Rover jostled across the rough terrain on the way to Alec's house. The beach at night was haunting and desolate in its gaunt, jagged coastline. A constant drizzle drenched the cold air as they traveled the winding private dirt road wrapping around the coastline. Natasha felt emotionally drained and sick at heart that she hadn't been able to say what Ian needed to hear from her. She wished she could, but she wouldn't lie to him. She had a commitment with the show and she had to return soon.

"We're almost there," Ian said, interrupting her thoughts.

Natasha glanced at him as he turned his attention back to the rocky trail. Her heart soared at the very sight of him, strong, stoic and so protective of her. He had been understanding earlier, even gentle, though he had looked like he wanted to tear the ground apart with his bare hands. He had agreed to her wishes today, but how long would it be before he lost patience...and trust...or worse yet, interest in her?

Ian pointed toward the horizon. "That's Alec's house up ahead."

"Wow, it's beautiful." Illuminated by the dim lights surrounding it, the two story mansion basked in a soft salmon pink glow and spread over a craggy cliff that dipped into the water's edge. "Tell me about Alec. What's his deal?"

Ian glanced at her with a quizzical lift of his brows. "What do you mean?"

"Does he have a girlfriend? Has he ever been married?"

"You want to hear the personal stuff, eh?" Ian said, smiling. "Alec got married young and they divorced a few years later. That was ten years ago."

"How old is he?"

"Thirty-eight. Why?"

Natasha hitched her shoulder in a half-shrug. "Maybe I'll introduce him to one of my girlfriends."

Ian shook his head. "Don't if your friend wants to get married. After his divorce, Alec vowed never to remarry."

She tilted her head. "Bad divorce?"

Ian gave a short laugh. "You could say that. He calls her wee Katie the shrew."

Natasha laughed. "Really? That's funny."

"Not to him. Kate is wee in size, but feisty as hell. Alec was mad about her, but they fought a lot. When he divorced Kate, his parents were unhappy about it, especially his mum. She used to say that Kate was perfect for Alec. Eileen thought so too."

"That's interesting," Natasha said, her curiosity piqued.

"Eileen and Kate are still friends. They've stayed in touch over the years." He snorted. "Even though Alec's not thrilled about it."

"Ha, I can see how that would annoy him. What about his parents? Have they stayed in touch with her too?"

"No, they're not alive. They died last year. First their dad died in a car wreck and three months later their mum died."

"Oh, that's so sad."

Ian nodded sympathetically. "Aye, Alec and Eileen have had many losses recently, including their granny's passing last month."

Shortly afterward, they arrived at the MacLeod home and were warmly greeted by Alec's sister, Eileen and a cute white Scottish terrier. One glance at the little dog made Natasha miss Evita terribly.

Eileen greeted Ian with a kiss on both cheeks and a tight hug. "I can't believe it's been years since we've seen each other."

"You're as bonnie as the last time I saw you, Eileen," Ian said, smiling at her warmly. "This is Natasha White. Natasha, meet Eileen, Alec's sister."

"Nice to meet you. And who is this adorable pup?" Natasha said petting the terrier's head.

"That's wee Brodie. I'm afraid he's spoiled rotten," Eileen said, shaking her head at the dog fondly.

Ian snorted. "Why must you lassies always spoil your dogs? Natasha has a dog named Evita and she's a wee diva," he said, grinning at her.

Eileen gazed from Ian to Natasha with a smile. "She should meet Brodie then."

Natasha studied Alec's sister with interest, remembering that Ian had told her earlier he'd had a school boy crush on her as a kid. With delicate features and a flawless complexion, Eileen had a slender figure and long, chestnut hair. Her manner was friendly, but more subdued than Alec's as she welcomed them inside.

Alec came up and grasped Natasha by the shoulders, kissing her on both cheeks. "Welcome to our humble abode," he said, eyes twinkling.

"This is humble?" Natasha said with a lift of her brows. "Your home is beautiful."

"Thank you. Come in," he said, leading them to his stately living room. Everything sparkled, from the large crystal chandelier, bisque colored walls, striped cream and taupe silk curtains to the exquisite oil paintings. A high-domed ceiling topped oversized French doors that led to an expansive balcony elevated directly above the sea. Natasha could hear the waves lapping against the shore.

Seated on the ivory silk sofa before a marble fireplace with an ornate mantle, she accepted a glass of wine from Eileen who passed them out with miniature salmon quiches.

"Thanks, looks delicious." Ian devoured the miniature quiche in one bite. "Especially after having canned soup for lunch," he said with a chuckle.

Natasha flushed, but she brushed feelings of inadequacy as she reminded herself they were roughing it with limited food options. Of course, Ian would be delighted with Eileen's special hors d'oeuvres.

Lifting his glass, Alec toasted, "To old and new friends."

Ian neatly swallowed his whiskey and set the glass down. "Have you told Eileen why we're in Skye?" he asked Alec.

Eileen's brows drew together in a worried knot. "Yes, Alec told me. If there's anything I can do, let me know."

"Thanks, but let's leave that to Alec," Ian said.

Alec nodded. "I spoke to Detective Carson this morning. She said the evidence on the flash drive is highly inflammatory."

"Why?" Ian said.

"There are a few dirty cops involved, including the police commissioner," Alec said grimly.

Natasha groaned. "Oh God. No wonder Tony was killed."

"Who's Tony?" Eileen asked.

Ian's face darkened. "He's the *scunner* who hid his flash drive in Tasha's suitcase and put her in danger."

Eileen's mouth dropped open. "How awful!"

Alec set his glass down on the marble coffee table. His burnished brows drew together in a furry line as he regarded them solemnly. "A man fitting the description you gave of Rico Gamberi rented a fishing boat at Arisaig. He arrived in Portree last night. Paid cash for the rental."

Natasha's stomach lurched. "That was the same man who came to Glenhaven looking for me. It has to be Rico!"

"No, Detective Carson said Rico is in New York," Alec said.

"Really? Wow, that's a relief," Natasha said, pausing to digest the latest news. "Then whoever is here must be a member of the Capelli family."

"Check your phone again, Tasha. Maybe it'll work here," Ian suggested.

Natasha fished her phone out of her shoulder bag and turned on the power. "My voice mail isn't connecting. It's so frustrating." She stared at Alec. "We didn't notice anyone following us, and I hid in the back seat on the ferry."

"Most folks know Ian around here. More than likely somebody saw him on the ferry," Alec said.

"It's just a matter of time before he finds us." Natasha clasped her hands so tightly her knuckles turned white. "We're not even safe all the way up here in Skye. How far do we have to go to get away from the mob?"

Ian exchanged a meaningful glance with Alec. "Maybe it's time to change strategy and let them know where we are."

Natasha gawked at Ian. "What do you mean?"

"Lead the guy into a trap and stop him faster," Alec said matter-of-factly.

"We become the predators not the victims," Ian said. "We'll make it known where we are and then wait for him."

Natasha's skin prickled with alarm. Ian wasn't a cop, he was a doctor—a brilliant and compassionate healer. He might know how to handle a gun expertly, but he was no killer. The mob was brutal, volatile and unpredictable.

"What if it's too late for that?" she asked, fear mushrooming inside her.

Alec snorted. "You wouldn't be here if it was too late. Once he finds you, he'll make his move."

Eileen's eyes glittered with determination. "I'll visit Mrs. Collins tomorrow. As soon as I tell her that Ian MacGregor is staying at the cottage with an American woman, the word will spread like wildfire."

Ian nodded. "Good idea, Eileen. How is the old gossip?"

"Fine, always eager for news. There's not enough excitement for her in Portree," Eileen said, smiling at him.

"Are you okay?" Ian asked, turning his attention to Natasha.

"I've been better, but I'll be fine." She swallowed against the nervous dryness in her throat and forced a smile. "Let's talk about something else."

Ian nodded and turned his attention to Eileen, "Are you still working at the clinic?"

"Yes, I love caring for my wee patients. They're adorable and bright as buttons."

"What do you do for a living?" Natasha asked.

"I'm a pediatric nurse."

"Oh. That's nice," she said politely.

"Would you be interested in working with me at the clinic?" Ian asked Eileen.

Eileen's face lit up. "Oh, yes. That would be brilliant. I'd love to help any way I can," she said, her amber eyes glowing enthusiastically. "But are you sure you need me?"

Ian's brows lifted in surprise. "Of course. I need you full-time. How soon can you start?"

Natasha watched their interaction with a pang. She should have been the one bursting with enthusiasm for his clinic. Ian had been so tied up in helping Natasha, they had barely discussed his future plans for the clinic. He seemed thrilled that Eileen was being supportive of him.

"I only need to give two weeks' notice so Dr. Sinclair can find a replacement," Eileen said. "I'd love to be a part of your charity clinic, Ian, but I heard all the hiring had been done."

"Where did you hear that?" Ian asked.

"From Dr. Parkhurst. When I sent her an enquiry, Danielle said there were no openings," Eileen said, her brow furrowed in confusion.

A muscle ticked in Ian's jaw as his features hardened. "She was wrong. We still have openings," he said in a taut voice.

*Ugh, Danielle again.* The thought of her having any influence in his life made Natasha's insides clench with possessiveness.

"Great. Well, okay then. Lovely," Eileen said awkwardly after a weighted pause. She turned to Natasha with an apologetic smile. "Sorry to get sidetracked there. We've been catching up and I haven't properly welcomed you, Natasha. It's nice to finally meet you. Alec and I always wished Ian had brought you up to Skye during your first trip here."

Ian cleared his throat and Alec looked at his sister with raised brows.

Eileen sighed and stared at them, round-eyed. "Oh dear, I probably shouldn't have brought that up," she said, shooting a worried look at Ian.

"Drop it, Eileen," Alec said, his mouth twitching. He turned to Natasha with a smile. "Are you currently in a show then? You're an actress, right?"

"Yes," Natasha said. Clearly, Alec had run a check on her too.

"Tasha sings like an angel and her dancing is gorgeous," Ian said, smiling at her.

"Aw, thank you, Ian. You're too kind," Natasha said, astounded by his generous compliment.

"I'm only stating the truth," he said. Anyone would think he was looking forward to seeing her on stage. She regarded him with puzzled eyes and he smiled back enigmatically.

Eileen beamed at her. "I love musicals. I always go to them on the West End when I'm in London. Which one are you in?"

"It's a new 1920's musical comedy called "The Bee's Knees," Natasha said.

"I would love to see you in it. Sounds lovely!" Eileen gushed.

"Well, Natasha, good thing you can sing for the two of you," Alec said pleasantly.

"What do you mean?" Natasha said, noting his teasing tone.

"Haven't you heard Ian sing, or rather croak? Laird MacGregor can't carry a tune in the bucket," Alec said, shaking his head mournfully. He turned to Ian with a merciless grin. "Remember when they sent you home from choir tryouts with a note saying you were more suited to science than singing?"

"I remember," Ian said dryly, "and thanks for bringing it up. The only reason I was in choir tryouts was because Mum coerced me into going. She thought it might help me sing better."

"Oh no. Did that really happen?" Natasha said, looking from Alec to Ian.

"I'm afraid so. The minute Ian sang the first verse, everyone covered their ears." Alec threw his head back and howled. "He sounded like a rusty pipe."

Ian chuckled good-naturedly. "Stop talking rubbish, Alec. You're making me look bad in front of Tasha."

"Aye, quit giving Ian a bad time. His singing isn't *that* bad," Eileen said, giggling. "Just because you have the lungs of a lion, Alec."

Alec flashed a generous grin. "Thank you, Eileen. I'll take the compliment. Blimey, I'm hungry as a lion too. Are we ready to eat now?"

"Aye, please follow me into the dining room," Eileen said.

"We're in for a treat." Alec straightened his large frame and patted his lean stomach as he rose from the couch. "Eileen is a fine cook."

Fine was an understatement. Eileen's cooking was Michelin star quality. They enjoyed a perfectly roasted loin of lamb, surrounded by glazed apples and accompanied by a homemade mint sauce. Dessert was poached pears in a brandy-laced butterscotch sauce. All deliciously prepared by Eileen and served by the freckle-faced, apple-cheeked housekeeper, Tilly, who bustled around them cheerfully.

After dessert, they retired to the balcony overlooking the sea. "Will you look at those clouds?" Alec said, puffing on a cigar. "It's already starting to rain. We're in for a big one tonight."

"Oh no," Natasha said, dreading it.

"I hate to cut the evening short, but we should leave before the storm hits," Ian said, slanting a glance at Natasha.

"*Dinna fash*. We understand. The roads aren't the best." Eileen paused and studied them for a moment. "Why don't you spend the night here? There's plenty of room and you won't have to deal with the storm."

"Thanks, but we'll be fine. We just need to get going," Ian said.

They said their good-byes and thanked Eileen for the superb meal. They ran to the car in the drizzling rain and made it inside mere minutes before it turned into a squalling thunderstorm. Water sloshed against the car as it chugged along the dirt road. Natasha clenched her hands in her lap and watched the lightning and thunder outdo each other. Her pulse roared in her ears like loud ocean waves as she strove to harness her panic. Staring out the front window, her eyes fixated on the wind shield wipers as they worked nonstop to clear the blinding rain.

They had only driven about a mile when the car hit something solid with a loud thump. Cursing loudly, Ian got out of the car to check what they'd hit.

"What's wrong?" Natasha said when he returned.

"There's a fallen tree blocking the road," he said, wiping his wet face on his sleeve.

"Can't we turn around and go another way?" Natasha asked, peering behind the car.

"No. The tires have sunk into the mud. We'll have to wait it out, then I'll call Alec to give me a hand."

Natasha closed her eyes to block the distressing childhood memory she always associated with lightning and storms.

"We're safer in a car than in a house, Tasha. The tires will ground us from the electrical currents," Ian said, guessing her fears.

Logically, she knew that, but emotionally was another thing. She took a deep breath and reached for a blanket in the back seat.

"Here, dry off," she said, handing the blanket to Ian. The moment he took it from her hands, a spectacular ray of jagged lightning lit up the sky. A loud crack of thunder propelled her into Ian's arms.

"I hate lightning," she said, burrowing her face in his chest.

"It's going to be fine, Tasha. What happened to you at summer camp won't happen again." He smoothed her hair and kissed the top of her head as they listened to the howling wind and driving rain.

"I feel ridiculous. I should've outgrown the fear by now," she mumbled, "but the minute I hear thunder and see lightning I'm right back at summer camp, bleeding on the ground." She shook her head. "One way or another, I have to get over it. Especially before I have kids. They can't have a mom who freaks out over storms." She wished she could say, before *we* have kids, but how could she? She had no commitment from Ian, save for his declaration of love.

Ian held her face and gazed deeply in her eyes. "You will, angel."

Her heart skipped a beat and the storm's danger was forgotten as she stared at him, imagining how their children would look.

Suddenly a bright light illuminated the car from behind and Ian's body tensed as he craned his head to look. Natasha pulled away and looked behind him too.

"What's that light?" she asked, the fine hairs on her nape standing on end. "It's so bright."

"Get down." He gently pushed her head below the dashboard and reached for the rifle in the back seat with lightning speed. "Stay there," he said before getting out of the car.

Natasha's head shot up when she heard the door slam. She strained to see what was happening, but the powerful light was blinding. Moments later, she opened the door and got out when she heard Alec's voice.

"Don't shoot, MacGregor! I'm here to help," he boomed with a loud chuckle.

Ian put down the gun. "How did you know we were stuck out here?"

"Eileen was worried you might have trouble returning to the cottage because of the storm. Get in the truck and I'll take you back to the house," Alec said. "You're both drenched and I'm sure you'd like a hot bath tonight."

"I don't know about Ian, but a hot bath sounds wonderful to me," Natasha said gratefully. "But what about the car?"

"We'll get it tomorrow morning," Ian said. "I need to buy a new tire anyway."

"Get in, get in. Eileen will be pleased to have you stay the night," Alec said.

When they arrived, Alec excused himself to check on a banging shutter outside of the house.

"I'll help you," Ian offered.

"No need to. Go inside. Eileen's waiting for you," Alec said.

"Goodness, were you sitting inside the car or out of it?" Eileen teased when she opened the door. "Come in and I'll fix you a hot toddy." She led them into the kitchen and added warm whiskey to hot tea laced with honey.

Afterwards, Eileen showed them to a comfortably decorated bedroom with access to a marble-tiled bathroom. A white porcelain tub with clawed bronze feet filled the center of the room. She handed Ian a large robe that probably belonged to Alec and a wine colored velvet robe and silk nightgown for Natasha.

"Let me have your wet clothes. I'll give them to Tilly and return them to you nice and dry tomorrow," Eileen offered.

"That's very kind of you. Thanks," Natasha said.

Eileen smiled. "You're welcome. Make yourselves comfortable now. Good night."

Ian showered first so Natasha could enjoy a hot bath. When she returned to the room, the lights were off and Ian was already in bed. She waited a few moments for her eyes to adjust to the darkness. As she came closer, she saw Ian's nude body was turned away from her, a sheet carelessly draped over his hips. Natasha admired his broad shoulders, the smooth muscles bracketing his strong spine and the shape of his compact buttocks beneath the sheet. When he turned on his back and flung an arm above his head, her eyes took in his corded chest muscles and the dusting of dark hair tapering to a V near his navel.

Just as she reached the side of the bed, he grabbed her waist and hauled her on top of him. She squealed and clapped a hand over her mouth, worried someone might hear them. "I thought you were asleep," she said, giggling. She slipped out of the robe and laid it at the foot of the bed.

"I thought you'd never get here," he growled, anchoring her on top of him. His hands slid beneath her nightgown and fondled the backs of her thighs and buttocks, stroking, squeezing, kneading as she moaned and wriggled against him.

Tremors of excitement shot through her and searing desire spread to every nerve of her body. Her nipples tightened at the feel of his hard chest rubbing against their tender peaks through the nightgown. Straddling his lean hips, she sat up and pulled the nightgown over her head and off. Ian tipped her forward and kissed her nipples as his hand slid toward the apex of her spread thighs, probing lightly to rub her tender folds with his thumb.

"You're dripping honey, angel," he rasped, his voice deep with a Scottish burr.

Natasha's thighs pressed either side of his hard hips, every muscle pulsating with delicious tremors as he thrust upward, entering her with deep, deliberate strokes.

She dug her nails in his shoulders and matched his rhythm. "Oh yes. Like that. Just like that!"

"You're in for a looong ride, darlin'," he promised wickedly, delivering a few lusty smacks on her buttocks.

"Watch it, Dr. Who," she said, tingling with pleasurable spasms. "You'll wake the neighbors."

The following morning, Natasha stretched and smiled, remembering Ian's sexy playfulness the night before. They were back to where they'd once been, comfortable enough with each other to tease and play, even during sex.

Gazing at him tenderly, she tickled his ear with a soft kiss on the lobe. "Wake up, Highlander. We have to get the car, remember?"

"What time is it?" Ian asked in a sleep-roughened voice. He buried his face in the pillow and didn't open his eyes. He looked so gorgeous and relaxed, she would have loved to stay in bed with him all day.

She glanced at her watch. "It's seven-thirty. I want to get back to our cottage."

"Go back to sleep," he ordered. "The stores don't open until ten."

She blew softly in his ear. "I don't want to sleep. I want to talk."

Ian turned over and gazed at her, his silver-green eyes slumberous beneath coal dark lashes. "About what?" he asked lazily.

She smoothed his tousled hair from his brow and drew in a steadying breath as she prepared to ask him a crucial question.

"Tell me about Danielle Parkhurst," she said, ripe with curiosity as she searched his eyes.

## CHAPTER EIGHTEEN

"Bloody hell. You woke me up to ask about Danielle?" Ian muttered, fully awake now and out of sorts.

Natasha's chin shot up. "It's a reasonable request. No need to get your feathers ruffled."

"I'll ruffle more than your feathers." Ian's voice rumbled out of his chest in a sexy growl as one strong arm snaked and pulled her toward him. He cupped her breasts in his hands and kissed the pink buds. "Beautiful," he breathed between kisses.

A wild shiver coursed through her, but she set her jaw and scooted away from him. "Not now," she said in a strangled voice, the moisture from his kisses teasing her tightened nipples. *Damn him.* Ian knew the power he wielded over her. If she let him continue, she'd melt in his arms and all talk about Danielle would be over. "You're playing dirty."

"What's wrong with playing dirty?" he said with a wicked grin.

"No playing until you tell me about Danielle," she said doggedly.

Ian shook his head. "Stubborn lass. What do you want to know about her?"

"Everything."

"I don't talk about previous relationships," he said stiffly.

"That's chivalrous of you, but she's also your partner. Isn't she?" she persisted.

"We're no longer involved and our connection is strictly business. End of story," he said firmly. Ian's unshaven chin stuck out belligerently.

Natasha rolled onto her stomach and propped herself on her elbows to study his face. "Why are you being so tight-lipped?"

"Let it go, Tasha," Ian said. "There's nothing between us anymore."

"Oh, never mind. Forget I brought it up," she said crossly. She yanked the robe over her shoulders and pulled the sash tightly as she got up from the bed. "Do you and I even have a future together?"

Ian shot up and was at her side in seconds. Grasping her shoulders, he grated, "Aye, we do, damn it. What brought that on?"

Her eyes flooded with tears. "I feel sick inside that I'm going to leave and you'll be here with Danielle," she admitted brokenly. "I know it's stupid and weak, but I'm jealous and it's eating away at me."

He gave her a little shake. "Haven't you been listening to me? I told you Danielle and I are over. Don't you trust me?"

"I don't want to share you with anyone," she said in a small voice. "I want to be with you, but you haven't said anything about…" Her voice trailed off uncertainly as she dashed hot tears from her eyes with her knuckles.

"What makes you think I'd let you leave here without a commitment to return?" he demanded, eyes blazing.

She hiccupped and looked down. "You haven't said anything about wanting me in your life permanently."

Ian lifted her chin and peered at her. "You're being daft, Tasha, and unfair. You asked me to take it one day at a time and I did." Sighing deeply, he leaned his forehead against hers and closed his eyes. "I should have followed my instincts and told you exactly how things are."

"What do you mean?" she said shakily.

He held her face between his hands and kissed her hard. "You're mine. Every morning I wake up and every night I fall asleep beside you, I'm grateful you came back to me." He kissed her tear-streaked cheeks and looked deep into eyes and straight to her soul. "You're not leaving until we find a solution. I'll work around your show, commuting back and forth, whatever it takes to be together until we can make definite plans for our future."

She stared at him in wonder. "Are you saying you're willing to compromise, to make concessions for my career?"

"Damn right I am. I'll move heaven and hell to make it work. If I'd done it years ago, we wouldn't have wasted so much time apart." His eyes glittered with fierce resolve. "I love you, and I'm not going to lose you again."

"You'll never lose me," she said, her heart bursting with so much love it hurt. "There's no one in the world I love more than you, Ian."

"And there's no one in the world for me than you, angel," he said, kissing her tenderly.

Later that morning after Ian left with Alec, Natasha went downstairs and found Eileen in the kitchen. "Good morning, Eileen."

Eileen turned to her with a warm smile. "Morning, Natasha. I trust you slept well," she said, eyes dancing.

Heat rose to Natasha's cheeks as she wondered if they'd been too loud in their lovemaking. "Yes, very well. Everything was comfortable. Thank you."

"Would you like a cooked breakfast?"

Natasha glanced at the fluffy scrambled eggs and kippers with grilled tomatoes and toast. "Looks delicious. I'd love some," she said, brimming with happiness over Ian's recent affirmation.

"Cuppa coffee or tea?"

"Coffee please. Just black."

Eileen served Natasha a mug of steaming coffee and set a plate of hot food before her. Brodie came up and begged charmingly on his hind legs, dancing for a morsel of food.

"Stop that, you wee rascal," Eileen scolded fondly as she lifted the dog on her lap and fed him a piece of toast. "The lads had quite an appetite this morning before they left."

"I'm sure," Natasha said, smiling at the image of Ian and Alec wolfing down Eileen's good cooking. "I'm not complaining because it's been wonderful staying in your cottage, but we've been roughing it with canned and dry goods."

Eileen smiled wryly. "Not exactly gourmet, eh? Do you like to cook?"

"I do. Although it's only me and my little dog in my apartment."

"What are your plans after Rico is caught?"

Natasha was taken aback by her candid question. She had spent a week avoiding that very question and now Eileen had uttered it quite calmly.

"I have to go back to New York. I'm under contract in the show," Natasha said.

Eileen fiddled with her napkin. "What about the danger?"

"I won't return until it's safe. Hopefully, that will be soon. But who knows?" Natasha stared at the food on her plate, suddenly losing her appetite. In all her euphoria over Ian's renewed love for her, she hadn't thought about Rico and the mob.

"What about Ian?" Eileen asked.

Natasha gave a dreamy sigh. "I adore him."

"And he adores you. It's plain to see."

"I'm thrilled we're back together again. It wasn't easy to regain his trust," Natasha said with a sigh.

Eileen nodded vigorously. "Aye, Ian is a force. He dominates any room he walks into. Like my fiancé, Callum," she said with a sly grin.

"You're engaged?"

"Aye, we're having a Christmas wedding."

"That's wonderful! How romantic," Natasha said with a sigh. "Will you be getting married in Skye?"

"Aye, then Callum and I will move to Edinburgh. It's lovely that Ian wants me to work at his clinic. He has always had brilliant ideas and plans."

"His plans for the charity clinic are impressive. I admire him so much for it. I just hope we can work around my career," Natasha said, surprised she was sharing the fears hidden deep in her heart.

"Anything is possible with love," Eileen said confidently.

"Ian is close to realizing his dreams. I want to be a part of them."

"You will. He just needs to get his inheritance back from that Anitra woman," Eileen said, shaking her head. "It isn't fair he's fought that battle for so long."

Natasha froze at the sound of her mother's name. "Wait a minute. What does my mother have to do with this?"

Crimson splotches stained Eileen's translucent skin on her neck and face as she gaped at her. "Your mother is Anitra?" she said, aghast.

"Yes, she is," Natasha affirmed. "How did you know her name?"

"I'm so sorry. I didn't know she was your mother," Eileen said in a choked voice. "I would have never brought it up. Please believe me."

"I do. What does she have to do with Ian's inheritance?"

"Me and my blasted mouth," Eileen moaned, clapping a hand over her mouth. "I shouldn't have said anything!"

"You can't stop there. I need to know. Please tell me," Natasha beseeched.

Eileen clasped her trembling hands on the table. "Late one evening, after a night of drinking and carousing, I overheard Ian and Alec talking. Ian was worked up and talking loud. He said he couldn't move back to Glenhaven until he got his half back from Anitra."

The blood drained from Natasha's face as she stared at Eileen, slack jawed. "What else did he say?" she asked, ignoring the rapid palpitations of her heart. "Tell me everything." As repugnant as it was, she had to hear the whole story.

"I don't remember anything else," Eileen said, bolting from the table. "You'll have to ask Ian."

*Ask Ian.* Natasha dreaded that conversation with every fiber of her being. "I have no idea why he didn't tell me about it," she fretted as hot mortification spread over her face and neck. She pressed her cold hands to her reddened cheeks and took a calming breath.

"I've really done it now. Ian's going to be furious with me. Alec too. I am so sorry," Eileen said.

"It's not your fault. Please don't feel badly. I'm glad I know. I had wondered who held so much power over Ian's estate." Natasha swallowed against the knot in her throat. "Knowing it's my mother makes me want to die right here."

Eileen hugged her. "Don't feel that way. We can't control what our parents do. You only have to answer for yourself to Ian. He must have had a very good reason not to tell you."

"I guess," Natasha said doubtfully. Her hands gripped the edge of the table, her knuckles white and sore. How could Anitra have gotten hold of such a large chunk of Ian's inheritance? He had said his father's mistress owned the other half. Something was off here.

Natasha sucked in labored breaths as her lungs tightened into a painful vise of despair.

"Don't take it so badly," Eileen soothed. "Ian loves you. It'll all work out in the end."

"From your mouth to God's ears, Eileen," Natasha said fervently.

"I'm going to take Brodie out for a walk. Would you like to come with us?" Eileen asked, eyeing her with concern.

"No, thanks. I need to make some phone calls," Natasha said. "I'm hoping my phone works better here than at the cottage."

"Good luck. If you'd like to use the landline, there's a phone right here," Eileen said, gesturing to the wall beside the kitchen door leading outside. "Tilly is off today. Help yourself to more coffee if you like."

"Okay, thanks."

When Eileen left with Brodie on a leash, Natasha pulled her smartphone out of her shoulder bag and called her lawyer. "Hi Saundra, I'm so glad to reach you. Do you have any news for me?"

"Yes. I tried calling you last night, but it went to voice mail."

"Sorry, my phone was off to conserve the battery. I can't access my messages here."

"No matter. I have good news for you."

Natasha's spirits lifted. "You do? What is it?"

"The police did a take-down at Rico's club and arrested a lot of people, including Rico."

Natasha gasped. "Oh my God, that is good news. What about my agent? Is he doing okay? I haven't been able to reach Marty and I'm worried sick about him."

"Don't worry. They sent Marty home this morning. He seems to be recuperating well. I'll call and let him know you're out of danger."

"Good. Thanks so much, Saundra. I owe you big time."

"You don't owe me anything, Natasha. I'm glad it all worked out for you," Saundra said warmly.

"I'm going to send you house tickets for 'The Bee's Knees'. Let me know what day you and Bill want to come."

"Sure, thank you. Can't wait to see you in it," Saundra said. "Safe travels. Bye now."

Natasha downed her coffee and stretched after she hung up. What a morning! First the shocking revelation of Anitra's hold on Ian's land; now good news about Rico's arrest. She couldn't wait to share the good news with Ian, the other about Anitra would wait.

She climbed the stairs and midway up, the doorbell rang. Turning, she headed downstairs again, wondering if Eileen had gotten locked out.

Natasha opened the door and her heart nearly stopped when she saw the man. He had grown a beard, but she recognized him instantly. Her heart pounded and her pulse roared in her ears as she froze, paralyzed with shock. She couldn't speak, couldn't breathe, only stare at him.

He pulled her forward and pressed a gun to her head.

# CHAPTER NINETEEN

"Oh my God! Tony! Please don't shoot," Natasha whispered, her voice raw in her suddenly constricted throat.

"Shut up. You're coming with me," Tony muttered in her ear. Holding her arm twisted up behind her, he propelled her down the stairs and pushed her in the car. Going around the front with his gun aimed at her until he got in the driver's seat. The mouth of the revolver pushed against her temple as he drove with one hand.

Quaking with terror, Natasha said, "I thought you were dead."

"Sorry to disappoint you," Tony sneered, tearing out of the driveway.

"But the newspapers, the—the television news reports," Natasha stammered through trembling lips. "Everybody said you were dead."

"I escaped from my car the night Dino Capelli ran me off the bridge, then I swam ashore."

"Have you been hiding under police protection?"

"Not anymore. The Capellis bought out the commissioner. The police think I was murdered."

"How did you find me?"

"I tracked you on your smartphone through spyware I installed."

Natasha gasped. "When? How did you do that?"

He grunted. "Easy. I did it when you weren't looking."

"What do you want from me? Is this about the flash drive?" God only knew where he was taking her. Her heart drummed so hard, she worried her chest might explode any minute.

"Give me your phone."

"My phone?" she asked suspiciously. "Why?"

"I've got important information embedded in there. Lay it here where I can see it," he said, indicating the console compartment between their seats.

With trembling hands, Natasha did as she was told, desperately wishing she could text Ian to alert him. "You have my phone now. Please let me go," she begged.

His mouth twisted. "You think I'm gonna let you go?" A deep-throated, nasty chuckle rolled from his chest. "You were a prude with me, but you've been fucking that doctor since you got here. I'm taking you to your little love nest and I'm gonna fuck you every way I can."

"No!" she cried.

"If you think that cut on your thigh was scary, wait till you see what I do with the rest of you."

"You were the one who cut me in Times Square?" she asked, hyperventilating.

"Yeah. When I'm finished with you, I'll dump your dead body for the doctor to bury."

She sucked in lungfuls of air. "Tony, please don't say that. I like you; it just didn't work out between us. Please don't kill me. I'll come to you willingly," she lied, frantically eyeing the door from the corner of her eye. *Should she fling herself out of it?* He had to be going at least 100 mph.

"Liar!" he snarled, pressing the gun harder against her temple. Tony's eyes gleamed like a madman's as he came to a skidding stop on the side of the road. "I'm not waiting anymore. I'm gonna take you behind those bushes now, bitch. Get outta the car," he ordered.

Petrified, Natasha's eyes bulged at him. "Please don't do this, Tony. I never meant you any harm."

"Shut the fuck up and get out," he bellowed, shoving her out of the car.

Natasha fell to the ground on her hands and knees. She scrambled to get up and twisted her head to look behind her, stunned to find two cars heading toward them from the opposite direction—Ian's white Rover and Alec's truck returning from town.

Tony saw them too. "Shit!" he roared and floored the accelerator, leaving her in the dust.

Natasha waved her arms and shouted, "Help!"

Ian's Rover did a U-turn and headed in her direction. Falling to her knees, she thanked God when he brought the car to a screeching halt and sprinted toward her.

"Get the bloody *scunner!*" Ian shouted to Alec when he drove up to them. Alec tore off after Tony's car.

Ian reached her side in seconds and searched her face with anguished eyes. "Who was that? Did he hurt you?"

"Tony...Tony," she babbled incoherently, gasping for air.

"What about him? Lower your head and take a deep breath, angel," Ian said, settling her on his lap, his arms surrounding her.

She sucked in shuddering breaths, safe in Ian's strong embrace. Tony was gone, but for how long? She had to snap out of it. "It was Tony Martin. He's alive! He kidnapped me from the house."

"Did he hurt you?" Ian asked in a low, choked voice. "I'll kill him if he did."

"No, but he was planning to. If you hadn't come along, I…I don't want to think of what he would have done," she said, tears streaming down her face.

"Hush, it's over now. Alec will nab the bloody bastard." Ian held her tightly against his chest and kissed her temple. He stroked her back and spoke in a soothing voice. "Thank God, he didn't harm you. I couldn't bear losing you, darling. I love you too much."

"I love you more," she said, her wiping her tears.

"Impossible." He tipped her chin up and kissed her with fierce tenderness. "Let's go home, angel."

"Where you are, that's home to me."

"Aye, me too." Ian kissed her again and lifted her in his arms, carrying her as if she were the most precious cargo. When they were safely in the car, he said, "Do you need to get anything from Alec's house?"

"No, I have my shoulder bag. That's all I had with me. I feel bad about not saying good bye to Eileen and thanking her, but I want to get back to the cottage."

"Me too. We can thank her later," Ian said, starting the ignition.

"Tony took my smartphone from me. He said he had important stuff embedded in it."

"Try to relax, darling, and don't think about it. If I know Alec, he'll have the *scunner* cornered soon."

The Rover trekked down the same winding road where it had stalled last night. The fallen tree trunk had been cleared away, but the road was strewn with multi-colored leaves of red, gold and orange.

"Skye is so beautiful," she said softly as she looked out the window trying to calm her jittery heart. She glanced at Ian's profile. He seemed lost in thought, his handsome features set in solemn lines as he drove.

"Aye, it is, but nothing compares to Glenhaven. It's been my family's paradise for centuries." His silver-green eyes glinted as he looked at her. "I'm intensely proud of my heritage and soon it will be ours," he promised.

A tremor shook Natasha to the core, but she summoned courage. Now that she was out of danger, there was only one thing marring her peace of mind. "Ian, I have to ask you something. It's been tormenting me since I heard it this morning," she said, her heart rising to her throat.

Ian's eyebrows drew together over concerned eyes as he regarded her. "What is it?"

"I heard that Anitra owns part of Glenhaven. Is that true?" she asked in a low voice.

"Oh God." Ian shook his head and eyed her compassionately. "You've just survived a horrible ordeal, Tasha. Do you really want to go into this now?"

"Yes." Meeting his gaze directly, she swallowed hard. "No need to sugar coat. I can handle it."

With a labored sigh, Ian slowed down the car, pulled over to the side and brought it to a stop. Facing her gravely, he drew another deep breath and expelled it forcefully. His broad shoulders slumped as if he carried the burden of the world on them.

"I'm afraid it is, Tasha," he said, the angles of his face tense. "How did you find out? I know Alec wouldn't have said a word."

Natasha met Ian's probing gaze even though it pained her. "It wasn't Alec. Eileen overheard you talking about it with Alec. She thought it was common knowledge."

"It isn't," Ian replied, shaking his head.

"Poor Eileen. She was horrified when she saw my reaction, but it was too late for her to take it back." Natasha laid a hesitant hand on Ian's fist, noting how tightly he clutched the stick shift lever. "How on earth does my mother own half of Glenhaven?" It only meant one thing and she couldn't bear to hear it, but she had to know.

Ian's mouth twisted bitterly. "She inherited it when my father died. I've been trying to buy her out for years, but she refuses."

Natasha's heart plummeted. "Why would he leave it to Anitra?" she asked despairingly. She held her breath, unable to process a coherent thought as she waited to hear the awful truth.

Ian stared at her for a long moment. "There's no easy way to say this and it pains me to tell you. They were lovers, Tasha. Until his death," he said at last. "Your mother and my father."

"Nooo. I don't believe it." Natasha clenched her hands into fists and pressed them to her temples as her eyes frantically searched his face. The look in his eyes told her the damning truth. "Oh God, oh God," she cried, her shoulders shaking with choking breaths. "Did my father know about their affair?"

"I don't think so. They kept it secret. I only found out when Malcolm's will was read. Anitra and I were the only ones told by the barrister that we share the inheritance of Glenhaven estate. I'm sure she never told Walter about her affair with my father."

Natasha lowered her eyes from his penetrating gaze. "I'm mortified and…and furious with her. Have you forgiven your father?"

"For his sins of the past?" Ian said scornfully. He shrugged and gave a wry twist of his mouth. "He royally screwed up my life with them, but frankly, who am I to judge? Everyone has a weakness." He gazed at her and said earnestly, "You're my weakness, angel."

"And you're mine," she whispered hoarsely, overcome by emotion.

"I plan to continue fighting for Glenhaven and I won't stop until I win."

"Why didn't you ever tell me? About her?" she added despondently.

"I wanted to spare you. Anitra is your mother and Walter is a wonderful father to you, a man we both respect. I didn't want to destroy your idyllic vision of their marriage."

She grimaced. "Idyllic? Their marriage was a disaster. All I remember was their bitter fights. They never divorced, but they live separate lives and are emotionally distant."

Suddenly, a lot of things began to make sense. Anitra must have had another motive for pushing her to refuse Ian's marriage proposal. It had nothing to do with Ian's desire for her to move to Scotland. Her mother had wanted her far away from him for selfish reasons. She hadn't wanted to risk her daughter finding out about her adulterous affair with Malcolm. The dawning realization made her sick to her stomach and wounded to the core. Natasha's soul burned with shame for her mother. She felt hopelessly desolate as she realized she'd never really had her mother's love and support.

"I'm sorry for everything she did. All the treachery and heartache my mother caused," she said, hot tears spilling from her eyes.

"Hush," he soothed, gently drying her tears. "Don't apologize. You're nothing like her."

"Daddy was her victim. If he'd known, he would have divorced her and he could have found happiness with someone else. When I think of all the years she deceived him, I feel sick inside. I don't understand why she didn't leave him and marry Malcolm."

"You'll never understand your mother's motives." The wrath in Ian's eyes scalded Natasha's soul. The man she loved more than anything in the world hated her mother with a passion.

She looked down. "I know you can't stand Anitra and I understand why, but she's my mother. I'm going to confront her and make her sell you her portion."

Ian lifted her chin and looked her straight in the eye. "Don't do it, Tasha, you'll get burned. I'll handle Anitra."

"I must get involved! I don't want her to come between us again," Natasha said, her chest tightening. She cupped Ian's taut jaw with her hand and she gazed at him, feeling vulnerable.

He turned his face and kissed her palm. "She won't," he said reassuringly.

A tingle slid up her spine at the determined look on Ian's face. He was not someone to cross; Anitra had sorely underestimated him. Natasha remained silent. She had every intention of confronting her mother and setting things right. Once and for all.

Ian started the car and steered it back on the road. His phone rang, startling Natasha.

"Alec, what do you have?" Ian said, glancing at Natasha.

"We nabbed the shitebag," Alec said.

"Fantastic. Hold on, I'll put you on speaker so Natasha can hear you too."

"Hello, Natasha," Alec boomed. "*Dinna fash*, lass. Tony is at the police station."

"Oh, thank God!" Natasha exclaimed as blessed relief poured over her frayed nerves like a balm. "How did you catch him?"

"He was in a stolen car and nearly ran someone over getting on the ferry. The police surrounded him and he gave up. It was that or be run off the ferry," Alec said with a snort.

"Brilliant. Good job," Ian said.

"The police are holding onto your phone. Sorry I couldn't get it back for you," Alec said.

"They can have it," Natasha said right away. "I don't want any reminders of Tony."

"What about your phone contacts and information?" Alec asked.

"No worries. I have everything backed up. Thank you so much, Alec!" Natasha said, giddy with relief.

"My pleasure. Where are you?" Alec asked.

"We're heading to the cottage," Ian said.

"Please thank Eileen for her hospitality," Natasha added. "You too."

"Will do," Alec said. "I'll keep you posted."

# CHAPTER TWENTY

A bit later, they ate the picnic lunch Ian had picked up in town. For the first time in what seemed like forever, Natasha felt completely happy and out of danger. Ian looked at ease as he stretched out beside her on a blanket beneath a clear sky and shining sun. The black Cuillin Mountains formed a magnificent background for their meal.

Natasha tore off a chunk of crusty bread and chewed it as she watched Ian slice an apple. His hands, strong and competent, were so precise that she could imagine his expertise with a patient. "Tell me about the clinic and how you plan to work on Arthur's face."

Ian looked up. "I'm inviting the top dermatology students for seminars at my clinic. They'll perform laser surgery as charity for those who can't afford it." He smiled. "Don't worry about wee Arthur, I'll treat him myself."

"I wish I could be with him during the treatments to hold his hand and ease his fears," she said, sighing.

"He'll be fine, it's not painful."

"Oh good. I feel guilty about leaving him behind."

Ian gave her a comforting smile. "Don't. He's in good hands."

"Yes, he is. In your hands," she said, smiling back even though her heart ached at the thought of saying good-bye to Arthur. "What will become of him once you've finished the treatments?"

"I'll find a good home for him."

"What if they don't love him enough?" she fretted. "He's been rejected already by his own mother. I would adopt him and take him with me to New York if I could," she said wistfully. "Arthur is special. He is so sweet."

"Aye, he is," Ian said pensively. His eyes softened as he gazed at her with heart-melting tenderness. "Shall we adopt wee Arthur then?"

"Do you mean it, Ian?" Natasha cried. When he nodded, she grabbed his face and kissed him exuberantly. "Does that mean—"

"That I want to marry you?" he said, smiling at her. "I do. Will you marry me, darling?"

"Yes! A million, zillion times yes," she cried, hugging him.

"Good. Now no more tears, just happiness," he said, molding her to him.

Natasha moaned as his thumb rubbed her lower lip provocatively. She bit the fleshy pad of his thumb and licked it.

"You're irresistible," he murmured, tilting her face and nibbling on her lower lip. Within seconds, he'd kissed her into a quivering, moaning, shameless heap of desire.

Natasha arched as he unclasped her bra and raised her sweater. Lifting her breasts in his warm hands, fingertips lightly pulled the tender tips. Her breath caught in her throat and wild lust shot through her, electrifying every cell of her body. She grabbed handfuls of his dark hair while he bent his head and suckled her nipples. His teeth lightly grazing them, sending jolts of pleasure straight to her sweet spot.

"Delicious," he murmured between kisses, "like winter raspberries."

Hot, blinding desire spiraled inside her, urgent and unbearable as wet lust pooled in her feminine core. Emitting a shuddering moan of surrender, she closed her eyes and let him feast on her achy breasts. Within seconds, she was writhing and quivering with pleasurable ripples as Ian worked his magic on her. Stretched beneath him on the blanket, she welcomed his solid weight as he bore her to the ground, his lovemaking demanding and tenderly fierce.

Much later, Natasha lay in his arms, shattered and speechless at the profound love they'd shared. She gazed at him and memorized every detail of his face to carry her through the time they'd be separated while she was in New York.

Ian stroked her hair from her forehead and kissed her eyelids. "Your eyes are the softest shade of blue I've ever seen." He hugged her close. "Loving you is tearing my heart out, angel." He tightened his hold on her. "Nothing will separate us," he vowed.

"Nothing," she repeated fervently. After a while, she said, "Can we go inside now? The temperature's dropping. And my behind hurts." She grinned impishly and rubbed her bottom where it had been ground into the blanket by Ian's vigorous lovemaking.

"Aye, you've taken a pounding and we don't want to damage the wee, delicate goods," he said, chuckling as he patted her bottom. He gathered everything up and took her hand.

Inside the cottage, they set about packing everything up. The gurgle of the rushing stream outside made her walk to the window to gaze through the open shutters one last time. Inhaling a deep, healing breath, Natasha savored the Skye mountain air and gave thanks for their happiness.

Later, as they drove to the ferry, Natasha called Maggie to let her know they were on their way. She related all the events leading to Tony's arrest, punctuated by Maggie's wild exclamations and grumbling interjections.

After convincing Maggie that they were out of danger, Natasha asked, "How is Arthur?"

"The wee lad is keeping me busy, that's for sure," Maggie said, chuckling. "But you won't hear me complainin'."

Natasha smiled at the fondness in Maggie's tone. "I'm glad. What about my little pom pom? Has Evita behaved?"

"Aye, she has," Maggie said. "Ranald's quite taken with her, so is Arthur. She rules them like the wee diva she is."

Natasha chuckled. "Maggie, I have wonderful news to share with you," she said, leaving the best for last.

"What is it, lovey?" Maggie said.

"Ian asked me to marry him and I said yes—of course!" Natasha said, smiling at him.

He winked and squeezed her hand.

Maggie let out a loud whoop of delight. "Ranald, come quick! The kids are engaged to be married. Praise God!" she exclaimed. "Have you set a date?"

"Not yet, but we will soon," Natasha said.

"I'm crying like a *bairn*. I have to go now. You've made me so happy, I need to find a hankie. Give my love to Ian and we'll see you soon."

When she hung up, Ian said dryly, "I take it she's pleased."

Natasha grinned. "She's pleased all right. Her squeal almost left me deaf. I've missed them, and Arthur and Evita."

"Me too. We have a lot of good news to share," he said, smiling at her.

When they arrived, Natasha was surprised to find a dark green sports car in the driveway leading to the castle. "Do you know whose car that is?" she asked.

"No. I haven't seen it before," Ian replied, his brow furrowed.

Natasha shifted uneasily as he walked around to her side of the car.

"Stay here," he said. "I'll find out."

# CHAPTER TWENTY-ONE

Just as Ian approached the front doors, Anitra flung them open and stepped out. Natasha gasped and ran out of the car toward her mother, noting her aggressive stance and sour face. Dramatically dressed in a royal purple wool crepe suit, Anitra's jet black hair was swept into an elegant chignon at the back of her neck. As she got closer, Natasha recognized the diamond and amethyst bracelet and earrings sent by a fan on one of her birthdays. Now she was certain the "generous fan" had been her lover, Malcolm.

Anitra braced one bony hand on her waist as the other clutched a cigarette. Narrowing her green eyes, she took a deep pull of the cigarette and exhaled harshly.

"What are you doing here?" Natasha asked the moment she reached Anitra's side.

"What are *you* doing here?" Anitra countered, eyeing her furiously. "I've been beside myself wondering when you were returning to New York. You've ruined your career by disappearing like that and now I find you with him!" She waved her cigarette at Ian with disdain.

"Are you here to talk business?" Ian asked Anitra bluntly.

Lips curled downward, Anitra threw her cigarette to the floor and ground it with her heel.

Anitra glared at Ian. "I told you to stay away from my daughter."

"Since when have I taken orders from you?" he said in a deceptively calm voice.

Anitra pointed a sharp nail at Ian. "I hold the cards here. Shall I tell Natasha of your plan to blackmail me?"

Natasha's eyes narrowed on her mother. "Stop it!" she snapped.

Anitra sniffed. "Last week Ian came to London and threatened to blackmail me."

"Good. I would have done the same in his shoes. Don't waste your breath criticizing Ian. Nothing you say could ever make me love him less."

"You shouldn't trust him," Anitra said with a twist of her mouth.

"I don't trust *you*. The last time you came between us, you managed to break us up."

"That's unfair. I did it to protect you," Anitra retorted.

"You did it to protect yourself. I know about your affair with Malcolm."

Anitra turned to Ian with venomous eyes. "So you told her anyway. That shows how much you love my daughter."

Ian took a step toward her and Natasha laid a hand on his rigid biceps. "Let me deal with her."

He nodded tightly; a muscle ticked in his taut jaw as his intense eyes blazed at Anitra.

Anitra drew in a sharp breath. "I was deeply in love with Malcolm and we had an affair for years. So what?" she spat. "The only reason he wouldn't marry me was because of his son. Malcolm promised Fiona he wouldn't remarry unless his son was in favor of it," she said, jutting her chin toward Ian. Her hands shook as she lit another cigarette and took a deep drag. "I adored Malcolm from the moment I met him until the day he died, and I don't regret one minute I spent with him."

Natasha glanced at Ian's grim face and wished her mother would shut up. "Spare me your love life, Anitra! I only want to hear that you're going to stop this selfish battle over Glenhaven."

Anitra's chin shot up. "Never."

Natasha took a deep breath and looked her square in the eye. "Never? Then here's what I'm going to do. If you don't sell your portion of Glenhaven to Ian, I am going to write a scathing, tell-all book about you."

"You wouldn't dare," Anitra said with a mocking laugh.

"Watch me." Natasha thrust her face within inches of Anitra's. "By the time I'm finished writing about you, *mommie dearest*, you won't have one fan left," she bluffed in one of her most convincing performances yet.

Anitra's mouth dropped open as she stared at Natasha. "You would turn against your mother? You're my only daughter. That book would ruin me and you know it! I didn't raise you to be so cruel."

"You didn't raise me at all. You say you only have one daughter, but I only have one parent...Daddy. And now I find out you cheated on him your entire marriage. It makes me sick. How do you think Robert will feel when he finds out?"

"Leave your brother out of it. Don't do this, Natasha," Anitra said furiously.

"If you don't want me to, then sign the papers agreeing to sell Ian back his portion. If you do, I won't write the book. I won't even tell your sordid secret to Daddy and Robert. Do we have a deal?"

Natasha had her cornered; she knew it the minute she mentioned her younger brother, Robert. Anitra's eyes narrowed into sharp slits as her jaw clamped down. Several moments passed as she opened her mouth and closed it, swallowing convulsively.

"Where's the blasted paper?" Anitra said at last.

"Be right back," Ian said, leaving the room.

"Don't expect me to accept Ian, because I won't," Anitra fumed when they were alone.

"Suit yourself. I don't care whether or not you accept him. I love him and we're getting married. That's all I care about," Natasha said, meeting her mother's eyes calmly.

"Are you crazy? Why would you give up your stellar career to move here?" Anitra said, gesturing around her. "When you snap out of his spell, you'll see Ian for the domineering, selfish man he is."

"You're wrong. He's the most understanding, generous man I know."

Anitra stared at her wordlessly. After a heavy pause, she said, "So he won the battle. Like father like son," she said shaking her head as realization dawned. "That's the type of passionate love I had for Malcolm."

"Spare me. I don't want to hear about your lust for Malcolm. What about Daddy? Why did you even marry him, if you never loved him?"

"Walter never made me feel like Malcolm did." Anitra grabbed Natasha's arm with a brittle, cold hand. "I don't want to lose you to Ian," she said through tight lips.

"Then you'd better be civil to him. I love him with all my heart and I won't let anything or anyone ruin it ever again," Natasha said fiercely.

Anitra deliberated Natasha's words and finally nodded. Several strained moments ticked by as they waited in silence for Ian to return.

He entered the room with a manila envelope clutched in his hand and withdrew a paper from it. Placing it on the foyer table, he indicated a line at the bottom. "Sign here," he said to Anitra in a flat tone.

Anitra signed the document and put the pen down forcefully. Without a backward glance, she lifted her head and strode out the door to her car.

Natasha waited until her mother's car turned the corner before shutting the door. Looking up at Ian, she said, "Triumph at last!"

He pulled her in for a tight hug. "You were formidable, darling. Were you really planning to write that dreadful book?"

"No, but I enjoyed turning the tables on her with my final Trump card."

He chuckled and tweaked her nose. "Don't ever think of using a Trump card on me."

Natasha grinned. "You, Dr. Who? Never," she said, tickling his lean waist until he burst out laughing.

The sound of tires crunching the driveway made them turn and stare at the door. "Now what?" Ian said grumpily. "I hope she hasn't come back."

"I doubt it's Anitra." Natasha opened the door and squealed with delight when she saw Maggie and Ranald drive up. She rushed out to greet them. When Ranald parked the car, Arthur flung the door open and ran toward her with Evita yapping at his heels. Maggie and Ranald remained in the car, watching from afar with broad grins.

Arthur threw himself into her embrace, almost knocking her over with the force of his eagerness. "Natasha! Dr. Ian! You came back!" he cried elatedly.

Natasha hugged Arthur and kissed the top of his dear little head. "Of course, we did! We love you."

Arthur pulled back and gaped at her, his mouth broadening into the smile she found so enchanting. "You do?" he asked, his dark blue eyes sparkling.

"Absolutely! Ian and I love you very much." *You're my baby now,* she thought as happy tears filled her eyes at the thought of adopting him. He would be their first child and very precious to them.

Evita barked and growled indignantly, her fur standing on end as she gave her a look that said, "What about me, Mommy?"

"You too, baby," Natasha said, lifting Evita in her arms and kissing her fluffy face.

Evita responded with guilt inducing whimpers followed by ferocious yips.

"She's a wee bit spoiled, don't you think?" Arthur said, shaking his head.

"Aye, she is, Arthur." Ian fondly rumpled his hair. "Do you have a hug for me too?" he asked, squatting down beside him.

Arthur gave him a tight hug. When he pulled back, Arthur's brows crinkled at Natasha. "Why are you crying?"

His worried expression tugged at her heart. "They're happy tears," she assured him with a wobbly smile. "I missed you."

"I missed you too. Especially at bedtime," he said, ducking his head shyly. "Will you sing for me tonight?"

"Of course. I'll teach you a song so we can sing together."

Gazing at Arthur's dear little face, she didn't want to think about leaving him. The excitement of performing for hundreds of strangers suddenly paled next to the joy of bringing music into his life.

Arthur wound his arms around her waist and hugged her tightly. She hugged him back, longing to hear him call her mum.

Ian cleared his throat and asked Arthur, "What did you do while we were gone?"

Arthur wriggled out of Natasha's arms and put his hands on his hips, mimicking Ian's stance. "Maggie and Ranald took me sightseeing every day. We saw lots of castles!" He tugged at Ian's arm. "When can we go fishing again?"

"Is tomorrow soon enough?" Ian's eyes crinkled at the corners as he watched Arthur.

"Aye, aye, aye," Arthur chanted, skipping into the castle. "Where's Dugie? I'm starving."

"I'm right here, laddie," Dugie answered, entering the foyer as she dried her hands on her clean apron. "Come with me, ducky, and I'll feed you," she blustered, ushering Arthur from the room.

Natasha hugged Maggie and Ranald warmly when they approached her with beaming smiles. "It's so good to be back. Thank you for watching over Arthur."

Maggie waved a hand at her. "Och, no need to thank us, lass. He's a joy."

"He looks wonderful. What have you been feeding him?" Natasha said.

"Plenty of food and double doses of love," Maggie replied with a smile.

Evita growled and snapped at them, reminding everyone that Arthur wasn't the only one who needed sustenance and love—not to mention attention.

Laughing, Natasha kissed Evita's head and made a snap decision. She turned to Ian and said, "As much as it pains me not to take my little Evita with me, I'll leave her here to keep Arthur company until I return."

Ian braced his hands on his hips, very much the laird of the land. "That's fine, the dog can stay, but you're not going anywhere until I place a wedding band on your finger. I made that mistake once before and I'm not making it again."

Natasha threw her arms around him and said, "Damn right, you're not!"

# CHAPTER TWENTY-TWO

*One month later*

Natasha stood on stage looking out into the dark theatre and listening to wild applause. She smiled and held hands with her co-stars as they bowed to the second curtain call. A year ago she would have felt ecstatic and fulfilled by the audience's reaction, but tonight she couldn't wait to go home and call Ian. It would be early morning there, but he had insisted she call him after the show.

"Happy Thanksgiving," she called out to the audience, waving as she left the stage. It didn't feel like Thanksgiving though. She hadn't even eaten turkey today. She had refused the kind lunch invitations from friends and spent Thanksgiving alone at home.

Back in her dressing room, she took off her auburn bob wig and placed it on the mannequin head on the counter. She hummed to herself as she peeled her fake lashes off and washed her face of her stage make-up before changing into her street clothes. After receiving great news earlier, she couldn't wait to share it with Ian. She'd wait till she was home where she could speak in private without anyone barging in.

She had much to be thankful for, she reflected, gazing at a picture of Ian and Arthur on her mirror. She still couldn't believe she was Ian's wife and Arthur's mother. Ian had insisted on a quick marriage and later they adopted Arthur. She had hated leaving them in Scotland and spoke to them daily via Skype. She loved hearing about Ian's clinic and how he had already performed two treatments on Arthur, whose face was responding well to the laser. Evita was always in the picture when they Skyped, preening and barking along with their conversation, making sure she got her share of attention.

Natasha took Ian and Arthur's picture off her mirror and kissed it, yearning to be with them on this holiday. With a sigh, she put it back and reminded herself not to get melancholy. She had too many wonderful things to look forward to in the coming year.

A knock on the door surprised her. "Come in," she said.

The door opened and Ian appeared holding a large bouquet of coral roses in one hand and Arthur's small hand in the other.

Natasha jumped up from her chair and ran to them joyfully. "Ian! Arthur! I can't believe you're here!" she cried happily, hugging her two favorite men at once. "When did you get here?"

"This afternoon. You were wonderful tonight. Well done, angel," Ian said beaming at her.

"Aye, you were brilliant, Mum," Arthur piped in. Dressed in a dark blue wool coat and sporting a tweed newsboy cap, Arthur looked utterly adorable as he grinned at her with twinkling eyes. Very much a little laird in the making sporting a MacGregor tartan wool scarf like Ian's.

"Thank you, King Arthur of the round table," Natasha said, bowing to him. "I am so touched you came, Ian, and that you brought Arthur with you."

"We couldn't let you spend Thanksgiving alone, could we, Arthur?" Ian said to him.

"No, Dad, we couldn't," Arthur said, grinning up at Ian in agreement.

"I told wee Arthur, we'll be coming to New York for Christmas too," Ian said.

"Oh no you won't. I'll be home for Christmas," Natasha said, enjoying the surprise on Ian's face.

Arthur's eyes widened. "To Glenhaven?"

"Is there any other home?" Natasha asked with a lift of her brows.

"That's great!" Ian beamed at her. "How did you manage to get the time off?"

"Just this morning, Marty confirmed that I can leave before my contract is up."

"I meant it when I said I was willing to commute until you finish the run of the show. Are you sure you want to do that?" Ian's brow knitted as he searched her eyes.

"Yes," she said with absolute certainty. "I refuse to spend another holiday away from you."

"How are you going to get out of the contract?" he asked.

Natasha smiled slyly and patted her belly. "Easy. I'm pretty sure Simon won't want Legs LaRue dancing on stage with a baby bump," she said, breathlessly awaiting his reaction.

Ian's eyes shot open. "We're having a *bairn*?" he shouted happily.

"Aye, we are, Dr. Who," Natasha said, affecting a Scottish burr.

He touched her belly in awe. "I'm so happy…and so proud," he said, husky with emotion.

Natasha's eyes lovingly swept over Ian's gorgeous features. Every nuance was indelibly printed in her heart and soul since she first fell in love with him. "I hadn't realized how empty my heart was until I saw you again in your office after all those years," she said with a hitch in her chest.

He gently rubbed her belly. "Thank God you came to me that day, darling."

Happy tears stung her eyes as she tilted Arthur's chin up to meet her gaze. "Are you ready to be a big brother?" she asked, smiling at him.

"Aye. I'll be the best," he said, puffing out his chest proudly.

"What about your career? You sing like an angel, Tasha. It seems a shame not to share your talent," Ian said.

She smiled through her tears. "I can't imagine living anywhere other than Glenhaven. With you and Arthur."

"You can always go back to performing if you want to," Ian said.

Natasha shook her head and dabbed her eyes with a tissue. "Not for a long while. Maybe I'll make a comeback when our children are older, but not now. I'm happy with my decision," she said with total sincerity.

Ian kissed her deeply. Her fingers pushed into the satiny thickness of his hair and she lost herself in his kiss, forgetting everything but him.

"Ewww, Dad, yuck," Arthur said, making a gagging sound.

Ian stopped kissing Natasha and laughed. "Someday you'll understand." He hugged Natasha and said, "Too bad you were cheated out of a wedding reception."

She smiled ruefully. "I wanted to share the happy moment with everyone I love, especially my Heart sisters. I was hoping for a party."

"Aye, with lots of cake!" Arthur cried eagerly.

"Who said anything about not having a party?" Ian asked, silver-green eyes twinkling. "We'll have a grand celebration at Glenhaven Castle and invite everyone."

"Oh, Ian, I adore you. Both of you," Natasha said, pulling Arthur into their tight embrace. The joy of having them so close filled her to bursting as they clung together.

"No matter where you are, here or in Scotland, you belong with us and nothing will ever change that, darling." he said, making her eyes well up again.

Ian smiled and her heart turned over. His passionate words, fierce and heart-wrenchingly beautiful, were sweeter than any music Natasha had ever heard.

The End

For new release and book party information,
sign up for my newsletter:
http://sophiaknightly.net/newsletter-sign-up.html

## Excerpt: Heart Raider

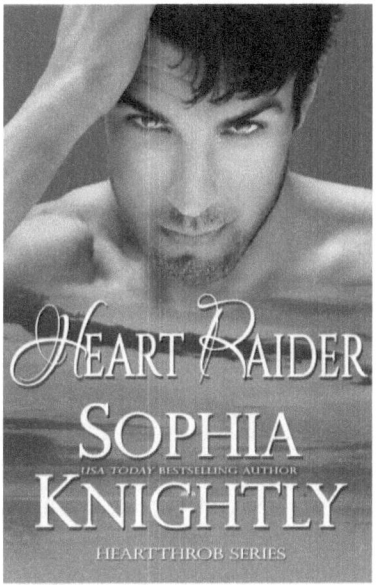

**by Sophia Knightly**

### Prologue

Thirteen-year-old Veronique Whitcomb gazed at the sparkly stars in the clear North Carolina sky and let out a frustrated sigh. Sitting cross-legged in front of the campfire, she swallowed against the lump in her throat and tried to smile. It was the last night she'd spend with her two best friends at sleep away camp and she wished it would never end. Tonight she'd enjoy their company...tomorrow she'd have to face the disaster called home.

"I hate that we're leaving tomorrow," Veronique said, grabbing each girl's hand. "I'm gonna miss you guys."

They'd first started coming to camp as little girls and none of them had sisters. Tash and Teddy would always be her Heart Sisters.

"I bet you'll miss Nick even more." Natasha White's blue eyes danced as she tossed her long strawberry blond hair. "You've been trying to get his attention all summer."

"I have not, Tash," Veronique retorted. *God, had she been that obvious?* The first time her eyes had connected with the deep blue eyes of the cutest counselor at Camp Merry Cascades, her heart had done a cartwheel and was never the same.

Theodora Behr clutched her heart dramatically. "Nick is sooo hot. I can't stop dreaming about him." She grinned and nudged Natasha.

"You can't have him, Teddy. I want him too." Natasha pretended to swoon. "Admit you like him, Ronnie. We all do."

"Cut it out, guys." Veronique's chest hitched at the thought of not seeing Nick again, but she rolled her eyes to hide her feelings.

Natasha smiled. "Hey, you don't have to get so defensive."

"Yeah, we're just messing with you. We won't mention him again. No more Nick—I promise," Theodora said, lifting her right hand in a pledge. "I'm gonna miss you too."

"We have to stay in touch after we leave," Natasha said earnestly.

"Pinky swear." Veronique raised her pinky with the bitten-down nail and ragged cuticle.

"I'm in." Theodora linked her suntanned pinky with Veronique's. "I plan to travel the world and marry a hot prince in a foreign land, but I'll always stay in touch."

"Me too." Natasha looped her bejeweled, manicured pinky with theirs. "I'm going to be a famous Broadway actress," she said dreamily. "Of course...if Nick proposed to any of us today, we'd say yes."

"You promised not to mention him again," Veronique reminded her. "Anyway, I'm gonna be too busy reporting important stuff to think about marriage. I probably won't marry anyone," she added with a touch of cynicism to throw them off.

"Unless it's Nick!" Theodora and Natasha added in unison and collapsed into giggles.

*Fifteen years later...*

## Chapter One

Veronique squelched a sharp intake of breath at the dangerous looking man whose wide shoulders filled the doorway. She hadn't expected to find him looking so untamed and ominous on this steamy August morning on Starfish Island, a barrier island off the Gulf Coast of Florida. He looked annoyed too. She couldn't blame him really—she'd stood there ringing the doorbell and pounding on the door until he finally answered.

Nick Cameron's cobalt blue eyes locked on hers, flashing with impatience. Veronique's stomach fluttered nervously as she lifted her chin and stared back, her lips unsteady with the effort to smile. The foreboding glint in Nick's eyes made her knees knock, yet she was not the knee-knocking type—not by a long shot. Veronique Whitcomb, intrepid reporter for Ace News, was not easily frightened. Still…Nick's sheer size and intimidating air gave her pause. She held onto the wooden balustrade and gaped at him. Dark stubble shaded his chiseled jaw. The angles of his face were sharper than she remembered, his cheekbones and jaw taut, his nose a hawkish blade. He was almost unrecognizable, save for the brilliant blue eyes pinning her with an intensity that made her smile falter.

"Ronnie?" Nick's searing gaze raked over her. "What are *you* doing here?"

Her heart lifted. Nick remembered her. Maybe this wouldn't be so hard after all. Maybe the large, scowling man would revert back to the childhood heartthrob she remembered. She'd flown into Miami two days ago from New York and driven across to the west coast of Florida in a rental car, stopping to do some interviews in Fort Myers before crossing over the causeway to Starfish Island. She would have driven *anywhere* to seek him out.

"Never mind. I know why you're here," he said caustically. "You're not getting an interview." He looked behind her, peering from left to right.

"Relax, I came alone," she said, guessing that he was checking to see if there was a camera crew waiting to ambush him.

"You're leaving. Now." His hand on the door, he began to close it in her face.

"Wait a minute!" She stepped up to the door ledge and he took a step backward. "How did you recognize me?"

He looked at her tousled, layered shag with narrowed eyes. "I've seen you on TV a few times—reporting. Your hair's still reddish brown, but you haven't changed much from the thirteen-year-old brat with long pigtails and freckles who raised havoc wherever she went."

"Gee thanks." Why was Nick making her feel like a gauche tomboy when she'd gotten all dolled up in a floral sundress and pretty sandals? She had even put on make-up, for God's sake. She did not look like the ragtag, wild Ronnie he remembered from Camp Merry Cascades years ago.

She drew herself up to her full five foot, five inches. "I *have* changed a lot in fifteen years and you know it."

Nick's steely gaze flickered over her flushed face. "Fifteen years or not, I'd recognize your freckles in a heartbeat, especially when you're blushing."

She wished her fair skin didn't turn bright pink under duress. It was one of those things a reporter could do without. Not even the self-tanner she'd applied before coming down from New York could hide her vivid blush.

"Fine welcome after all those years. Aren't you going to invite me in?"

"No." Nick towered above her with tanned, muscular arms folded across his chest and solid legs braced apart. His thick black hair was longer and shaggier than any businessman would ever have. She stared at his well-developed arms and the imposing chest straining his cotton T-shirt. His uncivilized appearance wasn't exactly what you'd expect of a billionaire corporate raider. He looked more like a muscle-rippling wrestler ready to take down his opponent. There wasn't an ounce of fat or flab on him.

Her pulse quickened as she took in every detail. Nick, at twenty when she'd last seen him, had been lean and lanky, but he'd put on at least fifty pounds of roped muscle since. He'd grown a few inches too.

"How did you find me? Nobody knows where I live and I plan to keep it that way," he warned, his voice low and tough.

Veronique lifted her hair up and fanned her neck. "Please let me in and I'll tell you. It's hot out here and these sandals are pinching my feet," she said, shifting from one foot to the other. Why had she even bothered to wear the strappy sandals? Oh yeah, to impress the grouch blocking her entrance.

"Make it brief and then skedaddle. Got it?" Nick opened the door and gestured for her to enter his plantation-style mansion.

Veronique nodded, even though she had no plan to skedaddle. Not when she'd managed to get inside his house. Delighted to pass the threshold of his reclusive digs, she followed him past a high-ceilinged portico and into his living room. As Nick ambled ahead, the play of taut thighs and well-formed butt muscles contracting and relaxing in his low-rise jeans snared her attention.

She forced her gaze away from his jeans and studied her surroundings. A mahogany staircase led to an upstairs loft and other rooms at the back of the house. The living room and dining room were decorated in greige tones, a relaxing combination of gray and beige. Other than basic, minimalist furniture and a few abstract paintings, the house was sparsely decorated.

The living room had a plush, square sectional surrounding an oversized travertine stone coffee table. The dining room, with a long sleek table and six chairs, looked like it was never used. A modern, diamond shaped crystal chandelier hung from a high beam ceiling over the table.

"Aren't you happy to see an old friend?" Ha, she was being delusional. Nick looked ready to throttle her.

His brows knotted over irate eyes. "I wouldn't exactly call you an old friend. More like a little rebel without a cause. I'm surprised they didn't send you home, with all the havoc you raised," he groused. "Especially the last summer you spent there."

*Why did he have to mention the worst summer of her life?*

"You forget I had famous, rich parents." Damn, this wasn't going as she'd expected...and hoped. She'd wanted him to take notice of the new, grown-up Veronique. "My thirteenth year wasn't exactly a happy one. After Daddy's death and Maman's nervous breakdown, I toughened up real quick."

From that low point in her young life, she had vowed never to feel so vulnerable again. Her father, Brett Whitcomb, a renowned TV news anchorman, had died of a lethal cocktail of drugs and alcohol the summer of her thirteenth year. Her genteel French *maman*, Helene, had always been prone to depression and bouts of paranoia. The more Brett had self-destructed, the worse it had become. She had worshiped her dashing celebrity husband and refused to acknowledge he was an alcoholic and drug addict. When reality finally set in after his death and Helene found out Brett had lost their family fortune in a Ponzi scheme, she spiraled down into a nervous breakdown, leaving behind her frightened, rebellious daughter to cope with the press.

"That was a rough time for you," Nick conceded in a quiet tone. He knew all about her childhood traumas, he'd witnessed them first hand—especially Helene's penchant for high drama and histrionics.

Her thirteenth year was the last time she'd seen Nick—until today. She'd kept tabs on him, rejoicing in his triumphs and success over the years. She met a lot of men in her line of work on a daily basis, but no one had held her interest long enough to build a relationship. Maybe she was "commitment phobic" as Maman often proclaimed gloomily...or maybe no one measured up to Nick. He'd been her hero then and still was, albeit a fallen one. Now that she'd found him, she wasn't about to let things rest until they were set back to right.

Veronique expelled a heavy sigh. "There's no use dredging up bad memories. Mind if I sit down?" she asked, eyeing the living room couch.

"Matter of fact, I do mind."

She paused, gathering courage before he booted her out of there. "I have a proposition for you."

Nick didn't respond. His gaze was so direct, she had to break eye contact and gather her wits. As the seconds ticked by, she realized he wasn't interested.

"Don't you want to know what it is?" She held her breath and waited. He continued to stare at her with a mixture of distrust and skepticism.

"No," he finally said. "But I have a feeling you won't leave until I listen to you. I already told you I'm not giving you an interview. What harebrained scheme are you cooking up now?" he demanded.

She thrust her chin high and narrowed her eyes at him. "I'm no longer a kid and prone to what you rudely refer to as 'harebrained' schemes. I'm all grown up now, if you hadn't noticed," she stated, throwing her shoulders back and puffing out her chest.

Nick's gaze lowered to her breasts and then back to her face. "I noticed." He shook his head as if to clear it. "Once a hellion, always a hellion."

"I don't remember you being so gruff. You were always nice to me." The Nick she remembered as camp counselor had been on the serious side, but kind and fair.

His upper lip curled. *Damn, how long was he going to make her stand there before him like a delinquent?* With his brawny hands braced on his lean hips and his wide-legged stance he looked like a tough detective interrogating a suspect.

Nick was being so patronizing, she felt like filling him in on the past years of her adult life, the ones filled with awards for investigative journalism and documentaries. But more than likely, he knew all about her recent public shame and how she'd been demoted from foreign correspondent to reporting fluff. She had once been renowned for her daredevil journalism, but given Nick's aversion to the media, it wouldn't be wise to bring it up now. Especially since he too had been publicly shamed in the media, but for vastly different reasons.

Given the way he was glowering at her, she wasn't about to tell him the reason she'd landed on his doorstep was to present Ace News with a prized story. An exclusive interview with Nick Cameron, the notorious, sought-after recluse whose fall from grace had landed on every tabloid would do wonders to revive her flagging career after the fiasco of her last assignment.

But that was only part of it; the real reason was to alert him to what she'd found while investigating his recent divorce from tobacco heiress, Elizabeth Remington.

"You still living in London?" he asked abruptly.

His question surprised her. "Nope, I live in New York now."

"Reporting for Ace News?"

She paused. "Yes. I've been reassigned to human interest stories." Her stomach contracted as she said it. The reminder of her recent demotion and near firing still smarted and she'd rather not get into details with him.

Nick cocked his head and quirked a dark brow, the gesture so arrogantly male, it reminded her of Sean Connery when he'd make a sardonic remark in old James Bond movies.

He was making her feel as welcome as a bloodthirsty mosquito. Veronique locked her determined gaze with his as they faced off standing rigidly apart, throwing sparks off each other. Neither spoke until she finally strolled over and plopped down on a duck white canvas sofa.

"Okay, I give. What will it take for you to stop frowning at me?"

"How about you march your little butt out of here?" he asked in a gravelly tone.

He was definitely out to rile her. "How about we make nice instead?" she said with a saucy grin.

Nick lowered his strapping frame into the big armchair across from her, elbows braced on widespread knees. He leaned in nose-to-nose, close enough for her to notice the thick jet lashes framing narrowed blue eyes. Wariness sharpened the hard edges of his jaw line as he watched her intently.

"Tell me. What is so important that you would disrupt my privacy?" he asked, not taking his eyes off her.

He was trying to intimidate her, but his closeness was making Veronique weak in the knees and she couldn't help but take a satisfying whiff of him. He smelled wonderful up close—clean and manly and so *delicious*. She exhaled heavily and looked away, willing her body not to react to him, but it wasn't working.

She couldn't tell him his hideaway was the perfect refuge for her while she tried to figure out who had shot at her in the Miami hotel parking lot, because he'd go ballistic. If no one had located Nick's whereabouts during the six months after he'd disappeared from public scrutiny, they wouldn't find her there either.

The shooting in Miami had happened so fast she hadn't been able to get the license tag number of the drive-by shooter's car. Adding to her frustration, there was no security video of the parking lot. The only evidence of a random shot was her word. She hadn't stuck around long enough to find out where the bullet had landed. The minute she heard the shot, she dove into her car, called 911 and drove to the nearest police station.

She was used to danger, but that random shot had rattled her. It could have been anyone out to get her after the type of investigative reporting she'd done in the past.

Or it could be the case she was currently investigating…

"Answer me," Nick prompted in a gruff voice.

Hunched over like a cagey jungle cat, he didn't look amenable to providing temporary refuge and definitely not an exclusive interview. He grabbed her chin and turned her face to meet his sharp gaze.

An electrifying spark passed from his callused fingertips to her chin. He must have felt it too because he dropped his hand to his knee. Her heart raced and she could feel her pulse throbbing in her neck. "

"I, um well…" She was interrupted by a bolt of lightning followed by a loud crack of thunder. The air between them crackled with more electricity than the storm outside. She ran to the large window to get away from him and get ahold of her bearings. "Must be the outer rain bands. Storm's almost here!" she announced breathlessly as the gusting wind swirled outside and the heavy rain pelted the house. "We're in for a downpour."

Nick lumbered forward and joined her at the window. His fingers closed around her elbow. "Time to leave," he said firmly.

"Haven't you been tracking Tropical Storm Abby?" she asked, disengaging from his grip. "It's sure to be the first hurricane of the season. When was the last time you ventured into town?"

"That's none of your business. Why did you show up here knowing it was heading this way?" His deep voice started off low and increased with each word. While he wasn't exactly yelling, he wasn't whispering either.

Veronique took a step back from Nick's imposing form. "Do you even watch TV?" she blurted out.

"Not if I can help it."

"Why own one if you don't watch it?"

She sucked in a nervous breath. Maybe he didn't know the reason she'd been hauled out of her high-status job as foreign correspondent in Ace TV's London bureau and sent back to the States to report filler stories. She could only hope. It hadn't been her fault that Eric, the fact-checker, had fed her erroneous information on a major political scandal involving a prominent, conservative Senator and a call girl reported to be a spy. When the truth was revealed that she wasn't a spy, but his longtime mistress, Veronique had been demoted and Eric fired.

She missed the excitement of investigative reporting. Not that she minded doing human interest stories, but they weren't as challenging or adrenaline-inducing as breaking a controversial case wide open. She'd had success in cases she'd worked on in the past including exposing a pyramid scheme among top senators, a child porn sting in a Bible belt community, and a heroin operation cover-up in a prestigious private university. The one case she'd tripped up on because of inaccurate fact checking from her trusted co-worker had sidelined her rising career and put her credentials in doubt.

*Damn the media and the public for their fickle ways.* One day she was at the top of her game and the next, kicked to the curb. Whether Nick realized it or not, she could relate to how he felt.

"I watch it once in a while, but not every day," he said, bringing her to the present. He frowned. "Quit stalling and get going. I want you outta here before the hurricane hits."

"Pfft. Hurricanes don't scare me," she scoffed. *And you don't either.* "They're pretty exciting. I covered a few and even went surfing just before Hurricane Olga hit. What a rush!"

Nick grabbed the remote control and switched on the news. Five seconds later, when the anchorman said the storm was strengthening into a hurricane, he flicked it off.

"Before you go—and you will soon," he promised curtly. "Tell me how the hell you found me. Nobody knows where I live."

"Well... I wouldn't say *nobody*..." Veronique hesitated.

He crossed his arms over his chest. "I know for damn sure Fred wouldn't give you my address. You must've done major snooping in your step daddy's office to find my whereabouts."

Veronique grimaced. "Who said anything about Fred? He's your lawyer, for God's sake! He would never divulge that information."

"Damn straight he wouldn't." Nick's deep voice rumbled out of his chest like thunder.

Veronique eyed the front door when he stepped closer. It was time to retreat and formulate another plan ASAP.

# SOPHIA KNIGHTLY - BIO

USA Today bestselling author, Sophia Knightly, loves to cook up hot romance and delicious humor in her feel-good stories. Whether it's romantic suspense, romantic comedy or chick lit, her books are fun and sexy contemporary romances that feature hot alpha heroes and strong, smart women.

A two-time Maggie award finalist and a P&E Readers' Poll finalist, she is traditionally published by St. Martin's Press, Kensington and Samhain Publishing. Her popular Tropical Heat Series books, *Wild for You* and *Sold on You*, have consistently been on multiple Amazon bestselling lists and sold over 100,000 copies.

When not writing or reading, she loves walking the beach, exploring museums, going to the theatre, enjoying good food, and watching movies. One of her favorite pastimes remains simply watching people, especially those in love!

Sign up for her "new release" newsletter at:
http://SophiaKnightly.net/newsletter-sign-up.html

Write to her at: SophiaKnightly@gmail.com

Follow her on Twitter @SophiaKnightly

"Like" her Facebook author page at:
http://on.fb.me/vGfJ5t

Visit her website at: www.SophiaKnightly.net

WILD FOR YOU Book Trailer:
http://youtu.be/XtVlFBdaHvs

SOLD ON YOU Book Trailer:
http://youtu.be/X20NbJElrvM

GRILL ME, BABY Book Trailer:
http://youtu.be/6Y07iUPt3rg

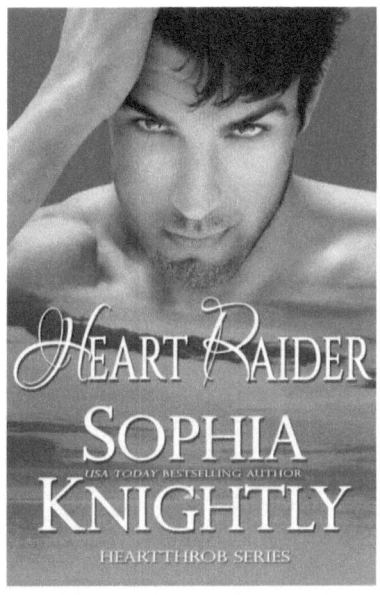

**HEART RAIDER (Heartthrob Series, Book One)**
**by Sophia Knightly**

*Stranded together during a rampaging hurricane...*

Hot passion explodes between a reclusive billionaire and a headstrong reporter seeking his exclusive story...a story that could get her killed.

*Hunted by someone desperate to silence her...*

Daredevil TV reporter Veronique "Ronnie" Whitcomb is charismatic, fun-loving, and loyal to a fault. Especially to the man she fell in love with fifteen years ago. He's now a self-made billionaire, and at the center of a public scandal so hot and juicy, Ronnie must get an exclusive interview...an interview that will vindicate him and expose the real criminal behind the scintillating headlines. Her life is in jeopardy, but her love for Nick might cause the real danger.

*He'll risk his life - and his heart - to keep her alive...*

Financial whiz, Nick Cameron rose from an underprivileged life to become one of America's youngest corporate billionaires. Now he's laying low on a barrier island, far away from the raging media storm that nearly destroyed him. When little Ronnie Whitcomb shows up on his doorstep, all grown up and heart-stoppingly beautiful, he tries to deny his feelings for her, but a hurricane strands them on the island together. Keeping Ronnie at arm's length becomes impossible.

\*     \*     \*

## WILD FOR YOU
## (Tropical Heat Series, Book One)

*To Love, Honor and Protect*

Detective Clay Blackthorne has his hands full when he promises to safeguard an old college pal's sister without letting her know what he's up to. He never imagines that lively Marisol Calderon will knock his socks off and put a ring on his finger--and all at his suggestion! Their marriage of convenience is meant to protect her and Clay doesn't plan on being hitched for long to the tempting beauty. But the honeymoon sure feels real to him...

Sassy Marisol is used to doing whatever she wants--and right now her plan is to shake up the hot detective's hard-edged demeanor. But the fun turns to danger when a mystery stalker bent on marrying her marks her as his prey. Temporarily becoming Clay's wife seems like a practical way to thwart the stalker. But as passion ignites and Marisol falls for the tender heart buried beneath the tough detective's chest, Clay's true identity is revealed and she begins to wonder who--if anyone--she can trust...

\*    \*    \*

**SOLD ON YOU**
**(Tropical Heat Series, Book Two)**

*Just Say Yes!*

Confirmed bachelor Dr. Marcos Calderon is in hot water. He needs to come up with a fake fiancée fast or he'll disappoint his beloved grandma who's arriving on the next flight to meet her. Proper social worker Gabriela Morales should fit the bill--but tonight, in that sexy, slit-to-there red evening gown, she looks anything but proper.

Gabriela only volunteered for the hospital's charity bachelorette auction to benefit a cause dear to her heart. Now she's reeling from the hot doctor's bid of fifteen thousand dollars for a weekend date with her! She's not sure what Dr. Handsome has in mind, but the smoldering look in his eyes is unmistakable...

*   *   *

## GRILL ME, BABY

*The heat is on...*

Raised among women who taught him to cook at his family's Buenos Aires restaurant, master chef Paolo

Santos deftly works his culinary wiles--and his gypsy charm--on posh Flamingo Island's female clientele.

The tastiest tidbit on the island, though, is cool, elegant Michaela Willoughby. The redhead's slender curves are as enticing as her rabbit-food menus are maddening. And she's his main competition for the chance of a lifetime.

Michaela overcame her own weight issues to become Flamingo Island's premiere spa chef. Now she has a chance to share her innovative recipes for healthy living on a new cooking show--if she can somehow outshine Paolo. His sizzling, Latin-lover looks are more heart stopping than his decadent cooking. And she'd love nothing better than to stick a fork in his outsized ego.

When the stage lights ignite, so does the competition...and a sexual chemistry no one--least of all Paolo and Michaela--saw coming. Suddenly, separating business from pleasure is as impossible as separating a scrambled egg. And the big question isn't whose knife cuts fastest...it's whose heart can take the most heat.

*Warning: Contains two hot chefs duking it out in a lively showdown of sexy rivalry. Mix in family drama, luscious recipes and spicy mischief, and there's more than just steam rising out of the kitchen. May cause lusty cravings for midnight indulgences.*

\*    \*    \*

## PAGING DR. HOT

*A love prescription so potent only the hottest doctor can fill it.*

Miami TV reporter Francesca Lake is on a manhunt…or rather, a doctor hunt. Frankie wasn't always a hypochondriac. Her motto used to be "Fear is not an option", but everything changed with her mom's near-fatal heart attack. Now a day doesn't go by where she isn't worried about something.

After a harrowing incident in the hospital ER, she has a life-altering epiphany. She needs to find a marriage-minded doctor ASAP—one who will calm her fears so she can get on with her life.

So begins a series of amorous escapades and startling revelations as she works her way through the list of eligibles: an outrageous Aussie sex therapist, a brilliant neurosurgeon (who's wired the wrong way), and a handsome Cuban cardiologist.

None of them compares to hunky Dr. Harrison Taylor…but there's a problem. Much as Harrison's rugged physique, forest-green eyes and warm smile make her senses wobbly, she needs a people doctor, not the vet for her miniature dachshund Romeo. Besides, Harrison's propensity for crazy stunts would only make her worry more.

Frankie is trying to be sensible, but her heart and her outspoken dog are conspiring against her…

*Warning: Contains juicy secrets and romantic misadventures between a loveable hypochondriac and three hot doctors. Side effects may include intense yearnings for a strong doctor, an adorable miniature dachshund, and an impromptu trip to sultry Miami.*

\*     \*     \*

## TROPICAL HEAT SERIES BOX SET

Two fun, sexy and heartwarming romances of Sophia Knightly's Tropical Heat Series in one bundled volume.

In *Wild for You* (Book One), Detective Clay Blackthorne has his hands full when he promises to safeguard an old college pal's sister without letting her know what he's up to. He never imagines that lively Marisol Calderon will knock his socks off and put a ring on his finger--and all at his suggestion! Their marriage of convenience is meant to protect her and Clay doesn't plan on being hitched for long to the tempting beauty. But the honeymoon sure feels real to him...

Sassy Marisol is used to doing whatever she wants--and right now her plan is to shake up the hot detective's hard-edged demeanor. But the fun turns to danger when a mystery stalker bent on marrying her marks her as his prey. Temporarily becoming Clay's wife seems like a practical way to thwart the stalker. But as passion ignites and Marisol falls for the tender heart buried beneath the tough detective's chest, Clay's true identity is revealed and she begins to wonder who--if anyone--she can trust...

In *Sold on You*, (Book Two) Confirmed bachelor Dr. Marcos Calderon is in hot water. He needs to come up with a fake fiancée fast or he'll disappoint his beloved grandma who's arriving on the next flight to meet her. Proper social worker Gabriela Morales should fit the bill--but tonight, in that sexy, slit-to-there red evening gown, she looks anything but proper.

Gabriela only volunteered for the hospital's charity bachelorette auction to benefit a cause dear to her heart. Now she's reeling from the hot doctor's bid of fifteen thousand dollars for a weekend date with her! She's not sure what Dr. Handsome has in mind, but the smoldering look in his eyes is unmistakable...